Praise for Sierra Dean's
Something Secret This Way Comes

"*Something Secret This Way Comes* has it all, suspense, erotic passion, and deadly danger—a great triple play."

~ *Joyfully Reviewed*

"Sierra Dean spellbinds the reader in her debut urban fantasy novel... *Something Secret This Way Comes* is a fast paced, original story with a fantastic heroine and a fresh take on UF, it is one of the best books I have read this year and I cannot wait to read more!"

~ *Ex Libris*

"This book was an outstanding read, one that I'd definitely recommend. As it had it everything a paranormal should—a heroine that hunts the things that go bump in the night, some deliciously sexy werewolves, some hot sex scenes, even a major cliff-hanger that sets up the next installment of this series. In fact what more could you want! Great job, Ms. Dean."

~ *The Romance Studio*

"This is Sierra Dean's first book, and what a marvelous debut it is. I found the world she created to be an intriguing place, an alternate New York filled with paranormal beings and happenings. The characters are rich and complex, and the action is fast paced and entertaining."

~ *Whipped Cream Erotic Romance Reviews*

Look for these titles by *Sierra Dean*

Now Available:

Secret McQueen Series
Something Secret This Way Comes
The Secret Guide to Dating Monsters
A Bloody Good Secret
Secret Santa
Deep Dark Secret

Something Secret This Way Comes

Sierra Dean

SAMHAIN
PUBLISHING

HUDSON BRANCH

Samhain Publishing, Ltd.
11821 Mason Montgomery Road, 4B
Cincinnati, OH 45249
www.samhainpublishing.com

Editing by Sasha Knight
Cover by Kanaxa

First Samhain Publishing, Ltd. electronic publication: May 2011
First Samhain Publishing, Ltd. print publication: April 2012

Dedication

To Jessica Cote and Jessica McCarthy, who continue to be the greatest cheerleaders a girl could ever ask for.

Chapter One

In the sullen hours before daylight, a thick dewy fog was settling over the deep green lawns of Central Park. A waning moon hung over the cityscape like a Cheshire cat's looming smile. It was cold enough in the spring air that an exhaled breath became a cloud with a limited lifespan. With enough of those escaped breaths, one could trace the path of the breather as they moved through the park and into the night.

Along the edges of the famous Great Lawn, just inside a jagged forest with a dazzling array of buildings creating an illuminated backdrop on the darkened landscape, one such trail was moving with great speed through the half-naked, outstretched branches, the clouds short and anxious. Always mere inches ahead of these markers, a young woman was running for her life.

I was not the woman in question, although I was also running.

Like a fool, I'd believed I might be able to take a nice, quiet walk through Central Park that night, enjoying the heavy predawn stillness, which is almost never available in a city like New York. Typically the only solitude I'm allowed is during the brief allotments of hot water my shower provides me, and even then the pipes in my building rattle and bang whenever they're in use. The shower is only quiet when the water runs cold.

Tonight I had wanted to be alone with the darkness before slipping away for my morning slumber, but that had been too much to hope for in the city that never sleeps. Even though a quiet night for me would involve getting harassed by a mugger or roughing up some drug addicts if they tried to scare rebellious schoolgirls, it still would have been preferable to what I was being forced to do now.

Too bad for me, and more specifically for the girl I was running after, she was being chased by something that wasn't peaceful, quiet or even human.

Fear was radiating off her in waves that were so strong the thing after her would be able to find her regardless of how fast she ran or how well she hid. Fear had a cloying scent to it, not quite sweet, more like aged cloves and copper. I knew that because I could smell it too. And the feeling that accompanied it sent shivers reverberating through the base of my spine. There was a predator in me that related to what her assailant felt as he tracked her, the primal part deep down that could empathize with the frenzied vigor of collapsing victoriously on your terrified prey.

I could feel him too, and could finally recognize for certain that it was, indeed, a male. I wouldn't go so far as to say man, because there wasn't anything in him that resembled what he once had been. The shell he wore still looked human, but what was now inside that skin suit could not be described as anything other than monstrous.

All I could feel off him was his overpowering hunger. That coupled with the fact I hadn't sensed from her any warning hints of anxiety escalating into fear. She hadn't had time to worry. Instead she slipped immediately into a wild, blistering terror as she was chased at a perilous clip by his animal hunger. That instant fear was the only reason I was running at all. Because the girl was very human, and very vulnerable, and he had taken her by surprise, which was against the rules.

Even though the thing after her was without a shadow of a doubt dead, I knew if I wasn't faster than him, the girl would soon be among their ranks. And once she was gone, his betrayal of the laws which governed the undead of the world would become my problem anyway, so a little preemptive interference was just saving myself and some vampire bureaucrats a lot of hassle.

At this point, I'd tell myself anything to justify the chase.

The girl broke free of the tree line and started making a wild, hobbling sprint across the Great Lawn. That was the first moment I realized I had actually passed him in our pursuit. I was still sprinting after them through the woods, holding out hope that his hunger would distract him from becoming aware I had joined his hunt. I could smell blood on the air and knew she must have cut herself somewhere in her escape.

As she limped across the field, I saw that one of her feet was bound in a broken stiletto and the other was dragging the mated shoe behind, strung to her only by an ankle strap. She was sobbing, choking out screams, and part of me swallowed those noises with deep pleasure. An animal hunger within wanted me to get to her first so I could rip her to shreds myself.

But that wouldn't do. I had never killed a human, not a pure-blood human anyway, and I wouldn't start tonight or any night, I hoped. I wasn't an undead killing machine like he was. I was something else altogether, and while what I was certainly wasn't any easier to believe in than vampires, it did allow me enough illusions of humanity to know killing people, at least those who didn't have it coming, was wrong.

I felt like my chance was now or never, and I broke free of the trees, sprinting after her. I didn't dodge the clever fingers of a branch sharpened by the storms of winter, and was clawed across the face with a painful swipe, but I just kept running. I ran until every muscle in my body burned and screamed, and then I ran faster. If I was human, I would have fallen down exhausted, vomited on the grass and lay defeated for an hour. But I was not human, and I could have completed a marathon at this pace if I needed to.

It took almost no time at all for me to catch up to her, but it felt like hours. He was out in the open now, following us both, and still I ran. I kept going until I reached her and grabbed her hard by the arm, dragging her behind me as I continued my pace. She was screaming and trying to shake free of me, unable to distinguish me from her actual attacker. As she clawed at me with surprising might for a girl of her slender build, I acknowledged there was only one way we were going to get out of this with her still alive.

I stopped running and slapped her hard and fast across the face. She replied with stunned silence, and we both stood staring at each other.

This girl looked so much like I would have if I had anything like a normal life. She was slender and petite, with blonde hair. But unlike me, she had an unnatural tan, acquired by spending hours in a light-box coffin, and she wore more makeup than I'd ever thought to own.

"You need to listen to me very carefully." He was coming, and fast. I only had seconds. "I can save you from this. I can keep you alive."

Terror vanished from her face and was replaced with the more frightening emotion of hope. I'd gotten through enough that she knew I meant to help her. Her grip tightened on my wrist as she began to come to terms with what I was saying. Her tear-filled eyes were wide and eager. Her earnest hopefulness made the bottom of my stomach lurch. It was my responsibility to keep this maladjusted socialite version of myself alive.

"But I need you to stay out of my way."

I tried to loosen her grip, but she wouldn't let go, and I could see him now, a blur of rage and energy heading straight at us.

"Let me go and you live. Let. Me. Go." I shoved her off me with a little too much force.

She stumbled and collapsed, but understanding seemed to sink in at last.

"Now run away as fast as you can."

She scrambled backwards and got to her feet. She shot me one last desperate look before she started to run again, and I had enough time to turn around before I was hit dead on by a vampire charging for me at full speed.

Chapter Two

I was flattened to the ground, the wind knocked out of me with a painful hiss and a thrashing vampire with his bared fangs going straight for my throat.

Just another day at the office.

For the time being, at least, he seemed content to believe that I was a more than equal trade for the girl he'd been chasing. Who could blame him? As far as he knew, she and I were both warm-blooded girls out in the park alone, waiting to be somebody's perfect victim. I may not have been bathed in the rich smell of fear, and my outfit was a far cry from her provocative dress, but when it came time for a blood-crazed vampire to feed, she and I might as well have been the same. All a vampire needed was a neck and a pulse.

The major problem with my current situation was that my gun was tucked into the back of my jeans, which meant, as a result of my being pinned down, it was now being crushed into the small of my back.

I needed to get on top of him. Oh, if I only had a nickel for every time that had been my solution for things.

His teeth grazed my collarbone, slicing the skin and jarring me out of my inappropriate musings. As luck would have it my intuition had been correct—he was a newborn and he was sloppy. A full-grown vampire would have tried to latch on at the first sight of blood, but this one didn't even seem aware of what he'd done. Unfortunately, the open wound also meant there was the smell of fresh plasma sitting right under his nose, and his ignorance was short-lived.

He stopped snarling and, in a moment of bewildered stupidity, stared at the wound he had made as if he didn't know how it had gotten there.

I took what might be the only opportunity I'd get and used his unguarded distraction to my advantage by punching him across his cheek as hard as my body would allow. That hit, if inflicted on a grown human male, would have broken his teeth out the other side of his face and turned the cartilage in his nose into pulp. As it was I heard the vampire's jaw crack, and he sat back off me, blinking with mute surprise.

He snarled and made to dive at me again, but I'd had all the time I needed. My gun was drawn, armed and pressed against his forehead before he even had a chance to cross the miniscule distance between us. I scrambled to my feet, the gun still trained on him, not wanting to remain on the ground if this went south.

The vampire had to cross his eyes to get a look at what I had fixed on him, and it would have been comical except for what followed. He gave a short, hoarse laugh, a sound that should be uniquely human if not for the icy edge to it.

"Do you know what I am, little girl?"

To anyone else, this dismissal would have been unnerving. I wasn't too concerned with his bravado, however. I was more interested in his reaction to my weapon. He wasn't frightened of my gun in the least, and that would prove to be his undoing. It was why I used a gun in the first place—vampires didn't see them as a serious threat and let their guard down. All it takes is turning one smug vampire's head into a pulpy red mass before the rest realize how effective a gun can be for killing almost anything.

"Enlighten me." I smiled with emphasized innocence, widening my brown eyes for a doe-eyed look that the vamps tended to love.

The truth was, as much as I'd like to kill him, I technically couldn't. But if it came down to it, I wanted to be able to face the shitstorm that would follow with as much useful information as possible. Since he was so new, there was a chance I might be able to pump him for a little information before I was forced to pull the trigger.

"I am your darkest nightmare. I am your death."

Wow, someone had definitely given him the Introduction to Sounding Like a Poncy Asshole seminar before sending him out into the world. I rolled my eyes at his speech, which reeked like an old Lugosi movie.

"You're a fucking baby," I said, not even a hint of awed, cowering fear in my words.

That got his attention.

"I will rip your head off and bathe in your still-hot blood." He didn't sound as arrogant this time, but I had to give him credit for his continued efforts.

"No. You won't." I said it as matter-of-factly as one might say *New York is a big city.* "You're what? Three days old, maybe? You're not even a blip. You're nothing. For all the vampire world cares, you might as well still have a pulse. Talk as big as you want, but I'm not the one who should be scared."

He stood up and I tensed, my finger tightening on the trigger a fraction of an inch. His new position brought him to almost a foot taller than me, but I didn't lower my weapon, and I didn't back down. He saw now that I was well aware of what he was. Most people didn't even believe in vampires, let alone utter their name with such nonchalance. He raised a brow at me and waited.

"Why don't you ask me what I am?" I pressed the gun into his forehead harder.

He scoffed. "You are my dinner. Or perhaps I will turn you, bind you to me and have you every day until you wished you were dead."

It was my turn to make a noise of disgusted annoyance and roll my eyes again. If he didn't stop with this ridiculous, ostentatious performance, I was going to strain something.

"You wouldn't know how to turn me even if you wanted to. You're so young, you wouldn't be able to stop. You'd drink too much and kill me before you could figure out which of your own arteries to open." The sun would be up in a few hours, and though the night was still on my side, I didn't particularly want to let this drag on much longer for either of us. "Now go ahead...ask who I am."

He ignored me and tried to bat the gun away. I brought my knee up with a hard thrust and caught him in the groin, which was still excruciating even if you were undead, and replaced the gun at his temple when he collapsed. "Ask."

"Bitch."

I smacked him with the gun. "Ask."

The part coming next was my favorite. It was a moment six years and many, many dead vampires in the making, and I never got tired of it.

"Who are you?" His voice was strained, though he would have his full strength back in an instant.

"My name is Secret McQueen."

His eyes widened for the briefest of seconds, and I knew he recognized my name. It had an almost legendary status among the undead. Newborn vampires came to know it right away, because to be introduced, in person, to the owner of it, meant that you were dead. Well and truly dead. The forever kind, not the fun, false-immortality kind of death that vampires luxuriated in.

Knowing who I was, he understood I meant business.

"He told me about you." And then, to my surprise, he smiled. "Oh, he will be so very pleased with me."

Chapter Three

Some people might wonder what would lead a girl to chase a vampire through the heart of New York City, and why that same girl would risk her own life to point a gun at a newborn vampire in the middle of Central Park.

This would also bring up the messy question of why I can outrun a vampire, and why I have the occasional unrealized urge to hunt down humans from time to time.

The all-too-easy answer would be to tell you that I'm a half-vampire bounty hunter who takes out rogue vampires at the request of the vampire council.

And, yes, that is the *easy* answer. Problem is, I'm a little more than just a half-vampire. While logic might suggest that my remaining half would be human, it is not. I am, to the best of my knowledge, the world's only half-vampire, half-werewolf hybrid. I was born this way; it was not by any choice of my own.

My mixed heritage was not of interest to the newborn vampire in front of me, because it was a well-guarded secret. What had piqued his interest was my name and the reputation that went with it. What had me worried, though, was how pleased he was to be making my acquaintance. I was willing to play along with him for the time being, as I was keen to know who had been telling him about me. The vampire in front of me was obviously not a sanctioned birth. The fact he was out in public so soon after rising and chasing an innocent girl through the heart of the city told me this.

So even though this vampire would not be considered a clean kill by council standards, he might be able to lead me to the one who made him, and that was who I wanted. That vampire was a rogue against the council and someone worth hunting.

According to a centuries-old law, all new vampires are turned only by decree of the vampire council. Becoming a vampire in this day and age is the paperwork equivalent to being sworn in to senate. The problem is rogues, those vampires who didn't respect the council and wanted to return to the old ways—the days when vampires were believed in and feared, and had the power to do what they wanted without yielding to the rules of a governing body. Rogues didn't like hiding from humans and pandering to the rules of a human society. They didn't seem to remember that there was never a time in history where vampires were an actual ruling class. Instead they had their own version of the good old days, of hunting peasants or living in legendary castles. The really old ones passed these golden-years stories onto the younger ones, and suddenly all these Enlightenment era and New Colonial vampires got it in their heads to challenge the governing laws, espousing ideals of a lifestyle they hadn't lived themselves.

They turned humans, buried them, and when the new vampires awoke, often sharing a coffin with a fresh dead body, they went mad, dug their way free and had all the urges and needs of an animal.

Then there's the other thing about new vampires that annoys me to no end—they're a lot like children. They're inherently curious, disrespectful unless taught to be otherwise and blissfully unaware of their own mortality. This one in particular had all the traits of a rebellious and highly irritating

20

little boy. The kind that screams in stores and kicks and bites. Only getting bitten by this child could kill you.

Child or animal, a newborn rogue vampire is no fun whatsoever to deal with. They cannot, under most circumstances, be reasoned with on any level. But I really wanted him to clarify what he meant when he said, *he will be so very pleased with me.* They say curiosity killed the cat, but I needed to know who made him. Guess it's a good thing I was part wolf and not part cat.

"What is your name?" I figured if I could at least get a little intel while he was momentarily at ease, I'd have something to bring back to the council. The Tribunal, the leaders of the vampire council, wouldn't be happy to see me a third time under these same conditions, and the feeling was mutual. If I killed this rogue, which I had no doubt I'd be forced to, I wanted an olive branch to bring to the Tribunal. Something good to justify my blatant disregard for council law.

He was still thinking about this question, his features clouded over with genuine confusion.

"Henry," he said after a pause that felt endless. "I was Henry Davies."

"Was. You do understand, then?" I never could figure out why, but a vast number of newborns did not understand that their new powers came with certain sacrifices, namely their pulse. Being a vampire was such a thrill until you realized you weren't actually alive anymore. That pesky blood-drinking thing was also pretty hard for some of them to swallow, no pun intended.

"That I'm dead?"

"Yes."

He rolled his eyes, clearly thinking me a moron for asking such an obvious question. "He told me it would all be different."

Sometimes I really hated vampires. It's ingrained in their psyche to be as vague as possible.

"Henry, who is *he*?"

"He is the one who made me."

"Thank you, Captain Obvious. Does your master have a name?"

Henry's gaze locked on mine, and there was a moment of hesitation when I thought he might be about to give me an answer. The flicker of humanity was gone as fast as it appeared, leaving only a dismissive sneer. I knew that look well enough. He was thinking about what I might taste like. He wasn't planning on answering me; he was more or less deciding on how long he would wait before he ate me.

Or, more specifically, before he tried.

"Henry, I suggest answering my question, because if I so much as see fangs, I will kill you."

He laughed. The son of a bitch actually laughed at me. Just further proof on how young he was. No established, educated vampire would ever laugh in my face, especially not when they knew for certain who I was. They might joke behind my back, calling me "little vampire hunter" and pretending I wasn't as scary as rumors would have them all believe. But when faced with me, a rogue vampire knew the end was near.

I may not look like much, but I don't have my job based on my appearances. I kill vampires, it's what I do, and not just any five-four blonde girl could pull it off. I get why he'd laugh, because at first glance I might come across more like a damsel in distress than a killer. In most cases it worked in my favor, but it got frustrating trying to intimidate vampires who refused to take me seriously.

In the distance I heard sirens, and I hoped to hell it meant the girl had made it to a pay phone or had at least found someone to call the police for her while she cried. And she would cry, for days most likely.

In the meantime, if those sirens were in fact for the girl in the broken heels, I didn't have much time to play games with Henry. Human police officers didn't handle supernatural stuff all that well.

The word denial comes to mind. They were always so willing to ignore the most obvious explanation in lieu of overly contrived answers which shut out the option of the irregular. Occam's razor did not appear to apply in the case of humans, especially human police.

"Henry, we don't have time for this. I need you to tell me who made you, or I let that girl identify you to the police and you spend the night downtown in a cell." This particular threat held more weight with new vampires. I didn't think Henry would really get it, but it was worth a shot.

"I'm not afraid of the police," he said with a snort. In this instance he was justified in his dismissal of law enforcement, and he and I both knew it.

Henry had a lot of cocky swagger for a new vamp, and it was beginning to narrow down the options in my mind for his sire, but I needed a name if I was going to get a warrant. Killing rogues was an awful lot like bringing down drug kingpins. It was one thing to get the lowest level thugs, but quite another to get the master sire. It's almost impossible to find a master's master's master. The council and I were both looking to find the names of the old ones, the ones we suspected but dare not accuse without evidence.

"You might want to consider the fact that all police-station cells now have windows."

"So?"

"So, you're not immune to sunlight anymore. And telling

me what I want to know is going to be a hell of a lot better than waking up as nothing more than a pile of ashes."

Henry was starting to get bored with our conversation. His eyes were wandering and he was licking his lips. Then a dark shadow of a thought crossed over his face, stirring the inky depths of his black eyes, making them glimmer in an unpleasant way. His brows narrowed, and he turned his attention back to me, smirking.

Henry chuckled. "He told me about you. Secret McQueen, big bad vampire hunter. He told me I shouldn't cross you. He said that you were dangerous." He was laughing with unrestrained scorn now, amused by his own joke. But he was also giving me clues. His direct sire was a rogue who knew me. Probably one I'd crossed before.

"You have a wise sire, Henry, now tell me his name."

"No."

In a flash Henry went from aloof to attack, and he had my free wrist in his hand, his gaping mouth going for my throat.

Idiot, the throat was such a clichéd move. Had he bitten into my wrist while he had the option, I might have been in trouble. The intensity of his attack did, however, manage to topple us, and his weight landed on me with hefty force once again. Henry, with his solid mass of vampire hunger, outweighed me by about a hundred pounds. I used a considerable amount more strength than he probably anticipated I had to bring the arm he was holding across my chest to block his attack on my neck. He was so certain of himself he bit his own arm by accident while gnashing for my skin.

He howled in sudden shock.

"Hurts doesn't it? Being bitten by a vampire when you're not in the thrall."

"You will know soon, girl," he snarled, spit flying from his mouth, his eyes deep black with rage.

He dove in to bite me again, but I dodged faster than he was prepared for. As he lunged to bite, I jammed my gun into his open mouth, a bullet loaded in the chamber and my finger trembling on the trigger.

"I already know what it feels like, asshole. Now tell me the name or I pull this trigger." I knew I was going to do it whether he told me or not.

His lips moved around the barrel. I pulled out the gun and pressed it in one swift motion under his chin. Henry licked around his mouth, tasting where my gun had been. He touched his fangs with the tip of his tongue, as if savoring the memory of something delicious, and choked out a laugh.

"My master will be thrilled to know that one of his own was responsible for the death of the great Secret McQueen. And he will be even more impressed to know that you died without ever knowing who he was. Because I will never tell you, not even when I eat your still-beating heart right out of your chest."

And then he spit in my face.

Chapter Four

The one benefit to having someone else's saliva on your face, if it's possible to find one, is that it makes it a lot harder for the blood to stick.

When the back of Henry's head came off and rained its contents over us, I was able to wipe the worst of it out of my eyes. I shoved his now literally dead weight off me and knelt next to the corpse.

If his sire was who I thought it was, there would be another way to tell. I only knew of one master sire who would be exceptionally thrilled to see me dead. I tugged down the neck of Henry's shirt, and sure enough, though scabbed over from healing, there was my proof.

A set of bite marks, ragged and painful looking, but with an unmistakable gap where one of the fang punctures should be. A gap which would match to a missing tooth. One that I had knocked out six years earlier while fighting for my life against the first master vampire I'd ever tried to kill.

"Son of a bitch." I sucked in a breath of cold air and cast a look behind me, a paranoid but somehow necessary gesture to confirm he wasn't there.

It all made sense now. The attitude and the smug certainty. The cocksure way he had gone right after that girl. He truly was his father's son.

"Fuck me. Shit." I was hissing now, forcing words through gritted teeth. If I could have been more intelligible, I'm sure something a bit more eloquent might be said, but right then all I could think of were curses, and I strung them together with blasphemous intensity. From inside my jacket I pulled out my cell phone and a small flashlight. I hit number two on the speed dial and flicked on the flashlight with my teeth.

"This is a late check in, McQueen."

"I need a pick up outside Columbus Circle. As soon as you can be there. Don't bring the nice upholstery. I'm messy."

A pause. "Who?"

"It wasn't sanctioned. I'm going to call Holden, have him alert the fucking Tribunal. But it doesn't matter, Keaty. You have no idea whose seed this guy was."

A longer pause. Francis Keats would not guess, but I suspected from the tone in my voice that he knew all too well who I was talking about.

I was looking through the grass with my flashlight, waiting for it to... There it was, a glint of metal. I picked up the bullet and put it in my pocket with the casing I'd already collected. There was no time for me to hide the body, so I had to hope the girl was too shaken to be specific about our location. Even if they did find him, the body would be nothing more than dust by sunrise. Bullets, however, did not simply disintegrate.

"It's Peyton. He's back."

"I'll be there in four minutes."

Keaty was waiting when I reached the street corner. The sidewalks were almost empty, with pedestrian traffic dwindling in the hours after all the bars had closed but before reasonable citizens would be awake again. It used to be known as the witching hour, and in some circles it still was.

I slipped unnoticed into the black car, its tinted windows blocking out all questions and suspicion. After all, what would people think if they saw a blood-splattered blonde being driven around by a serious-looking man in glasses?

Keaty must have left in one hell of a rush if he was still wearing his silver-rimmed bifocals. I wasn't sure if he thought they made him look weak, or if he knew they would sully his badass reputation, but Keaty never let anyone see him with them on.

Anyone but me.

The seat squeaked beneath me, and I realized he'd put a plastic slipcover over the leather. How pragmatic, he decided to save the car rather than put in contacts. At least I knew where his priorities were.

We drove in silence for awhile, my breath returning to normal after I had blitzed across Central Park to meet his car, and my sense of panic reducing. I felt safer now being this close to him.

Francis Keats, best known to me as Keaty and to everyone else as Mr. Keats, was the closest thing I had to a certainty in my life. He was my partner, as in business partner only, thank you. I'd met Keaty six years earlier, when I was sixteen and had come to the big city to chase my demons, both figurative and literal.

Keaty had been the one to save my ass when I got in way over my head with a vampire I hadn't known was a rogue. Back then, I didn't work for anyone and was foolishly hunting any vampire I could find. Sixteen years old and I'd almost gotten myself killed on one of my first outings. The vampire had seemed young, and I thought he would be an easy kill. I had been so very wrong, and now it was coming back to haunt me.

No one had feared the name of Secret McQueen then, I can tell you that much for certain.

But Keaty, who was a solitary man by trade, must have seen something in me, because after I refused to go back home, he took me under his wing. Keaty was one of five people who knew what I really was, and I was one of only two who ever called him Francis and lived to tell the tale.

"Is any of that yours?" he asked, indicating the blood on me. His voice was calm, showing no concern if he had any.

"No." The scratches on my face and clavicle were already healing. One of the benefits of my dubious bloodline.

"Going to tell me what happened?" Keaty passed me a towel and a few wet-naps.

I recapped the story of the girl in the woods and an almost-feral Henry Davies. Then I told him, without sparing any details, of what Henry had said to me and of the healing bite marks I'd found on his neck.

"You're absolutely certain?" Even he sounded certain, but I knew he had to ask.

"Yes, I'm sure."

"Well." He parked the car in front of an old brownstone with one light burning on the main floor and a painted name in the frosted glass that read *Keats and McQueen Private Pest Control.* "We always knew he'd be back. It was never a question."

"But why wait this long? Why now?" We got out of the car and hiked up the steps. An old woman passing by with a small pug gave us a second glance and frowned with disapproval. A twenty-two-year-old girl with a forty-year-old man at this time of night? I knew what she was thinking, even before she shook her head and hurried along. At moments like this I had to fight the urge to put my hand in Keaty's pocket and lick his cheek, or something equally silly. That had never and would never be the

29

relationship I had with him, so it bothered me when that was what people assumed of us. Of him.

"Six years to a vampire is hardly a long time, Secret. Especially one as old as Peyton." He unlocked the door and let me in. I made a beeline for the upstairs bathroom, and Keaty followed me. "As for why now," he continued, as I started up the taps in the old clawfoot tub, preparing to wash vampire brains out of my hair, "I believe he must have bigger plans in town than just your death. I think you're a small perk in a much larger scheme."

I had been thinking along those same lines. "You think he has something to do with the number of rogues going against the council?"

"Probably, and maybe more than that. I believe Peyton may be responsible for a lot of the Tribunal's current headaches. He may even be one of the masters we've been hoping to find."

"I shudder to think that Alexandre Peyton is that high in the vampire food chain. I know he's powerful, but at three hundred and change, I sincerely doubt he'd be considered worthy by those in charge."

"Maybe he would if he killed a certain vampire hunter." He jutted his chin out to me. "A certain half-vampire, vampire hunter."

I sighed. "A certain half-vampire, half-werewolf vampire hunter?"

Keaty's jaw clenched. As a man who made his living killing monsters of all makes and models, he'd always had some difficulty dealing with the vampire half of my heritage, but he had even more trouble accepting the werewolf half. That made two of us. "He doesn't know that. None of them know that."

"They know I'm not human, Keaty. They can smell it. The wolves can too. They all know something isn't right, they just haven't been able to put it together yet. All it takes is one wolf to tell one vampire that I smell furry, and one vampire to tell one wolf that I smell undead, and the pieces will fall together. It's all a matter of time."

"Then I guess it's a good thing that vampires and werewolves aren't exactly having weekly brunches."

I put my hair under the water, my blonde curls unraveling in the warm stream, streaks of red washing out and circling down the drain. My heart pounded as I thought about Peyton and the vampire council.

I still needed to call Holden.

Holden was my vampire liaison with the council. Like a caseworker, I guess. Whenever a baby vampire or the rare non-vampire was brought into the fold, they were assigned a liaison from within the council. A lower level vampire, most of whom were younger than two hundred. They were all wardens, a title assigned to trusted vampires, but those who had no real power in the hierarchy.

Wardens needed to prove themselves at that level before being promoted to sentries, governors, then to tribal elders, and finally, if the possibility presented itself, to Tribunal lords. Since there were only three Tribunal lords at one time, unless you challenged one in a fight to the death, the only way to advance that high was to wait.

I was proving to be a much more difficult challenge than the elders had expected when they assigned me to Holden, and I often worried that I was keeping him from gaining ranks within the council. His bicentennial had come and gone during the six years I'd known him, and yet he remained in his lowly warden position.

Both Holden and the vampire council knew about my vampire half—there was no hiding it from them—but only

Holden knew about the other half, and he had kept it a secret, even from the Tribunal lords. Holden, like Keaty, had known me since I was sixteen, and they were both guarding me without being asked, like overprotective brothers.

"I think, maybe, the Tribunal will go a little bit easier on me this time than last."

"You mean the time you killed three rogues on a subway platform, without sanction, in the middle of the evening, with a hundred people watching?" A chuckle lightened his voice and could have almost gone unnoticed. "Yes, I imagine that one vampire, in a dark field, would be a shade easier for them to swallow than headlines in *The Post* about a maniac girl with a sword and bodies that turned to dust in the morgue."

"*The Post* is a joke anyway. *The Times* didn't even touch it."

"And you made a valiant attempt of explaining the difference to the Tribunal, didn't you? They loved that, as I recall."

I pulled my hair into a wet ponytail, the thick, loose curls already returning, all the red gone from the gold.

"I just think they'll see the significance of Peyton's return more than the death of one rogue."

Keaty sat on the edge of the tub and offered me another towel to wipe the stubborn bits of brain out of my ear. "You still don't understand them at all, do you? They're your people, part of your heritage—"

"Don't," I warned, shooting him a humorless glance.

"And don't keep denying it. You can't just pretend it isn't true. Their laws apply to you because you let them. You asked to be allowed into their fold. I was killing vampires for the council for ten years before you ever tried it, without ever meeting them face-to-face. You were in the city three months and you were begging for an audience. What you fail to recognize is that a death to them is always a loss. When they sign over the warrants to us, they are allowing us to kill their children. Their brothers and sisters. Their parents. Vampires are not as abundant as you like to pretend, and they won't ever take a death lightly, not even when you see it as a reasonable kill."

I held the towel and looked at myself in the mirror, pale, exhausted, but otherwise no worse for the wear. I listened to what he was telling me, and he was right. To the council I was both an aid and an abomination. They would not kill their own but knew Keaty would because he was human and also lacked a moral compass when it came to killing monsters.

Then I showed up, a half-vampire, blood kin to their history, and I demanded that they let me kill my own people. And I wondered why they had so much trouble accepting me. I couldn't even accept myself.

"I'll call Holden," I said again, still no closer to actually wanting to do it.

"I'm sure he'll be thrilled."

Chapter Five

Holden, like most vampires, did not answer his phone. He always let the machine get it, believing that any caller with a real reason to contact him should be willing to leave a message and willing to wait for a reply. Vampires are patient to a point where it wears thin on anyone around them, which is one of the reasons they spend most of their time with their own kind.

I recapped the events of the evening as best I could over the limitations of voicemail. "Hey, Holden, it's Secret. I killed an unsanctioned rogue in the park tonight. He had it coming. Send the Tribunal my love."

I was in an all-night café near Keaty's, waiting for my nonfat no-foam latte while I left the message. The barista behind the counter, who appeared to be about fourteen, gave me a concerned look.

I flashed him my well-practiced innocent smile and said, "My dungeon master." A spark of revelation lit upon his zitty face. "I just needed him to know the outcome of a campaign he missed." I winked and took my drink out of his hand while he muttered something about rolling twenties.

It was late spring, and there was still a chill in the air, but the café had seen fit to set up its sidewalk patio a week or so after the snow melted. I pulled my jacket around me, though the cold didn't really bother me, and sat on one of the wrought-iron chairs. My cell phone was securely in my pocket in case Holden called, but I expected I wouldn't hear from him right away. I was also in no hurry to go back to the office and talk to Keaty about the state of affairs I now found myself in. I'd told him I was getting a coffee and then calling it a night.

Dawn was only an hour or two away, and there was nothing I could do to change what I'd done tonight. I would have to face the consequences when they came.

I tried to enjoy the hot, bitter sweetness of the latte, in sharp contrast to the coolness of the night, but my mind was reeling from what had happened. It took a lot to scare me, mostly because almost anything that went bump in the night I had killed at some point, but my encounter with Henry Davies had really shaken me.

The unshakeable, calm and centered Secret McQueen had been knocked on her proverbial ass by the impression of a bite mark. Maybe I had been mistaken. There was a chance part of the bite had healed faster or maybe I had been anticipating it so much I had imagined the missing tooth mark.

I prayed that I was wrong. In the six years I had been doing this, the closest anyone had ever come to truly killing me was Alexandre Peyton, and he had promised me that next time we met he wouldn't fail. If I was right about it being his mark, I was going to need to be on my guard more than usual until things either came to a head or blew over.

As I sipped my coffee I was overcome by an unexpected warmth which had nothing to do with the drink. It was like a humid summer breeze was blowing down 81st Street, only it crawled over my body and into my pores. My mouth felt thick with musky, dense flavor. The sensation was invasive and overwhelming, and what scared me the most was how comfortable I felt with it. I licked my lips and tasted cinnamon.

My latte was vanilla.

It was then, with a ripple of electric pinpricks up my spine, I felt a man pass. He approached from behind me and seemed to be wholly unaware of my presence until he turned towards the café door. He paused before entering, his close-cropped ash-colored hair tousled by the cool night air, and fixed his radiant azure eyes on me. There were two men with him, one on either side—a brunet who was the same height, just over six feet, and another who was my height and blond. The one who was watching me looked as puzzled as I felt, but he snapped out of it after a brief period of stunned silence and took a step in my direction.

"Hello?" he said, the way people do when they believe they already know you and simply cannot place the who and how.

If I'd been on my game, I'd have a snappy shoot-down or roll my eyes and tell him to get lost. I might have ignored him under any *normal* circumstances, because as a general rule I try to avoid men who might try to flirt with me. I did not date, although I had tried once or twice in the past. I had no time or patience for it, not to mention there were certain aspects of my life I could never explain to a human boyfriend.

But I could not look away, and nothing about this felt normal.

Not only could I not tear my eyes from him, something inside me pulled closer, dragging me nearer like a leash being tugged. There was a piece of me that wanted nothing more than to go to him. He was beautiful, I couldn't deny that, but he was a stranger, and this reaction was strange to say the least. This was more than magnetism; it was practically a law of attraction. The pull knotted inside me, fluttering in my stomach with the feeling of a thousand desperate moths crowding together to seek the light of a single bare bulb. My body demanded I go to him, and I realized I was now standing. My chair was several inches behind me, and I held my drink in trembling hands. When had I stood?

His friends were watching me too, like they knew what was happening between us. They were both interested and unconcerned by my reaction. I bet none of them had to make much of an effort to attract the ladies, considering all three were picture-perfect male specimens. The man in the middle smiled, a flash of white canines, and it dawned on me what I was smelling below the cinnamon and electricity. It stopped me dead in my tracks.

"Wolf," I said. It was almost a hiss, the sound an animal makes when threatened.

My stupid werewolf half was being lured by him, and I wasn't about to have any part of it. I had no intention of letting some animal dupe me with werewolf lust. I'd heard about this, weres using their powers to overwhelm newer or lesser wolves. I'd been dealing with my lycanthrope half since birth, which was a lot longer than most adults with the affliction. Just because I'd never shifted as an adult didn't mean some twenty-something who'd probably been turned last week was going to get the best of me.

I tended to shut out my werewolf half far more than my vampire half. Vampires, for all their flaws, were still primarily human in their behavior. I could accept that and relate to it. Their society had laws, structure and regulation. They were very political in their hierarchical organization.

Werewolves left me feeling more unsettled. They were animals. Primal beings. They were willing to abandon the human aspects of themselves to embrace something wild and reckless. I'd never tried to learn about their world because I didn't want to be a part of something that catered to such careless freedom. I did not have the luxury to let myself lose control in that way. If I did, I risked releasing much more than my inner wolf.

I turned away from him, and his face fogged with confusion again. I was not going to play his games. Heading towards the back entrance of the patio, I made a break for it. I was almost at the corner of the block before I hazarded a glance back. They were gone.

I stopped walking, still clutching my latte. Maybe he'd been willing to let it go when he saw I clearly wasn't interested. I breathed a sigh of relief. One less thing to worry about for the night. My plate was already overburdened as it was. The last thing I needed was to fend off some pushy frat boy's puppy love.

Turning back to the corner, I walked smack into the tall brunet who had been with the man. A small sound of surprise escaped my lips.

"What the—?"

"I'd like you to come with me, miss."

"Like hell." I dropped my drink and was reaching for the gun at the small of my back, but he grabbed my arm first.

"That won't be necessary. We only want to have a quick word with you about what just happened at the café."

Before I could find the proper string of profanities to explain I had no intention of going anywhere with him, he was dragging me none too gently towards a waiting car. He pushed me into the backseat as the door opened, pulling the gun from the back of my belt as he did.

And I thought my night couldn't get any worse.

Chapter Six

"What the hell do you think you're doing?" I was in the back of a sleek town car sitting next to the handsome man from the café and loving tinted windows a lot less than I had earlier that evening.

"My name is—"

"Look, I don't care who you are, pal. You don't go around sending out your lupine mojo to random girls and then kidnapping them when you get rejected! I don't care what bit you, that's just not how it's done."

He regarded me with careful silence for a moment, then ignoring everything I'd said or perhaps because of it, he smiled. "Lupine mojo?" Chuckling, he shared an amused glance with the brunet. "Is that what you think that was? You think you were attracted to me because of *wolf magic*?" He said the last two words with a sarcastic flourish, spreading his palms wide to mimic casting a spell.

"Don't flatter yourself. I wasn't attracted to you." My arms were crossed and I was pressed so hard against the door there would be an imprint of the handle in my hip later. I wanted to be as far from him as possible in such a small space. His face was half hidden by the dark interior of the car, so I only caught glimpses of him when we passed under a light. "This next corner will be just fine." This was directed to the blond driver, the other man who'd been with him.

"Oh, I'm afraid not," my objectionable companion replied.

I was steadily going from put out to pissed off. "Please believe that you *will* be letting me out of this car."

"I plan to let you go, no harm done, but there are some things that you and I need to discuss first."

"I have nothing to discuss with a man who uses his goons to throw me into a car. Where I'm from, if a guy wants to get to know a girl he buys her dinner first. Kidnapping went out in the caveman era."

"Well, perhaps if I bought you dinner..."

"You have got to be kidding me." My mouth hung open. I was unable to suppress my shock at the shift in his methods.

"No. I'm entirely serious."

"Pull over the car."

"Dominick, you heard the lady. Would you please pull the car over?"

"Yes, Mr. Rain." There was something forced about the way he said it, like it wasn't typical for such a formal address to be used between them.

The car rolled to a stop, but when I went to open the door it was—big shocker—still locked.

Continuing the farce of a pleasant conversation, Mr. Rain said, "I take it that you were not close with the one who bit you."

"I was never bitten," I snapped. "Don't try to pretend like you know what you're talking about when it comes to me, puppy. You have no idea who I am."

"You are wolf, though. I can smell it on you."

I tried the door again. So far he was just talking; he hadn't tried to touch me or move closer. The tangible, electric vibe was still filling the backseat like an invisible twilight fog, and it made it hard for me to be there. The hairs on the back of my arms and neck rose being near him.

"What do you want from me?"

"I just need to ask you a few questions. Perhaps answer some of your own. You seem willfully ignorant of what it means to be a wolf, otherwise you wouldn't be fighting this so hard. I believe I may be able to put right the negative opinion you have of your own kind."

Questions? I had never known what it meant to be a wolf, and sure I had questions. But was I really going to trust a stranger? One who had kidnapped me, no less. Did I really have a choice?

"I'll answer your questions, on one condition," I offered.

"Name it."

"I get my gun back."

From the front seat I heard two very different reactions. Dominick, the short blond behind the wheel, let out an abrupt laugh. I was getting mightily sick of being laughed at tonight. The dark-haired one who was in possession of my gun was utterly humorless. He let out an almost inaudible growl.

"You promise to sit down and have a conversation with me if I return your weapon to you?" the handsome, mysteriously named Mr. Rain asked me. And why did I feel like that name should mean something? I was too distracted to rack my brain for where I might have heard it before.

This guy was good. I didn't want to agree, but something about the way he was talking to me made it difficult for me to refuse him.

"Promise me," he repeated.

"Yes. I promise. Now give me my gun." I held my hand out to the front seat expectantly.

"Desmond, please oblige the young lady."

I stared at the brunet wolf, my eyes locked on to the odd-colored pools of his own, and saw the unspoken threat there. His eyes told me if I stepped out of line he would be on me. Deep inside a part of me bristled, the internal-organ equivalent to a dog's ruff going up when alarmed. What was it with these guys? I'd been with them less than fifteen minutes and they'd already gotten more reaction out of my wolf than anyone had in the past twenty-two years combined. I'd been so careful to keep my inner dog collared, I often forgot it was there at all. But it was awake now, and everything happening had it both snarling and wagging its tail.

Traitorous beast.

The wolf named Desmond handed me my gun, and once I was holding it I resisted the urge to point it at anyone. It wouldn't do me any good anyway. The bullets in the weapon weren't silver. While vampires were just as prone to silver injuries as werewolves were, I'd learned that when you were using the gun to blow off someone's head it didn't matter what kind of metal you were using. My job description almost never included hunting werewolves, so using silver bullets for everyday jobs was an unnecessary expense. It was experiences like this that made me think maybe I should splurge and use silver bullets all the time.

I didn't point the gun at Mr. Rain or either of his men. Promises were promises after all, so the gun went back into the waist of my pants. Why I hadn't considered wearing my holster today was beyond me. I'd wanted a quiet night, but it was no excuse for being so unprepared. If there were a Boy Scout motto for bounty hunters, it would be *Always Be Armed.*

Dominick had left the car and was opening my door from the outside. Desmond and I exited at the same moment, and I had no doubt he would stick to my side like a stretched-out shadow for the rest of the evening. His attitude was doing a lot to tell me that he liked this situation even less than I did. He was taking great efforts to stay close without actually touching me.

Mr. Rain let himself out and rounded the town car to stand next to me. He didn't have the same apprehension as Desmond about touch. His hand pressed against the small of my back, his deft fingers avoiding my weapon and angling me forward with a gentle nudge. The contact of his fingertips, even through the leather of my jacket and the flimsy cotton of my shirt, sent a shimmering thrill up my spine and all the way down into my groin.

The unexpected intensity of the lust brought on by such a small touch terrified me. Certainly this wasn't normal. I was not in control of my own desire, and I hated being out of control in any way.

Sandwiched between Desmond and Mr. Rain with Dominick following at our rear, there was no easy way out. We walked towards the building that Dominick had parked in front of, and I immediately recognized its high-gloss black exterior and the cascading wall fountains on either side of the twelve-foot glass doors. The building had been featured in both *Architectural Digest* and an episode of *Lifestyles of the Fabulously Wealthy*. I had only seen it in passing, on my way to or from killing something.

Rain. Rain was the name of this six-star beast of a hotel, where room rates started at eight hundred dollars a night and only went higher from there. Realization began to dawn on me, but I still hadn't put all the pieces together. I knew enough to know that when I fit in the last few bits, I wasn't going to like the big picture.

A doorman stood in the entrance, looking unfazed to see one small woman being flanked by a pack of men. Pack? Poor but appropriate word choice.

"Good evening, Mr. Rain. Will you be needing the car again tonight?"

"That remains to be seen, Carl. Please have it at the ready," Rain instructed. The doorman nodded, and I felt a pit building in my guts. "Tell Melvin to ensure that no phone calls are forwarded to the apartment until further notice."

We crossed the massive lobby in a few quick strides. It didn't allow me much time to marvel at the slick black and silver details, but I did notice that the interior walls, much like those outside, were made of black marble waterfalls. The polished elevator doors slid open, and I was ushered inside the mirrored box.

Elevators were a conundrum for me. The vampire in me did not blanch at being encased in a tight space, as the undead are programmed to accept this as a survival requirement. Though I had never been inside a coffin myself, vampires were predisposed to like tight, dark areas. The oft-overlooked werewolf part of me, however, longed to claw at the doors until I was allowed out.

It felt like we rose for an eternity. Mr. Rain's hand slid under the base of my short jacket and shirt and grazed my bare skin. I wanted to slap him for his forwardness until I realized that the tension had completely drained from me just at the thrill of direct content. His faintest touch had soothed the beast within. My wolf was no longer panicked.

Boy did I ever have questions for this guy.

I'd met werewolves in the past and had killed two out of necessity, but none of them had created this surreal wave of tranquility in me.

"Who are you, anyway?" The words slipped from my mouth in a breathless whisper, all of my abrasive rage lifted from my voice. The other two wolves exchanged a glance.

"I am Lucas Rain," he said, as if it were just any normal name and he was just any normal guy introducing himself to a girl for the first time.

A breath caught in my throat, and I swayed from the shock of learning his true identity. How stupid could I have been to miss it? Mr. Rain? Rain Hotel? God, I was slipping. This was *the* Lucas Rain, an intensely private billionaire real-estate magnate.

He had, as rumor held, bought the Boston Red Sox as a twenty-first birthday gift to himself. He never showed his face in public. Page Six only published blurry photos of him in baseball caps or hooded coats.

Models constantly insisted on having bedded him, but none of their stories aligned well enough to establish where he kept his permanent residence. The only thing they could all agree on was he was a vigorous and gifted lover, and never asked for second dates.

Conjecture and mystery surrounded everything about the Rain family. Lucas's father, Jeremiah, and his father before him, had each been just as secretive and shut-in as Lucas now was. The only Rain descendant who relished the spotlight was Lucas's sister, Kellen, who put the Hilton sisters to shame with her debaucherous public antics. Lucas was like a ghost, nothing known about him for certain. But here I was, standing side by side with him, and if his touch was any indication, he was more real than any ghost I'd ever encountered.

I also knew the reason he cherished his secrecy as deeply as I did my own. There was something that Lucas had kept hidden from the prying eyes of humankind for his whole life, and I was already in on the secret.

For a werewolf native to New York state and specifically New York City proper, the name of Lucas Rain was held in reverence for a completely different reason, one that would never be published in the tabloid columns.

I was in an elevator with Lucas Rain, the werewolf king of the East.

Chapter Seven

The elevator doors opened with a sigh, and I stumbled out away from Lucas and Desmond. Dominick stayed in the elevator, waiting to see what was about to unfold. I had not previously been afraid for my safety, but it was now occurring to me that if anyone wanted to make me disappear with no questions asked, it was Lucas Rain. He had the wealth and the power to make it happen. I broke into a cold sweat.

This did not go unnoticed.

"Why are you afraid? That's not the reaction I'm used to getting. Unless of course someone has done something to wrong me. I don't even know you, so I don't think you have a reason to fear me." He looked genuinely puzzled.

The doors had opened onto a private floor, and I was all alone with these men. Having my gun offered me little comfort, apart from knowing headshots would kill werewolves. But the memory of the threat in Desmond's eyes, and knowing how easy it had been for him to take the weapon once, left me unsure of my chances against three creatures whose individual skills nearly equaled my own.

On a good day I was stronger than the average werewolf, but I wasn't stronger than three male wolves in their prime. I reached down into the depths of my psyche and tried to yank my vampire awake to no avail. Outside, the pale gray hues of the warning dawn were painting the sky, and the vampire part of me, for all intents and purposes, was dead to the world. Fuck. That left me with werewolf instinct and the training Keaty had given me.

Lucas stepped forward and looked at me the way a human observes a caged animal that was in danger of hurting itself.

"Would it make you feel safer to be here if you could call someone and tell them where you are before we continue?"

The man was a born politician and problem solver. It was little wonder that at only twenty-six he was the CEO of a Fortune 500 company and, more impressive than all that, was the sole monarch to a secret civilization of thousands. The offer was so simple. It was the exact right thing for him to say.

I was unaccustomed to civility in my line of work.

"Umm, yes, actually." I cocked my head to the side, trying my best to understand what he really wanted from me. Outright asking him seemed too...obvious?

"I'm afraid your cell won't work up here. Everything gets routed through the landlines. Desmond will show you to the study. We have a phone there. You can have all the time and privacy you would like. Then you can join me upstairs."

"Upstairs?" I gazed around, getting a better look at my surroundings, not grasping the full size of his living quarters.

"Yes. I own the building, so I took the top three floors for myself. An oasis above the city. It makes it easier to stay home when home is this size, I guess."

"And no cell phones is a big factor in maintaining your oasis?"

"I just don't like them. I have one, but I find it's more of a distraction than anything else. My personal time is limited for obvious reasons, and I've taken measures to make sure I can enjoy it in peace."

"I see." I wasn't sure I did.

"Before I leave you I have to ask, and I hope it doesn't seem rude coming so late in the game. What is your name?"

I almost laughed. At this point it felt like I'd been with him for days, and it was an adjustment for me to find someone who didn't guess who I was within moments of meeting me.

"Secret." Then to assure him I wasn't just coyly avoiding telling him my name, I added, "Secret McQueen."

"McQueen," he repeated, casting a glance at Desmond. "Well now. Isn't that interesting?"

"Makes sense." Desmond shrugged. But I saw his color pale.

I hadn't encountered that many werewolves in my time in the city and had only been formally introduced to one of them. Funny that Desmond's reaction was almost identical to that of the other wolf I'd met—cavalier but uneasy. It didn't bode well. If they had any intention of explaining what the revelation meant, it didn't show. Instead, Lucas bid me a temporary farewell with a nod, and Dominick trailed after him into the depths of the apartment. The main floor was a labyrinth of locked doors and long black hallways. I had not yet seen a window, and the whole area was lit by majestic stone chandeliers.

Desmond set off down a hallway, anticipating that I would follow.

"So..." I began, not sure if he would be open to conversation. "Are you and Dominick his...bodyguards?"

Desmond stopped in front of an open doorway, his tall, lean body filling its frame. He gave me an assessing look like he wasn't sure what to make of me. "It's true, then, what Lucas said. You really are ignorant of the ways of your own people."

I bristled. "Wolves are not people."

His eyes locked on mine in the unnerving way he was proving to be a pro at. "Wolves are just better versions of people. At least, unlike ghouls or vampires, we are still alive." I knew this wasn't an attack because he didn't know what I was, but I took offense anyway.

"At least vampires don't feel the need to burst free of their own skin once a month to go chase rabbits in the moonlight."

He raised the corner of his lip, hinting at a smile but not fulfilling it. "You're going to prove to be a complicated addition to the pack." Then he sighed. "I am not Lucas's bodyguard. Dominick *is* his personal protection, yes. I am Lucas's second-in-command. His lieutenant."

I didn't need to be a part of the werewolf pack to know this was a position of great importance. I also wasn't stupid enough to ignore how I'd insulted him with my naivety.

"Desmond, I'm sorry. If I've offended you or your position in any way, it was unintentional."

He seemed to relax a little.

"You have my word that any future insults will be much more personalized and meant only for you," I added with a smile so wide he could not mistake my joking for malice. For reasons I couldn't name, I didn't want Desmond to dislike me.

How strange this night had become.

He moved from the doorway to let me enter the study. "I hope you're given the opportunity to insult me again in the future. From whatever position you'd like."

As he left the room I couldn't help suspecting he was flirting with me.

I placed two phone calls before leaving the study. The first was to Keaty, who answered after only two rings. I spared the details of how I'd come to be in Lucas's hotel room, but informed him I was having a *tête-à-tête* with the werewolf king. He understood the gravity of the situation and told me if I didn't call him before daybreak he would personally dethrone Lucas. In a permanent way.

The second call was to my friend Mercedes Castilla. *Detective* Mercedes Castilla, she often reminded me. Cedes was one of the few cops who actually believed in the things that went bump in the night. She was smart enough not to share her liberal beliefs with those around her, but it gave her the unique advantage of calling a spade a spade. Or in this case, a fang a fang.

It also meant that she understood when human justice would not prevail and would call me to do the dirty work.

Mercedes did not fully understand what I was. Explaining my genetic makeup to her would have confused and terrified her, so I had bided my time until I knew which of my monsters was the lesser of two evils to her. For the first year of our friendship I had only let on that I was a bounty hunter who was, perhaps, not altogether human. After a rogue slaying in which I'd needed her help covering up some evidence, she called me to say, "Bloodsuckers had it coming. They weren't even alive anyway. Good for you."

Crestfallen that the forward-thinking Mercedes was so willing to pigeonhole an entire race, I begrudgingly confessed the *other* half of my bloodline to her instead. The half I was not so willing to embrace.

While she didn't get how one could be half werewolf, and I could do little to better explain it, she accepted my lycanthrope half was a part of me, like her Puerto Rican half was of her. It also meant I had to grin and bear it when she lambasted vampires as being mindless killing machines, which she was a fan of doing. She was especially displeased about the constant nocturnal presence of Holden in my life, after I'd admitted that he was my undead liaison.

Telling her I was in Lucas Rain's penthouse, however, thrilled her to no end.

"Ohmigod, is he as handsome as they say? As rich? Have you slept with him? Are you going to? What does he look like?" This string of tween-girl gibberish was coming from a hardened detective who was, as much as she loathed acknowledging it, several years past her dreaded thirtieth birthday. This year would be her fourth twenty-ninth birthday, meaning she'd been twenty-nine as long as I'd known her.

And she thought vampires had issues.

"Cedes, breathe please. If I was here to get it on with Lucas Rain, I don't think I'd be on the phone with you." It was at this unfortunate moment Desmond chose to return. A smile tilted the corner of his lips, and it vanished as quickly when I said, "I just want you to know that if I don't call you by dawn, something bad has happened to me. Tell the police to look here first."

"Bad? What do you mean? Secret, what's going on?" If I was willing to involve the police, she knew it had to be serious. "Did you call Mr. Keats about this?"

I assured her everything was fine and I was only being careful, but something else had already occurred to her.

"Before you hang up, do you happen to know anything about a girl who got attacked in Central Park tonight? She's in a holding cell right now because they're worried she's lost her shit. She keeps saying something about how a skinny blonde woman rescued her from a monster. She's using the V word."

I tensed. I wasn't worried the police would believe the girl's story about a vampire assailant. Other people had made the same claim, and nothing ever came of it. But she wasn't the first to mention a vigilante blonde saving the day. At the police stations across New York, a less-than-pleasant nickname had begun circling.

"The boys are saying it's Buffy to the rescue again." She was teasing me, well aware this would get my goat. I gripped the handset so tightly the strong plastic began to buckle.

Desmond must have felt my agitation because he stepped farther into the room, keeping a watchful eye on me in case my annoyance manifested itself more aggressively. I raised my hand to let him know I was fine.

"Cedes, can you please do what I've asked?"

"Was Mr. Keats worried?"

"Keaty never worries unless I worry. I'm not worried, I'm just being smart."

She chuckled. "You need to learn to enjoy life more. You're at a billionaire's *penthouse* and you're calling to check in. You don't need a chaperone. Get your freak on!"

I sighed.

"Okay, okay. But call me if tonight turns into a weekend getaway to Ibiza."

It would be unwise for me to tell her that she would never see me in the daylight, let alone roasting on the sand with the UV worshipers, and I couldn't tell her that a trip to Ibiza's sun-kissed beaches would kill me. That was if the werewolf king didn't kill me first.

I hung up the phone and faced Desmond. "I'm ready."

Boy was that the biggest lie I'd told all night.

Chapter Eight

I followed Desmond up a circular staircase, allowing my mind to drift as we moved towards the upper floors of Lucas's lair. In the well-tailored dark denim jeans Desmond was wearing, I could appreciate what was on display, and the rear view was definitely worth a good long look. He walked with the self-assured grace that all lycanthropes, myself included, possessed. I often took my own agility for granted but always marveled at it in others. His every step was light and easy; his feet barely touched the stairs. By the time we reached the top step I had almost forgotten what awaited me, I was so mesmerized by his butt.

But there it was, a long hall leading to a large set of open double doors made of a dark wood. The instant I saw them they made me uneasy, because I associated doors like that with bad news. Within I could see the flickering light of a fire. My heart caught in my throat, my mind racing with questions.

"Go ahead," said Desmond, and then he left me.

I walked down the corridor with halting, heavy footsteps. I was fighting the urge to draw my gun as I entered the room with more than a little apprehension. Calling it a *master* bedroom would have been such an understatement that I bypassed the word in lieu of more spectacular synonyms. The room was palatial. Its size eclipsed that of my whole apartment, which wasn't actually a big accomplishment given that I rented a one-bedroom basement suite.

An Olympic swimming pool could fit in there with space to spare. The scope of the suite was overwhelming, and it was just one room of many.

"Welcome," Lucas greeted me, rising from a large, beautiful and expensive-looking mahogany desk. The room contained a sitting area in front of the fire with two couches, as well as a bed that looked wider than king size, but instead of ushering me to either of them he motioned to the leather chair across from his desk. We both sat.

He wanted me to know this was all business, and I appreciated that. Given the reaction he'd caused in my groin earlier, any place where lying down was an option was not somewhere I wanted to have our conversation.

I didn't trust myself around him when it came to my more primal urges. I was at obvious risk to giving in to him. I just had to look at him and I knew he could easily have any woman he wanted. He had the charming allure of a man who was accustomed to getting his way.

In spite of all his wealth and responsibility, Lucas Rain had an easy, unaffected smile. His eyes were the color I imagined a noontime sky in August to be—bright, blue and almost cheekily cheerful. If he was burdened by his money, his title or any of life's daily troubles, it didn't show.

He had undone a majority of the buttons on his crisp white shirt and was flashing his well-toned chest and abs at me as if it was the most normal way possible to greet a guest.

Werewolves were more at ease with nudity than humans. It must have had something to do with being naked with others at least once a month. Nudity was the sort of pleasure I tended to enjoy alone in bed. Sleeping. Alone. Did I mention the alone part? I didn't mind being naked, but I also didn't make it a habit of getting naked around company.

Vampires, regardless of how European a lot of them were in other respects, were more socially proper in situations like these. Although they would boast in private about their centuries of sexual prowess, none would dream of greeting a visitor in such a state of undress. Well, okay, that was a lie. I knew at least one very powerful, old vampire who often wore less than Lucas currently was.

I wished I were more accustomed to seeing men naked because then the beautiful smooth expanse of his chest wouldn't be so distracting. As it was I felt the tug of desire building and had to look down at my hands. I swear to God I was blushing. How pathetic. The taste of cinnamon was on my lips again, with no reason to be there.

He got down to business. "I'm going to share some things with you tonight I expect you're not really willing to hear. I apologize in advance if any of it is difficult to understand. You're the first of our kind I've met in a long time who is so unaware of the ways of our people. I'll try to help you through this the best I can."

I stared at him. It sounded like the buildup to a cult initiation. If he was expecting that by my coming here I would agree to join his pack straight off, I had to put that dream out of his head before we began.

"Look, Lucas. Mr. Rain. Your Furry Highness, or whatever it is I'm supposed to call you—"

"For you, Lucas will be more than acceptable."

For me? Why was I so special? I momentarily lost my train of thought. "Lucas, then. I appreciate that you thought I was in such need of an education you kidnapped me off the street." At this, he smiled. "But I want you to know I only agreed to come here because you left me no other option, not because I want to join your hunting party. I'm not really a team player. And in case you missed it, I'm not the biggest fan of *being* what I am."

He was quiet for a moment, folding his hands with their gloriously long fingers across his taut stomach. My indignation faded as my mind wandered with thoughts of the places and things those fingers could find and do. I blushed more.

"Before you saw me on the street tonight you felt me, is that correct?" he asked.

After a moment's hesitation I ventured, "Yes."

"You felt me specifically, not Dominick or Desmond. When you saw me for the first time you understood right away it was me you felt?"

I thought about it before answering, then again said, "Yes."

"What did I taste like?"

"Cinnamon." The answer was too quick. I hadn't thought, I just opened my mouth and out it came. My eyes widened with the horror of what I'd said. Admitting that he'd left such a sweet taste in my mouth felt too intimate to share.

He smiled, leaning forward against his desk, resting his chin on his folded hands. "Very good."

That was a *good* thing?

"How much do you know about how werewolves are made? How we are governed? Do you know anything of our history?"

"I know my mother was a werewolf. I don't know much else. I was raised by my *grandmere*, my mother's mother, and she usually changed the subject when I asked about any of it. My mother abandoned me after birth, and I guess *Grandmere* blamed it on the wolves."

This was only partially true.

I was leaving out gaping holes in the story, like how my

57

werewolf mother had been seven months pregnant with me when the human man she loved—my father—was bitten and turned by a vampire. A rogue vampire no less. In the blind bloodlust of his newborn state, my father hunted down the most vulnerable prey he knew of. He'd almost drained her before some flicker of humanity sparked in him and he gave her his blood, which she'd fed on to survive. The blood had saved her life and mine. Because she was a werewolf and already had one blood-borne infection, she was protected against being turned into a vampire.

I was not so lucky.

The blood she had taken from him infected my developing body. As I understood it, because I carried her lycanthropy, half of me was already predestined for a life among the furry. But there was also a human piece of me that was destroyed and rebuilt into something new. Had I not been part werewolf, it's likely the vampire blood would have killed me in her womb. Instead I was spared death, but when I was born it became apparent to my mother that there was something wrong with me.

Without fully grasping what had happened to her baby, she brought me to her mother's house and left me there with a note telling my *grandmere* the whole story and explaining that the pack would never allow an abomination like me to be raised as one of their own.

Grandmere had studied biology and genetics in her youth and was the one who recognized the impossible combination of commingling supernatural infections that had led to my unusual existence.

Explaining all this to Lucas was out of the question.

"Do you know how werewolves are made?" he asked.

"Get bit. Turn furry. Seems pretty basic to me." I'd always

thought the process of turning someone into a werewolf was grossly uncivilized in comparison to the perilous tightrope act of siring a vampire. Spitting your infected saliva into someone's open wound and then waiting until a full moon lacked the mystique and the marvel of self-control vampires exhibited in suppressing their own hunger and sacrificing their own life essence to create a new being.

"Not exactly." I could tell the brute simplicity of my answer aggravated him.

He started again, slower, as if speaking to a child. "You're aware that lycanthropy acts like a virus. It can only be transferred via a wound that exposes the blood of the recipient to either the blood or saliva of the host."

"Uh-huh." Any idiot who'd seen a wolf-man movie knew that. I was blonde, not retarded.

"But what most of the world at large, at least those who believe in our kind, are unaware of is that not everyone can catch lycanthropy."

"Excuse me?" This was news to me.

"No one understood it at first. The consensus among our kind for a long time was that those who were bit but did not turn were simply not worthy of the gift."

"Gift? You think of lycanthropy as a gift?"

"Yes, and I hope that in time and with deeper understanding so will you. Especially given your...unique position."

I flinched. Did he know? He couldn't. Yet what did he mean by my *unique position*? I was too afraid to ask and he was already continuing.

"We once believed that those not strong enough to join the pack were unable to integrate the virus into their system.

Usually, due to the wounds that led to the initial infection, those who did not turn succumbed and passed on. Over time, though, as medicine and science advanced, werewolves and other lycanthropes who worked in genetic fields began doing private research into the matter. About forty years ago they discovered it was a genetic anomaly that determined whether or not a recipient, once bitten, would inherit the gift."

"Wait. So you're saying genetics determines whether or not someone becomes a werewolf rather than carrion?"

He cringed. "These days werewolf attacks on humans are almost nonexistent. Almost all new wolves are either turned in accidents or as part of the cycle."

"The *what*?"

Lucas let his head fall back and looked up at the ceiling, his teeth grinding together while he regrouped his patience. "You understand that I am King?"

"Yes. I understand that about a quarter of the werewolf population in this country considers you to be their unelected leader."

"Good. Then this should be easy to follow. The genetic trait that allows our kind to carry the gift is hereditary, so over the years, before we knew the scientific reason for it, entire families contracted lycanthropy. Across the country many of the families that carried the virus generation after generation became acknowledged leaders. The knowledge they had of the ways and rules of the generations before them was invaluable. First they were alphas—pack rulers—but as more people contracted lycanthropy the need for regulation and laws grew as well. Four families in particular rose to almost mythic positions. They came to be considered royalty among the wolves because of their wisdom, fairness and long histories."

This was a lot to take in. I had never known werewolf

society to be so structured.

"Within those families and almost all families that carry the gift, it has become a rite of passage to initiate the new young into the pack. It is *very* rare indeed for a child to be born with active lycanthropy, even if both her parents are wolves. If you were never bitten, as you claim, then something very traumatic must have occurred during your mother's pregnancy. Something that caused her circulatory system to share the virus with you rather than block it out as is normally the case. Because of that, you caught the virus years before you were meant to. It makes you very special."

"You have no idea." Sarcasm seeped from every word.

"Oh, but I do. You are special for many reasons, more than you can imagine yourself. You see, among our kind there is a tradition known as The Awakening. When a child reaches the cusp of adulthood, they are presented with a choice—continue to live a normal human life or accept the inheritance of our forefathers and join the pack."

"I don't understa—" Then it clicked. "You mean you wait until they're old enough to weigh the options, and then you bite them if they say yes?"

"If they accept, then they are initiated, yes. This is how the old families have done it for centuries. It's how we carry on our legacy. It's also how we've stayed so well hidden from the public. Keeping ourselves a secret is the most important rule we live by."

"If this is all so secret, why share it with me? I was never 'Awakened'." I made little air quotes around the word. "Never initiated. I'm a freak by your standards, aren't I?"

"Far from it. A born wolf is the thing of legend among our people. You would not be shunned, but revered. That is not, however, the reason I've brought you here."

"It's not?" Why the hell was I here, then? I was gaining new respect for the werewolves, but the whole situation had me missing the political simplicity of the vampire world.

"I didn't know until you told me you'd never been bitten that you were more special than I had first thought. I brought you here because of what happened on the street, and when you told me your name downstairs it confirmed something I suspected from the first moment we met."

Ah, here was my chance for some enlightenment about their earlier discussion. "You and Desmond said something about my last name being interesting. How it made sense. The last time I told a werewolf my name he got really uneasy about it, but never explained why. I'm starting to think there's more to it than just a name, unless werewolves in general hate *Bullitt*. But I'm betting that's not it."

"While there are better Steve McQueen movies, I'm partial to *Papillon* myself, it's not the reason your name makes wolves uncomfortable. I mentioned that mine is not the only family with a royal legacy."

"Yes."

"In the East the wolves are ruled by my family, the Rains. In the West they are ruled by the Cavanaughs. The O'Shaughnessy family rules the North, and do you know who the kings and queens of the South are?"

"Obviously not." His little spiel was leaving me with a pretty good idea, though, and I didn't like it.

"The royal family of the American South is the McQueens."

Chapter Nine

"What the hell are you saying?"

"You are royalty. Your grandfather... His name was Elmore McQueen, wasn't it?"

Grandmere most often referred to her now-deceased husband as *that awful man*, or more colorful Creole phrases as I grew old enough to appreciate them, but his Christian name had been Elmore. I nodded to confirm his assumption.

"Then your mother must have been either Savannah or Mercy McQueen."

"Mercy." I cast my eyes downward. Her name brought bile to the back of my throat and the sting of tears to my eyes. In spite of the large fire, I now felt cold.

"Your mother must have met with a lot of difficulty for settling with a human man."

"My *grandmere* approved of it, and I don't think Elmore really said much about it since he'd married a human girl himself. At least before he left her with three children to raise so he could bed down with a new bitch." I let my tears turn to a fog of rage. I needed to push the sadness away if I was going to be able to look at him. The insult had a different sting to wolves. If there was a werewolf equivalent to the c-word, *bitch* was it. Lucas flinched to hear me say it.

A long pause filled the room, broken only by the sound of a log settling in the fire. We stared at each other across the desk, and I ached to touch him so badly my fingers tingled, but I couldn't understand why.

"Regardless of your grandfather's second family and your mother's abandonment, you are by blood and birthright a princess to the Southern line. It all became clear to me when I learned your name."

"What became clear? At the moment nothing is clear at all here." I waved a hand around my head to illustrate my continued confusion.

"Let me try to phrase this in a way that won't frighten you."

"That's probably not the best way to start."

At least he wasn't speaking to me like I was a child anymore.

"The thing is, while we have genetic explanations to make things easier for us to understand, there is still something primal and magical about being a werewolf. I was Awakened when I was thirteen, and it was like having a light turned on. I was roused from a sensory-debilitating sleep that day, and I haven't looked back since. I see and hear better, I taste things more purely, and my sense of smell...well, you know how our noses work."

In truth, since I was born this way I really had no frame of reference for what human senses were. I also had difficulty telling my werewolf and vampire abilities apart as some of them were so similar. I just nodded.

"As wolves, we feel things on a deeper level than humans. Connections between members of the pack are richer and more intense than anything human couples could understand. Within the old families in particular these bonds are almost unbreakable. We have come to understand it as a unique matchmaking system, one that has been built into our bodies."

Now I was not only confused, I was getting nervous about the look in his eyes and the heat in his voice. As he spoke, something inside of me began to uncoil and rise in response to his words. I was drawn to the edge of my seat as though the thing within me wanted to carry me right across the desk.

"I don't understand." My breath was raspy and confessional.

"Among the oldest werewolf families there is a phenomenon known as soul-bonding. It is a measure by which the kings of our race pick those who they can truly trust. There is a call put out by the beasts inside of us that is meant for a select few to hear. It was how I chose Desmond to be my second. His wolf answered the call of my own when we were still very young, before either of us had even been turned. The call is the reason you felt me on that patio tonight. You knew who I was without having ever seen my face. It is why you could taste me in your mouth without having ever had trace of me there before." The last part was said in the tone of a familiar lover, and I licked my lips.

This felt powerfully intimate, and I was leaning up against the desk now, as was he, the both of us swaying towards each other like trees whose branches longed to intertwine.

"You're saying we're soul mates?" As much as I would have liked to smother that last word with sarcasm, my voice would not allow me to.

"Soul-bonded," he corrected. "I'm saying your body wouldn't have reacted to the simple touch of anyone else in the world as it did to mine."

"Y-you felt that?"

"The more you embrace what you are rather than shutting it out, you will find you can also feel what I'm feeling when we are together. I have been told it can make certain situations incredibly fulfilling." His tone left no doubt of what he meant.

I shivered but felt the urge to remove my jacket. Leaving it on meant I could get up and walk out of the room at any moment, and my life would stay the same. I could ignore all this new information and choose to go on living my pseudo-normal, pedestrian existence. That life, mind you, was filled with executing vampires and other ghouls, and regular meetings with both a vampire liaison and my more frightening partner. My life was anything but typical. I could not deny that it was also very lonely.

If I removed the jacket, it meant I wanted to stay with him longer. To stay meant I had to accept some of the things Lucas was telling me. I would be allowing this man, a relative stranger, into my life simply because he told me we were meant to find each other. That we were destined by a mistake of birth and blood-borne pathogens to be together. Staying or leaving should have been such a simple choice.

But as Lucas rose from his chair, his eyes never leaving mine, I knew nothing would ever be simple again. I couldn't deny the effect he had on me and I no longer wanted to. I'd been spending so much time with the dead I had forgotten what it felt like to be with the living. I'd ignored my own physical desires to such an extent I often forgot I had them.

He rounded the desk and moved towards me, and I was painfully aware that not only did I have the same desires of any sane woman looking at a man this beautiful, I had urges equal to those of an animal who had just discovered her mate.

He stood next to my chair and spun the seat so it turned to face him instead of the desk. My knees grazed his shins. He looked down at me, one hand on either armrest of the chair, and my breath caught in my throat. Heat radiated off us both, making the air between us stuffy.

I believed in vampires and werewolves, so why not believe in soul mates?

I took off my jacket.

Chapter Ten

I had told Mercedes that I hadn't come here with the intention of bedding Lucas. I reminded myself of this over and over as he ran his beautiful, long fingers down my bare arms. Everywhere his skin touched mine it felt like fireworks exploding under the surface. I'd been with enough men in the past to consider myself a woman of average experience, but this was unlike anything I'd ever known could exist. I worried, perhaps foolishly, that I might be brought to the edge of orgasm while sitting in a chair as he grazed my arms.

He smiled as if he'd heard my thoughts. Maybe he had? I had no idea how this soul-bonding thing worked. His hands cupped my face, one trailing fingers through the loose curls of the ponytail on my shoulder as the other traced my jawbone with one thumb. He lifted a handful of my hair to his nose and smelled it.

His thumb stopped moving, breath catching in his throat and eyes growing wide.

"You smell like death."

My whole body coiled like a compressed spring, ready to burst from my seat and away from him. I was terrified that he could tell what I was. If he could read my thoughts, the guilty rambling occurring there at the moment wasn't helping my case any.

Then I remembered my gun. I remembered Henry Davies. I had a perfectly reasonable and somewhat honest explanation for smelling the way I did.

"I'm a bounty hunter." I wrapped my fingers around his wrists and pulled his hands away from my face. After the next bit of my speech I didn't think he'd still want to jump my bones. "Most of the work I do is for the local vampire council, executing rogue vampires."

He took a step back, and I noticed for the first time he was barefoot. He tilted his head to the side as I spoke, a habit that made me picture him in his furrier form.

"Vampires aren't the only thing I hunt. I also do private contracts." I searched his eyes, hoping he understood the meaning of the statement.

"You've killed werewolves."

He was a smart one, at least. It pleased me to know werewolf matchmaking hadn't saddled me with an idiot for a soul mate. Although I was certain this confession period was going to make him less fond of me.

"Yes."

"Were they killed because of someone's hatred towards our kind? Some private vendetta?" His expression shone with rage.

I shook my head solemnly. I didn't want to tell him the next part. "I've killed two werewolves. The first was the pet of a rogue vampire, and he tried to rip my throat out when I came for his master."

Lucas sat on the edge of his desk. It did not escape my notice that he was now outside my reach. "And the second?"

"The second..." I looked around the room, like I might find the right words floating overhead. "I told you earlier I'd met another werewolf who knew my name. That's part of what makes the second kill so difficult to explain. I want your word that what I tell you doesn't leave this room and you won't retaliate." I could tell he didn't like it, but he nodded, his mouth fixed in a grim line. "My second werewolf kill came at the request of an alpha in Albany."

"Marcus?" Lucas was taken aback at this. I, for my part, was shocked he immediately knew the man who had hired me, though I suppose any good king would know who worked under him.

"Yes. He came to me because a new wolf within his territory wasn't abiding by the laws. Your laws. This wolf was using his newfound strength in human form to force himself on local women. Marcus was worried it would bring your people to the attention of local authorities. When the boy attacked Marcus's human daughter, things came to a head."

"Oh God." Lucas looked away from me. "Why didn't he come to me? We have ways to handle these things."

"Marcus didn't ask me to kill the boy, I need to make that clear. He asked if I could use my *unique* abilities to make the boy leave the Albany territory. The boy sealed his own fate by thinking he could best me in a fight."

The tension in his jaw and the furrow of his brow told me my news had hit him harder than either of us had anticipated. I had been killing my own kind for six years. I'd seen the look of betrayal and grim determination on the faces of the council as they placed death warrants in my hands and sent me to kill their brothers. I was a suitable means to an unhappy end, but everything was handled in a businesslike fashion.

When Marcus asked me to deal with the werewolf in his territory causing such trouble, I didn't see it as a business arrangement. I had only seen the father of a ruined daughter. Not until now, looking at the despair on Lucas's face, did I realize the death of one wolf could impact the entire pack. That the king himself would mourn the death of one. Or that Marcus's vendetta would hurt him as well.

Neither of us said anything for a long time. Muted tones of early sunrise had started to filter in under the blinds, and I was thankful they were closed. The sunlight wouldn't kill me the way it did a real vampire, but it would be difficult to explain why I had third-degree burns rather than a tan.

In spite of the drawn curtain I felt a familiar sense of panic. I needed to go home. I had to get back to the safety of my basement apartment, with its thick gloomy shades, where daylight never penetrated.

"Lucas..."

He raised a hand to silence me. I could imagine what he was thinking. I had the right smell, the right taste and the right name. For all intents and purposes the only thing keeping me from being his perfect soul mate was my own stubbornness. Then I dropped the bomb—*Oh by the way, dear, I kill monsters.*

"Do you remember his name?"

"Pardon?"

He fixed a hard glare on me, his sorrow overcome by anger, and his voice quivered with an uneasy mixture of the two emotions. "The boy you killed." It sounded so filthy the way he said it. "Do you remember his name?"

The way he asked it told me a lot rested on my response, possibly my very life. I might not be human—I was paid to be a killer and I could be more of a monster than those I killed—but I was not without a soul.

"William Reilly. His name was William Reilly."

Lucas nodded. He must have already known the name. I didn't remember the names of everyone I'd ever killed, but I remembered the ones I felt bad about.

This had gone from precoital intensity to feeling like after-school detention in the span of seconds. I for one was ready to be done with it.

"If there's nothing else, I mean, if you're done with me..." I inclined my head towards the door.

"For tonight." He kept watching me as I rose to leave. "I'm sure this has been more than enough for one evening." His phrasing implied he hadn't totally written me off, but I was going to get out of here while I was still in his good graces.

"Secret?" He apparently wasn't quite done.

I stopped halfway to the door, turning to look at him. He padded towards me, and I admired the flashes of bare stomach his open shirt granted me. As he approached, once more the taste of him filled my mouth. I wondered what I tasted like to him. I sighed in spite of myself when he placed one large hand on each of my shoulders.

His blue eyes were so close to mine I saw a circle of gold around each iris, and I imagined again what he must look like as a wolf. I felt the urge to eliminate the distance between our mouths.

Only in the company of supernatural beings is it normal for moods to shift so suddenly.

"I forgive you," he said.

It wasn't forgiveness he was giving me as much as a royal pardon. The proud part of me wanted to tell him to stuff it, but the Secret who was accustomed to the rigid formality of the vampire council nodded with mute acceptance. He'd needed to do it, and as his subordinate I needed to accept.

I turned again to leave, but he held on to me, his hands stronger than I'd anticipated.

"You will have dinner with me. Tomorrow night." He looked at the watch on his wrist and laughed, then corrected himself. "Tonight."

"Umm." It hadn't sounded like a request, but the look on his face told me he was still expecting a response. "Okay?"

The coming night was shaping up to be as relaxing as the previous one had been. Meet with Holden and the Tribunal. Explain to Keaty about my new puppy fan club. Deflect Mercedes's questions about Lucas. Have dinner with my billionaire soul mate in his penthouse.

Yup. Sounded like a totally average Thursday.

Chapter Eleven

The sky was dark gray and overcast when I got outside. I still needed to find a cab in a hurry, but at least I didn't have to hide the smell of my own burning flesh. While the driver shuttled me westward to Hell's Kitchen, I called Keaty to tell him I was fine and asked him to call Mercedes for me.

Safe in my apartment, I staggered into my bedroom, which was a promising pitch black. Because of the danger posed by even one errant beam of sunlight, I couldn't trust curtains to protect me during the day, so I'd bricked the small window closed, telling my landlord it was to keep burglars out.

Collapsing onto my bed, overwhelmed by the daytime exhaustion that rendered vampires dead during daylight hours, I fell asleep straight away.

I was back in Central Park.

I knew the moon was full without seeing it, because I had the unsettling sensation something liquid and hot was burning under my skin, looking for a way out.

I heard a low growl but could not pinpoint its location. It came at me from every direction and never from the same place twice. Through the thick fog of trees the growl was coming closer, and I realized it was not one growl but many.

A pack.

My instinct was to run, and who was I to ignore my fight-or-flight reaction? My feet moved to escape but became tangled in the long dress I hadn't noticed I was wearing. The only dresses I owned were short and low cut, designed to titillate vampiric thirst. The garment I now found myself in had layer upon layer of rustling tulle skirts cinched together at my waist in a breathlessly tight corseted top.

A wedding dress.

I tried not to focus on why I was wearing a wedding gown in the woods. Instead I turned my attention back to the pack of growling wolves I could hear but not see. My heart pounded against my sternum as I grabbed armfuls of fabric and started to run through the woods. The smells and surroundings became more and more familiar as I fled. Branches pulled at my hair and dress, and I realized I was following the same path I'd chased Henry Davies down the night before. It meant the Great Lawn couldn't be far. My dress caught a low exposed root, and I toppled to the ground, cutting my hands on rocks and sticks as I braced my fall. I got to my feet and picked up the hem, where I accidentally smeared blood from my palms on the perfect white.

I felt guilty for ruining the fabric.

The wolves drew nearer as I began to run again. This time I made it to the lawn, where I could see someone who looked human standing alone on the empty field. I tore across the grass with all the speed I could muster. I didn't think anyone could save me from the monsters at my heels, but just seeing another living person felt like finding salvation. As I got closer I saw that my mysterious savior was Lucas.

He wore a tuxedo cut so well James Bond would be jealous, and smiled when he looked at me.

I reached him in a panic, out of breath, collapsing in a

foamy white pile at his feet with my arms covering my head, braced for the gnarling teeth of wolves to rip me apart.

But there were no teeth. The growls, too, were gone. The only sound in the night was a soft chuckle from above. I looked over my shoulder and confirmed that there were no wolves in the field.

I felt a strong hand on my shoulder and was soothed by it.

"Lucas, you must think I'm an idiot."

The hand squeezed and the chuckle became a low, menacing laugh.

"Secret McQueen, *mon chéri*, I believe you are no man's fool."

The voice didn't belong to Lucas, but I knew it all the same. It was pure Cajun loathing. A bone-jarring shudder rolled over me, and my head was slow to respond to my body's fearful commands, but I finally looked up.

Just in time to see Alexandre Peyton, vampire in my wolf's clothing, lunge for my throat.

Chapter Twelve

Waking up wasn't as dramatic as the dream. I didn't scream or sit bolt upright; I merely awoke with my breath stuck in my throat and a layer of icy sweat on my skin.

It was dusk again and my senses were at their prime. It didn't take long for my eyes to adjust to the gloom, and it took less time still for me to recognize someone else was in the room with me. He was sitting in the plush armchair next to my bedroom door.

My pulse leaped a little, which made me feel stupid because once I recognized who it was I knew he'd heard the change in my heart rate.

Though neither of us needed the light to see, I turned on the lamp next to my bed and propped myself up on a pillow.

"You're out awfully early, aren't you?"

Holden frowned, which was not all that unusual since he rarely smiled. "As you must have anticipated, the Tribunal would like to have a word with you."

"Oh, Holden. I think you and I both know they will have a lot more than *a* word for me."

I noticed he wasn't looking directly at me, and when I looked down I understood why. During my fitful sleep I had stripped off all my clothing, and the only thing covering me was a thin floral sheet.

"Oh." With the sheet still pulled close, I grabbed my silk robe from the foot of my bed and slipped it on, cinching it around the waist. "Better?"

The wolf part of me wasn't shy about nudity. But I respected that Holden came from another time. An era in which having a conversation with a lady who was naked would be unheard of.

I also knew well enough that he wasn't always this shy when it came to being up close and personal with women. It made me wonder if me putting on the robe protected his sensibilities or subdued his desires.

"Thank you." He turned to face me.

I wanted to point out that while he'd been watching me sleep the sheet hadn't been pulled up at all, but I let him have the illusion of his modesty.

"They want to see me right away?" The clock on my nightstand told me it was seven thirty. The growl in my belly told me I needed to eat before I went.

He must have heard it because he gave me a slight nod.

"They requested I bring you at nightfall. Do you have food or will I need to take you to the Oracle?"

I looked at the clock. I had enough food in my fridge, but given the events of the last twenty-four hours I wouldn't mind a visit with Calliope.

Calliope, better known among the paranormal community as the Oracle, was the fifth and final person who knew what I was. She owned a large mansion in the middle of the city, which existed on a plain outside human reality. Only those of the supernatural persuasion walking into the Starbucks on West 52nd and 8th in genuine need of help would find their way into

Calliope's home. She insisted the location was arbitrary, but I knew she had a sweet tooth for caramel macchiatos.

And the blood of male virgins.

Calliope was a true immortal. Vampires used the phrase *immortal* because they could not be killed by age, disease or random accidents the way humans could. But a stake to the heart, exposure to sunlight or, as I often demonstrated, a bullet to the brain could all kill them beyond revival.

Not Calliope. She was the daughter of a fairy queen and a god.

I had laughed in her face when she'd told me that the first time. She had politely reminded me most people would scoff at my parentage as well. Gods, she'd explained, at least in the Greek, Roman and Norse tradition, were not as divine as they'd have mortals believe.

There was a level of truth to most of the popular myths that came out of the polytheist religions. She told me that in the ancient years of Earth's history, true immortals were not as publicity shy as they became in later centuries. They used their power and influence to achieve a godlike status and began to believe they truly were as divine as humans believed them to be. This delusion of divinity led true immortals to use the word god to describe themselves long after polytheistic religions fell out of popularity.

Fairies, on the other hand, prized their privacy. They existed in a separate reality, only deigning to cross over when something caught their curiosity or they found babies or women to steal.

Fairies never stole men.

Calliope's mansion was a border station between human reality and the realms of fairies and immortals. It was a fascinating and terrifying place to visit. Calliope herself was part of the appeal. She had once lived among the mortals, using her particular gift for being the center of attention to its full advantage.

She had taken over the life of a small-town girl who had died without anyone's notice, and reinvented herself as the ultimate blonde-bombshell glamour icon. When she'd had her fill, she left the body without further explanation. It remains one of the greatest mysterious Hollywood deaths.

To see Calliope now, she looked exactly like the icon once painted by Andy Warhol, only her hair was no longer short and blonde but restored to a long, smoky black. Her figure was bodacious, her pout still as alluring. I did a double take whenever I saw her.

Looking the way she did it was strange to hear her tell me what my future held. True to her title, Calliope was an oracle and could see the future of those around her. Her visions were often vague, but she was always right.

She also dealt in blood. Food for vampires without fangs or those still too young to hunt without being dangerous. The council sent all sanctioned newborns to live in Calliope's care until they could be trained to behave.

I went to her because although I had fangs, I could not bring myself to feed off humans, willing or otherwise. It would cross too many lines for me. I could eat human food and enjoyed coffee and the occasional alcoholic beverage, but they did nothing for me nutritionally. I liked caffeine and booze because the acceleration of my metabolism meant I felt their effects almost instantly, and they burned off too fast for any lingering unpleasantness afterward. The downside was, going on a bender after a bad week was pretty much impossible because I was never drunk longer than an hour, and I couldn't blame my bad judgment on impaired sensibilities. And while I could eat, I still needed blood. In a pinch I could eat blue-rare steak, or even raw meat, as they appeased the hunger of my wolf. But both monsters craved blood, so that was the only thing that really satisfied me.

I had my fridge well stocked, which meant we didn't need to see Calliope tonight no matter how badly I wanted to.

"I've got some O neg in the fridge. You want?"

Holden grimaced. He'd attempted, and failed, to understand my aversion to drinking from the source.

"No, thank you." He rose from the chair and straightened his blazer. He tried hard to look as if he belonged in this century, and for the most part he succeeded. He was tall and slim with a narrow waist and a well-built upper body. From what he'd told me of his youth, he'd come from a poor farming community. His build came from hours of hard labor with little to eat, making him strong and lean.

His face was chiseled with a strong jaw and lips suited for pouting. His hair and eyes were both dark brown, and depending on the mood of the evening often passed for black. The eyes defined classic vampire—deep, focused and brooding. His mouth usually set itself in a pensive angelic frown with his brow furrowed. Holden's hair tended to be a bit too long, owing to the uncut look favored by farmhands two hundred years earlier, which he had opted to maintain. He liked to be consistent about that rather than trying to keep with the changing styles of the decades. Tonight he had pushed it behind his ears and gelled it enough to keep it there. It stopped just shy of the collar of his jacket.

It was no wonder Holden didn't have any difficulty feeding. Human women found him irresistible. His looks combined with the vampire gift to enthrall humans, better known as the thrall, meant he could feed on as many women, or men for that matter, as he pleased.

Under the charcoal blazer he wore a plain white shirt that in spite of simplicity looked to be on the offensive side of expensive. The ensemble was completed with a pair of dark indigo jeans and black shoes polished to a high shine. It hadn't come as a surprise to me when I learned Holden had once been an editor-at-large for *GQ* magazine.

All immortals, true or otherwise, feel the pull of the spotlight from time to time, even though their secretive nature compels them to stay away from it.

"I'll fix your drink while you dress."

I took my wardrobe cues from his ensemble, dressing in dark jeans, black ballet flats and a purple top embellished with Victorian touches of lace at the neck and buttons down the back. Through the lace, the top peek-a-booed an alarming amount of cleavage, which was impressive given how little I had to begin with.

I pulled my hair into a high ponytail and wore no makeup. Unless I was working I never wore any. Drinking blood flushed my cheeks and gave my lips a natural stain. Anything extra made me feel ridiculous.

From the kitchen my microwave beeped and I smiled to my reflection in the mirror. Ever the gentleman, Holden had thoughtfully heated my blood for me.

My light steps were noiseless as I walked down the carpeted hallway and met him in my tiny kitchen. When I'd visited the basement suite for the first time, the landlord kept apologizing for how small the space was, fearing the lack of cooking space would be a deal breaker for a lady such as myself. He must have thought I looked more domestic than I really was.

I had been more swayed by the old brick fireplace facade

and the bedroom big enough for a queen-sized bed. Both were luxuries for an apartment in my painfully limited budget.

Now with both Holden and I in a room too small for a two-seat table, the dining space was feeling extra cramped.

He handed me the warm blood in a wineglass, which was a touch too elegant for me, but I appreciated the gesture. As I drank the blood I tried not to meet his eyes. It unnerved me for anyone else to observe the pleasure I took in this, because it was like admitting that I enjoyed a part of what I was. Acknowledging that I liked drinking blood, that I relished the sweet, coppery tang of it or that I took pride in how much sexier I felt afterward, would mean that I embraced being a vampire at least on that small level. It would mean that one of the monsters was winning. But using that same logic one could argue that the wolf would win if I gave into Lucas's advances and let myself become his mate.

I assured myself the wolf could only win if I transformed at the full moon. I'd been able to fight that change for almost my entire twenty-two years, and I wasn't about to give in now.

Holden was watching me drink with great interest. He'd only seen me drink in close quarters once or twice before, and it had an unusual effect on him. His own hunger, coupled with a kind of desire, was laid bare in his eyes. Though his facial expression didn't change, I noticed a telltale darkening in his irises. With each swallow his eyes deepened from a milk-chocolate brown to an oily black, and a glimmer of intention filled them. His jaw was tense and stiff as I took the last gulp, eyes transfixed on my neck.

"*Holden.*"

The hunger vanished and he was himself again. "I apologize. In spite of your connection to us it is sometimes difficult for me to ignore that you are—"

"Alive?"

That was a bit cut and dry for his taste, but he nodded anyway. With the blood coursing through me, I felt very alive at that moment. Strong and self-assured.

"Well, let's hope that's still true when this night is over."

Chapter Thirteen

Meeting with the vampire council on their turf would never be something I'd get used to. When they delivered warrants to me it tended to be either via Holden, or another messenger would meet Keaty and me at our office. Perhaps I had difficulty adjusting to the council because I usually only visited them when I was in some kind of serious trouble.

I had killed other vampires without sanction. I had not yet killed one who hadn't had it coming, though. Every vampire who met their fate at my hands was a rogue themselves or consorting with one. Or, as was often the case, they happened to be making a dive for my throat.

Holden led me up the stairs of a beautiful old building that had once been a grand train station. I could see it for what it was, but the building was enchanted to appear to humans passing by as if it were in a decrepit state of disrepair. Even the most daring mortal would feel a terrible sense of dread upon venturing too close. Anyone who got past the front steps after those warnings was fair game as far as the vampires were concerned.

There was a very good reason vampires had been able to keep themselves a secret for millennia. They knew all the tricks and techniques to make it appear to the outside world as if they did not exist. Over thousands of years they had honed those techniques into an impenetrable web of secrecy. This was why they dealt with rogues in such a grave way. One rogue with a grandiose sense of self-worth who believed vampires should rule over humans rather than hide from them was all it took to put their entire society at risk.

It was one of the few things vampires and werewolves had in common, actually. They understood all too well that to be exposed to the scrutiny of the human public would be a disaster beyond repair. Society in general had enough trouble turning on the news every day to witness the atrocities committed by other humans. If people knew supernatural beings existed, it would result in mass genocide. Humans would always outnumber those in the paranormal community, and no amount of good PR or damage control could spin monsters in a positive light.

Even though I wasn't human I felt the foreboding aura of the enchantment upon reaching the building's top step. I tried not to let it show in my face, but any color I had from drinking the blood had long since drained away.

"Perhaps it won't be as bad as you fear," Holden suggested. Optimism didn't suit vampires.

"Yeah, sure. And maybe you and I will go to the beach and get some color this weekend."

"*Touché.*" Holden knew as little as I did about what to expect this evening. As a warden he was on a need-to-know basis about the goings-on of the Tribunal, and all he needed to know tonight was they wanted to see me.

We entered the building. Its busyness surprised me given the illusion of quiet from the outside. Vampires bustled about, but none of them noticed us, or at least they pretended not to. We walked through the wide-open hall that could easily be mistaken for any busy office building or bank on Wall Street.

Workers carried paperwork in manila folders and moved in the clipped, efficient manner of honeybees. These wardens monitored all other vampire activity in the country. The agents in this building, be they wardens or sentries, would be sent across North America to deal with any number of problems or complaints that arose. While most rogue activity occurred close to home, they had sent me to different states on occasion. What I wouldn't have given right then to be in Iowa or Oregon, or home across the Northern border with my *grandmere.* Of course none of those options were a remote possibility, so I followed Holden across the parting sea of fangs.

The building was resplendent on the inside. Much like Grand Central Terminal, which had been constructed as a sister building to it long before, it had vaulted ceilings with windows now covered over so no sunlight could sneak in. To make up for the missing light, panels of green and gold glass were inset in each window and illuminated from behind with soft yellow incandescence, giving the whole room a midday warmth. A short staircase descended into the main atrium, where the floors were tiled in black and white marble, creating the dizzying illusion of a giant chessboard. Brass posts divided the room along a far wall. Where in Grand Central they would have been ticket booths, here they designated private offices. The brass was polished to a high shine, winking false sunshine back at me.

Apart from the offices, there was a main common area that filled the majority of the atrium, where a maze of old wooden desks spread out like a corporate ocean. Everything that made a successful business operation was at work here, from the office drones to the executives. Vampires had long ago learned that organization made any good civilization run smoothly, and theirs was no exception. Phones rang at low tones throughout the room, and wardens spoke in hushed voices. Holden and I walked past all the lovely, modern edifices until we arrived at an innocent-looking door marked *Private*. My hands trembled as I pushed it open and stepped into the darkness.

The Tribunal was old school about their lair. It was reminiscent of a dungeon or medieval war room. Everything was kept dark with only torches on the walls to provide light, and a dampness that never went away clung to the air. We walked down many flights of slick stone stairs, traveling ever farther into the bowels of the city, before we reached our final destination.

I was thankful for the added gift of my supernatural agility, otherwise I would have slipped down the stairs on my ass.

We arrived at a set of double doors, the ones that often figured into my nightmares and were the reason I had a distrust of any that looked even remotely like them. Beyond them were the three vampires who held my life in their hands. This time Holden stood back to allow me to enter first. He could not follow me beyond this point. Only the Tribunal and a select handful of tribal elders were allowed to enter the decision room. The only other time you were allowed in was if you were up for discussion.

I sucked in a deep breath that tasted like mold and pushed open the doors, stepping into complete darkness.

"Welcome, Miss McQueen." The voice was a soft, airy soprano with a delicate touch of a French accent making *miss* sound like *mees*. The greeting came from the only female member of the Tribunal, Daria. "We are pleased you could meet with us on such short notice."

Their formality always unnerved me. If they were planning to kill me, did they need to be so pleasant about it?

"Tribunal Leader Daria, the pleasure is mine. I am at your council's service." I had to stop myself from saying *beck and call.* I knew the steps to this particular dance all too well. My eyes had adjusted to the total black of the room, and I could see her lovely face above me.

The Tribunal sat on a raised platform in handcrafted chairs that were too elaborately detailed to be thought of as anything other than thrones. Daria wasn't the actual leader, so she was seated to the left of center. To the right was a man I'd never get used to looking at. Juan Carlos might be the most alarming creature—human or vampire—I'd ever encountered. His hair was the color of pure jet and cut shorter now in an attempt to look more modern, but it maintained some of its wild curl. No matter what efforts he made, Juan Carlos could never blend in with humanity.

Once a Spanish Conquistador, he had sustained a variety of irreparable scars during his human life. One old injury had split his upper lip, and it had healed into a menacing sneer, which curled up towards his cheek and showed one of his formidable fangs. The rest of his face remained beautiful, but it was hard to notice when you could sense his desire to devour you.

"Tribunal Leader Juan Carlos." I couldn't bring myself to tell him it was a pleasure to see him because, to be honest, he terrified me.

"Secret McQueen." My name sounded as if it were on par with the likes of Mussolini or Stalin. His sneer deepened.

I turned my attention to the true leader of the Tribunal and all my terror slipped away. It wasn't that I found him any less terrifying nor was he less powerful, but part of his gift was to put anyone around him at ease.

Where Juan Carlos's beauty was an afterthought to his monstrous snarl, anyone who looked upon Sig could not help but fall in love. I did not know Sig's full name, but I knew he was Finnish, or claimed to be now. He was older than Finland, and from what he'd said the country he was born in no longer existed. He'd never claimed to be a Viking as so many other Scandinavian vampires did. If anyone asked, he rolled his eyes and called the plunder and pillage of the Vikings *that Norwegian occupation.*

Sig was also the only member of the Tribunal who I saw to any great extent outside of these meetings. While Daria would occasionally show me some general interest, in the way one might visit a puppy or kitten they were thinking of adopting, Sig seemed to consider me more than a pet project. It was he who decided my targets and he who had assigned Holden to be my liaison.

I often suspected Sig knew exactly what I was because of the interest he showed me, but I had never been brave enough to ask.

Instead of allowing myself to be intimidated by Juan Carlos, I looked into Sig's eyes. He smiled at me, the kind of smile given by a man who knows what he wants. Between Daria with her perfect straight blonde hair, who was wearing an original Coco Chanel evening suit, and fearsome Juan Carlos in his tailored Armani suit, Sig looked out of place.

He was splayed back in his throne, fingers laced together across his taut stomach, and his long, long legs stretched straight out in front of him. He wore nothing but a pair of brown leather pants. His feet, like his chest, were bare. His skin was so pale it practically glowed in the dark, and his blond hair light enough it was only a shade more golden than white. Daria's, by comparison, looked almost brown. Like Juan Carlos, he'd cut it short to help him blend, but had bangs brushed across his forehead which had grown too long and were beginning to obscure his ice-blue eyes.

"My dear Secret." He sounded pleased I was there. Juan Carlos made a noise of disgust. He had never approved of the interest Sig showed me. "As Daria has said, we are very glad you could join us this evening."

I bowed my head, enjoying the cadence of the accent that remained in his deep, marvelous voice. I understood, deep down, the effect Sig had on me was not entirely real. While most of their psychic gifts helped enhance the thrall over humans and did not impact other vampires, Sig was a rare case. His persuasive charm was the reason he was in a position of such power. Other vampires trusted him.

I hoped that my trust in him would not be the death of me.

Sig's smile faded when he moved the meeting along. "You know the reason we've brought you here this evening, yes?"

"I made an unsanctioned kill in Central Park last night." I knew better than to explain the details of the slaying without being asked. If they wanted to know something specific, they bring it up. Any other information did not matter.

When you've been asking people questions for centuries, you learn to get the information you need with as little effort possible.

"Do you feel the slaying was justified?" Daria probed.

"I do."

"Were you in immediate danger?"

"Myself and a human female."

"Yes, a human female who was allowed to escape. She is telling the human media all about a woman who saved her from a *vampire*," Juan Carlos interjected.

Sig raised a hand to silence him but remained reclined in the chair.

"I don't believe the media found her very credible," I offered.

"Need we reminisce over the subway incident, Secret? The media had plenty of sources that seemed very reliable indeed in that situation." Sig spoke the words Juan Carlos was surely thinking.

I stiffened, a chill sweeping through my whole body. If Sig was bringing up the subway-platform incident, I was in serious trouble. It was in my best interests to remain silent until one of them asked me another question.

"Holden has given us some of the details of your report, and we confess we are curious." This from Daria, who had her porcelain-doll face rested on a manicured hand. "Please tell us the story."

I relayed, with as much brevity as possible, the events of the previous evening, leading up to the slaying of Henry Davies and the bite marks I associated with Alexandre Peyton.

The Tribunal, even Juan Carlos, looked pensive upon completion of the story. Sig sat upright in his chair, crossing his leg at the knee and leaning forward as though to get a better view of me.

"You are absolutely certain?"

"I am."

"We discussed what to do about this matter prior to your arrival, and as is often the case with you, Miss McQueen, the Tribunal was not unanimous. Both Daria and I agreed we will overlook the events of last night. Juan Carlos, as usual, wanted to eat you."

My gaze darted to Juan Carlos and I paled. The three of them began to laugh heartily, as though Sig had just given the punch line to the funniest joke they'd ever heard. I would never understand vampire humor.

Sig continued, "In light of the development you've presented, however, we will need to alter the arrangement somewhat."

"Meaning?" I knew this would sound indignant, and sure enough, anger flared in Juan Carlos's eyes. Sig gave me a shrewd smile.

"We have a new job for you, my delicate flower." He and Daria exchanged a loaded glance. "You will find Peyton and you will bring him to us."

To the Tribunal, this directive meant bringing them a steaming pile of ashes that had once been one of their undead brethren. Bounty hunter may have been my official title, but none of the targets they'd sent me after returned in anything larger than a coffee tin. They expected me to kill one of the nastiest and most challenging vampires I'd ever faced? Did they honestly think he'd be like any other target? Killing Alexandre Peyton was going to be next to impossible.

"Oh, and, Secret?" Sig interrupted my internal diatribe.

"Yes?"

"We would very much like him alive."

Chapter Fourteen

Before I could register what the Tribunal had told me, I was back in the hall with Holden and we were winding our way back up the mile of wet stairs, my feet making the motions automatically. He must have seen the shock on my face or the stumbling way in which I was taking the steps, because his unwavering frown had deepened to a look of concern.

"Secret? What did they say?"

"Peyton," I muttered, and stopped walking to lean my face against the cold wall. The rough brick against my cheek lured me back to reality.

"I don't understand."

"They want me to bring them Peyton. Alive."

His eyebrows shot up and I almost chuckled. It's so rare for a vampire to be surprised by anything, it's a treat to be the cause of one of those alarmed looks. Unfortunately I couldn't really enjoy it at the moment.

"Why didn't they just kill you?"

This time I *did* chuckle. "And get their precious hands dirty? Isn't it so much easier to send me to a certain death? This way they aren't the ones who killed me, but they don't have to deal with me anymore. Juan Carlos will be thrilled."

"Yes." We began to walk again. If you're looking for comfort, a vampire didn't have the best shoulder to lean on. The only kind they could offer was a cold one. "But certainly Sig doesn't want to see you die?"

Both Holden and I were aware of Sig's special interest in me, though neither of us knew what it meant, and Holden *really* didn't like it.

"Maybe he thinks I can do it." I wasn't sure I believed that, but it was a pleasant thought, so I held on to it.

We didn't speak again until we were back out on the dark New York sidewalk.

"Do you think you're capable of bringing him in?" A nice vote of confidence from my vampire liaison. But he had reason to be doubtful. I certainly was.

I sighed. "I don't know."

We had arrived at a busier street and were standing in front of an upscale SoHo boutique shop. It became difficult to continue our conversation with all the modelesque Barbies carrying out their shopping bags turning to get an eyeful of Holden. I also had somewhere to be, and as luck would have it we were only a few blocks from Rain Hotel.

"Can we discuss this later? You need to, uh, feed?" I nodded at a healthy-looking brunette who had walked past us and none-too-subtly winked at him. "And I kind of have a date." I paused. "Maybe. I think?"

"With the wolf king?"

I drew to an abrupt halt in the middle of the sidewalk, causing a meaty wall of a man to walk directly into me. He skirted around me muttering something about *stupid women*, but my focus was on Holden, fire blazing in my eyes.

"You were following me last night?"

"After I got your message. Yes."

"And you didn't think to, oh, I don't know, help me out when some strangers threw me into a car?"

"They were only werewolves. You were fine," he said dismissively.

I snarled at him, and it was so inhuman a sound there was no doubt at all which half of me made the noise. Holden stiffened and took a step back. His face flashed with unease to hear something so animal coming from me.

"I'm not your bodyguard, I'm your liaison, and sometimes I think I am your friend. But don't pretend you wouldn't have been angry with me for rescuing you like some misguided white knight. As you are very fond of pointing out, you are perfectly capable of taking care of yourself. I did not believe you to be in any danger and I was right." He gestured to me to indicate I was alive and as well as could be expected.

We glared at each other in the middle of the sidewalk. Just another Manhattan lovers' spat as far as the people filtering around us could tell. If I had a dollar for every time Holden and I looked like a dysfunctional couple, I could buy a nicer apartment.

After a long silence and obviously feeling he needed to speak first, he tested the waters with an apology. "I'm sorry?" It sounded more like a question, and I doubted his sincerity.

"Fine. Whatever." I waved a hand at him and walked away in the direction of the hotel.

He did not follow.

I was glad I'd worn something at least moderately dressy to meet the Tribunal, but I regretted not bringing a purse, heels or anything a normal girl would have with her for a date. Would Lucas think I was slighting him because I was wearing jeans and flats?

I reminded myself that when he'd first met me I had been significantly more dressed down than this. I also decided that if we really were soul mates, he was going to have to accept that I wasn't the ball-gown-and-stiletto kind of princess he might have had in mind.

A princess, me. Man that was a lot to wrap my head around. Maybe I should have told Holden I was werewolf royalty. Hell, maybe I should have told the council. *Oh hey, Sig, I know you want to send me to certain death, but just so you know, I'm half werewolf and a princess at that, so show a little respect.*

Right, that would go over brilliantly.

I took the opportunity of being alone to have a good look at the lobby of Lucas's hotel. From the main foyer two hallways extended in either direction, one leading to a world-class spa, the other to a sushi restaurant. In the center of the lobby was an intricately sculpted crystal chandelier that looked to weigh several hundred pounds. To each side of it was a matching smoky-quartz chandelier, and beyond those, towards the end of each hallway, obsidian mates rounded out the tri-colored set.

The interior walls glistened like they were alive, lights from the chandeliers dancing on the moving surface of the cascading waterfalls that poured over black marble. At equal intervals down each hall were pedestals with large bouquets of exotic, fragrant flowers. In a corner, hidden from view, someone was playing a harp. Everything was alluring to the senses, and I breathed it all in, letting it soothe my rattled nerves before I walked up to the front desk.

My new Zen state was obliterated when I caught the attention of the desk clerk and asked to visit Mr. Rain in the penthouse. He took one look at my jeans and ponytail and his frown set so deep *Grandmere* would have warned him a bird might poop on his lip.

"And *who* are you?" he inquired, condescension dripping from every word. He smelled like a were but not a wolf. There was something weaselly about him in both scent and demeanor.

What to say? That I was Lucas's date, his soul mate? Dinner?

"My name is Secret McQueen."

He rolled his eyes before he picked up the phone next to him and pushed a large red button. The name on his tag said Melvin, and I planned to remember it. Just like I knew he'd remember mine after tonight.

"There is a woman here *claiming* she's here to see Mr. Rain. She says her name is Secret McQueen, and—" He listened for a beat and then all the color seeped from his face. "Yes, Mr. Alvarez. My sincerest apologies. Yes, I will be certain everyone at the desk is made aware of that." He hung up the phone and angled his head in my direction in a sort of half bow. "Miss McQueen, I apologize for my rudeness. You must understand a great number of women attempt to visit with Mr. Rain without his invitation."

"You're just doing your job, Melvin. I'm sure this will never happen again."

"No. Absolutely not." He slid a black card across the desk to me. "This is an elevator-access pass. Mr. Alvarez is on his way down to meet you, and he will help you program a code so you can reach the penthouse directly."

I wasn't sure who Mr. Alvarez was, but I took the card from Melvin's trembling hand. "Thanks."

The elevator dinged behind me, and I turned to see Desmond exit through the doors. He was wearing a soft gray sweater and some *very* well-fitting khaki trousers. His dark hair was a tousled mess, and he did not look pleased to be in the hotel lobby at nine in the evening on a Thursday. Especially not with me.

"Secret," he said with a nod. So we were on a first-name basis, then.

"Desmond."

"I trust Melvin gave you an access card?"

"He did."

"And I trust he has made his apologies?" He shot a meaningful look to the man at the counter. Melvin cowered and I couldn't blame him. Desmond was an intimidating force, even with bedhead.

"Yes, he did."

"Good. Follow me."

In the elevator he swiped my card and had me enter a four-digit code of my choice. He explained the card was now mine to keep and would grant me direct access to the penthouse floors. I knew he wasn't thrilled about this, because he also added that my card and code could be canceled at any time.

In the quiet that followed, there was an unmistakable change in the atmosphere of the elevator. Not to say he became more relaxed, or I less wary, but the sensation of unfamiliar tang bursting in my mouth had returned. At first I thought it was because we were getting closer to Lucas, but then it dawned on me that this flavor was altogether different. Instead of the heady cinnamon taste Lucas left in my mouth, I now experienced something brighter, more citrusy.

Lime. It was the puckering flavor of limes, and the only place it could be coming from was Desmond. I didn't know what to make of it and didn't know how to ask him what it meant, so instead I changed the subject. "What kind of were is the desk clerk?"

"Ah, you smelled him." This seemed to put him in a better mood. "Melvin is a wereferret."

I let out a loud, short cough of a laugh. "He's a *werret!*"

Desmond found this at least passingly funny, because he chuckled, a low, pleasant sound. "Yes, I suppose that would be one way to put it."

We arrived at the penthouse more relaxed than we'd been on the main floor.

"He's expecting you." Desmond nodded to the spiral staircase. He gave me a gentle nudge, and I couldn't help but notice how his hand lingered on my back a little longer than was necessary. I turned to see if there was any explanation on his face, but he was already walking away.

The subtle burst of lime diminished with his every step.

Was this a werewolf thing, leaving tastes in each other's mouths? No, that was impossible. I'd been around other weres and never tasted a single one before Lucas passed me on the street last night.

It was more than a little disconcerting. Lucas had told me it was an indication of the soul-bond I shared with him, so why could I taste Desmond? Surely it wasn't possible to be soul-bonded to two people. And why did I suddenly want a margarita?

It seemed like every moment spent with Lucas and the wolves was going to present me with a dozen new questions.

Chapter Fifteen

I found Lucas in the same place I'd left him the night before. Now, instead of bare feet and jeans, he wore the most exquisitely tailored pair of gray trousers, the same color as the sweater Desmond was wearing. I stopped to admire the way they hugged his bottom. I wanted to shake the hand of the tailor who made pants for the men of this pack. Had I been a were-feline of some variety, I would have purred. As it was I let out a fluttery sigh.

He turned to look at me with a bright, toothy smile. He had on a long-sleeved black shirt with a slight V-neck that gave me a teasing glance of his smooth chest.

"I thought you might not come."

"Well, I figured I'd see what you're like when you're not kidnapping me." I couldn't help but smile back. "Um." I looked over my shoulder, worried Desmond might suddenly appear behind me, which he did not. "Why does Desmond taste like spring break?"

From his place next to the massive fireplace, Lucas's brows knit together, but his reaction was slow and the shock seemed forced. Interesting.

"You can taste Desmond? The way you taste me?"

"Yes. Only you taste like Christmas. Cinnamon. Desmond tastes like lime." I licked the back of my teeth, chasing the lingering flavor.

Lucas furrowed his brow. "How peculiar."

Something about the way he said it further proved to me he wasn't all that surprised by my revelation.

"What does it mean?"

His face relaxed and he waved a hand in the air as if swatting my question away.

"It's irrelevant. Just a quirk, nothing to be concerned about." He stepped away from the fire and came to stand in front of me. He put his large hands on my waist, and I allowed him to do it. It didn't escape my attention that he was hiding something, but I also didn't think the situation with Desmond warranted over-thinking at the moment.

"You look lovely." He was all smiles once again.

"So do you." The taste of Desmond was gone, and now I felt as if I'd been sucking on cinnamon hearts. I wondered if being around Lucas would give me fresher breath.

I also wondered, if I kissed him would I find out what I tasted like to him? Could I lap up my own flavor by tracing my tongue over his? Before I finished thinking it, I rose on my tiptoes and closed the gap between us. I hadn't been consciously aware I'd made the decision to kiss him, but suddenly his lips were against mine.

He must have been surprised by the abruptness of my action, because for a second he hesitated.

I began to pull away, my cheeks flushing red as I muttered, "Sor—"

I didn't get a chance to say more than the first syllable before he drew me back into a tight embrace, holding me fast. I was literally swept off my feet as he kissed me—he was so tall my toes weren't even touching the hardwood. If I'd been human, the force of his grip would have threatened to squeeze the air out of my lungs.

But I was not that fragile, so I draped my arms over his shoulders and parted my lips to answer the imploring request of his tongue.

His hands slid lower, cupping my ass and lifting me fully off the ground. I responded with uncharacteristic eagerness by snaking my legs around his torso. The kiss deepened. His mouth slanted over mine and his tongue brushed along my own, the hypersensitivity making my head swim. He moved his hands, squeezing my thighs firmly, and my flurry of demanding kisses pleaded for him to continue. The inside of his mouth tasted sugared, the sweetness of something like cotton candy or toasted marshmallow. That something was me.

A coiled tightness stirred in the pit of my stomach like stiff fingers coming out of a fist. It twisted, unfurled and grew larger. Liquid heat spread through my body, starting in my guts and filling me until it prickled along every inch of my skin and threatened to spill over. I moaned into his open mouth.

Lucas's skin under my hands and against my body grew equally hot. Everywhere there was skin-to-skin contact I was sure we must be burning each other. He growled, but it had nothing to do with fear.

Where my legs were wrapped around him, even through layers of clothing, I could tell he was prepared to take this much further. It made me wonder what the heat of him would feel like inside me.

Gasping for air, I ripped away from the kiss, my palms pressed against his chest. My legs were locked around his waist, and I was so shaky I let him hold me there. I took deep, ragged breaths, unable to meet his eyes. He hadn't given up on his pursuit of pleasure, and his mouth was against my neck, kissing, licking... I pulled him closer, and we almost fell back into our heated embrace when his teeth grazed my neck and closed down on the tender skin.

My pulse raced and I could feel a familiar elongating and sharpening of my fangs. My vampire side was wide awake tonight, and we were on the verge of bringing it out into the world. His jaws tightened just a little. I made a small animal noise and abruptly came back to my senses.

"Stop." There was no hesitation or uncertainty in my voice. My eyes were on his neck, and it wasn't sex at the forefront of my mind. That is until I saw the big bed and realized that my libido was not as willing to stop as my common sense. My urges were divided between devouring him and letting myself be consumed in other ways.

He responded immediately to the command, releasing my neck and lowering me to the floor, where I staggered.

"Wow," I said once I'd caught my breath and my fangs had retracted. "Just...wow."

He licked his lips, and I noticed his eyes were no longer solid blue. The ring of gold around his pupil had doubled in size, and they did not look human. "That was unexpected," he said, his voice husky.

As the wolf inside me returned to her dormant state, my skin cooled to its normal temperature. The flush in his coloring faded as well. Never before had both of the monsters inside me woken at the same time. The wolf had wanted to mate, the vampire had wanted to feed, and both desires had felt like one and the same.

"I'm sorry." Heat flooded back, this time only to my cheeks.

"Why on earth are you sorry?"

"That was *so* inappropriate."

He laughed. It was an exuberant, booming, honest laugh. He put an arm around me, and I flinched before realizing there was no sexual overtone in the gesture.

"If you hadn't done it, I would have. Just being in the same room with you makes me dizzy."

"Me too." Though *dizzy* should have been substituted with *horny as sin*, his phrasing seemed more polite.

"You'll get used to it."

"I hope not."

"This is how it's meant to be with us. Is there any better evidence that we're supposed to be together?"

"I don't know if an irresistible urge to shred your clothing and molest you is really evidence that we're soul mates." I managed a smile. I still wasn't so certain we were destined to be together, but I couldn't deny there was something remarkable about our physical connection.

"I hope this hasn't put you off having dinner with me."

"No." I bit my lip in contemplation. "But if you don't mind, I'd really like to eat out." I faced the door so as to not look at the bed.

"Don't trust me?"

"I don't trust *me*." That was the God's honest truth. "I think it'll be a lot safer with a table between us."

I got a mental flash of him pushing me down on a large dinner table and ripping my shirt apart with his bare hands. I turned my face away.

"If you think that'll help." I knew from the chuckle in his voice he'd been thinking the exact same thing.

Chapter Sixteen

The elevator ride down was silent and tense. I was wedged between Lucas and Desmond, and it created a bizarre flavor combination in my mouth. On Desmond's right was the blond werewolf who, at only an inch or so taller than me, looked short compared to the other two who were each over six feet. With all the oddness of meeting with Lucas, I'd forgotten his name, but he reintroduced himself as Dominick. He had the carefree smile and glinting eyes of a troublemaker. I liked him instantly.

Desmond had returned to being surly and stared at the elevator doors with a steadfast scowl. From this angle I could see his hair was longer in the front than in the back, and he constantly pushed it out of his eyes. Against my better judgment, I decided the way his eyes squinted in frustration was actually rather attractive. What the hell was wrong with me?

As I contemplated Desmond's profile, Lucas took my hand in his. I didn't shake free in spite of the fact that I normally loathed any kind of public display of affection.

It felt odd for me to allow it since we weren't really a couple. But I couldn't deny I liked the way my hand felt when it was wrapped inside his large, warm palm.

We exited, not in the lobby but one of the basement levels. The parking garage was lit by scattered fluorescent bulbs, giving it a cold, blue hue in sharp contrast to the warm light of the hotel. The shadows were abundant, providing plenty of ideal locations for people and things to hide themselves. I found myself wishing I'd gone home to get my gun after meeting the Tribunal. Weapons of any kind were forbidden inside the council headquarters. I thought it was unnecessary to ban them considering the vampires themselves basically *were* weapons.

A familiar black town car was waiting for us. This time Dominick held a door open for me to enter on my own, rather than me being forced into the back. I sat far enough from Lucas for another person to fit between us, looking out the tinted window as we drove into the light-dappled night.

There was a feeling of unease in my gut that had nothing to do with my wolf or what had happened between Lucas and me upstairs. I kept seeing Sig's face and hearing him say, *we would very much like him alive.*

I'd like to go on a Dominican cruise and get a tan. I'd like to not wrestle with a monster who threatened to burst out of my skin every full moon. Both of those things seemed about as likely to happen as my capturing Alexandre Peyton alive.

It also brought back the nagging question, what was Peyton doing here in the first place? His vendetta against me was secondary to whatever brought him to New York. Keaty and I had established that last night during our post mortem.

Peyton wouldn't have crawled out from whatever rock he'd been hiding under unless he had a damn good reason. He was old and smart, and you don't get to that age without a strong survival instinct. For him to emerge as a known rogue in the city where three of the most powerful vampires in the Eastern U.S. ruled, though? It was more than just bold, it was a declaration of war.

But I still didn't know why that war was starting. I also wanted to know how high *Kill Secret McQueen* was on his to-do list.

Lucas, ever the gentleman, allowed me to stew on this as we drove, until he placed his hand on my thigh. "Secret?"

I turned my unfocused gaze from the window to look at him.

"We're here."

Here had brought us to the front of a club known as the Chameleon Lounge. Depending on what circles you ran with, it was either the most famous nightspot in New York or you had never heard of it.

The Chameleon Lounge was run by weres for weres, and like the council headquarters, humans did not see the club in its true form. To human eyes the building had become so run down even bums refused to sleep there. To a were, it was a posh and lavish place to see and be seen.

If Lucas was bringing me here on our first date, he must not be too ashamed to be spotted in public with me, because by tomorrow morning every wolf in Manhattan would know we'd been here together.

I got nervous. I'd honestly been expecting us to dine at a nice human restaurant. One of the places he wined and dined models and movie stars to the delight of local gossip seekers. Part of me had hoped to be called a mysterious blonde in the weekend edition of Page Six.

This was serious. Not just to our relationship, either. This meant I was about to flaunt my newly discovered royal status to a room of full-blooded weres. Inside the club the name Secret probably didn't hold water, but the name McQueen did. And Lucas Rain walking in with a McQueen implied something huge.

Everyone in the club knew more about soul-bonding than I did, so while I might not understand it, the deeper meaning would be evident to them.

I avoided spending time with werewolves because, just as Lucas had the night before, they could smell death on me. He had accepted it as a side effect of my chosen career, but what conclusion would a room of strangers draw? And how long would it be before someone pieced together my association with the vampires and the scent lingering on me?

I gave this courtship until my first full moon with him. When I didn't change into a wolf, I had no doubt Lucas would be done with me.

There was no way this could work.

I grabbed his arm as he began to exit the car, and he gave me a quizzical look. His blue eyes gleamed in the interior car lights.

"Didn't you want to go somewhere else? Like Nobu or something like that?"

I knew sushi didn't appeal to either of us as wolves tended to crave more substantial meals, but I ate out so rarely—blood-bag takeout from Calliope's alternative-reality Starbucks didn't count—I said the first restaurant I could think of.

He smiled and patted my hand like I was a nervous child. The gesture was mildly condescending, but I doubted it was intended in that way.

"I know this must feel like I'm throwing you into the deep end right after your first lesson, but *trust me*"—he emphasized the last words by squeezing my hand—"this is the best way."

With my stomach planted in my shoes, I let him draw me out of the car. Dominick held the door open and gave me a conspiratorial smile. Though he was a wolf, and just as near in proximity to me as Lucas or Desmond had been, he left no taste in my mouth. It confirmed what I'd thought at the hotel. I didn't react to other werewolves the way I reacted to those two.

Desmond was waiting by the entrance doors, and when he opened them a wave of warmth and noise swept out into the cool spring evening. Holding my hand, Lucas passed through the opened doors and into the club.

For a few moments my dread kept me from breathing. My lung capacity was substantially greater than that of most girls my size and was the only thing that kept me from turning blue and passing out. One of the many benefits of not being human. I had to admit, in spite of my reservations and complaints about what I was, there were definite perks.

Sadly neither of those perks, vampire nor werewolf, could get me out of this situation.

The unique feeling of being near a fellow werewolf was amplified by the presence of so many being together in one room. The warm, comforting feel that made the beast inside me respond like she was home washed over me, and all the hairs on my body rose with a shudder. It was the most overwhelming and electric sensation I'd ever experienced—standing this close to so many who shared one half of my curious heritage. When I was with vampires there was a cool silence. Being among the wolves was like getting dropped into a nest of fur and live wires.

I wanted to rub my face against the tangible energy in the room.

I also really wanted to be wrapped around Lucas again. Hoo-boy he hadn't been kidding when he used that deep-end metaphor. I had begun running my hand up and down his arm and had to force myself to stop. I put my free hand in my pocket to keep it from shaking. What was happening to me? One day with the wolves and already my control was slipping. It scared me.

The din in the room quieted to dead silence and all eyes were on us.

A beautiful woman with dynamic, curly red hair strode up to us, wearing a skin-tight violet bandage dress that hugged her ample curves more dangerously than a mountain road. Her heels were six inches high, which made her calves look like they were sculpted by razors. In a dress that tight with heels that high, any other woman would be relegated to standing still and looking pretty.

This woman, with her audacious body, approached us in a manner that brought the word *slink* to mind. She moved with a grace that would make supermodels insane with jealousy.

"Lucas." Her soft, husky voice turned his name into a delicate purr.

Even I wanted to sleep with her. How could I hope to compare or compete with someone who looked like sex squeezed into human form? Lucas nodded to her and placed his arm possessively around my waist, pulling me in closer. The redhead had cunning green eyes with smoky purple makeup that made them smolder, and now they were focused on me.

"Genevieve," Lucas said, "this is Secret McQueen."

I wish I had a photo of the way her perfectly groomed brows shot up. I'd been right in expecting my name would carry weight. It was nice that it had a different meaning here than it did in a vampire bar.

Genevieve eyed me incredulously, then a smile twitched across her red lips.

"Has the wolf king found himself a queen?" The casual, almost teasing manner in which she addressed Lucas was a definite sign she was not a wolf, and therefore not under the thumb of his leadership.

I did not smile back. She made me uneasy in a way I

111

couldn't quite put my finger on, especially when she was looking me up and down like a new menu item. Maybe I didn't need to worry about her taking Lucas after all. I didn't like how she said *queen* either. There was nothing special about her tone, but the word alone gave me a chill. The only queenly title I ever wanted was the one already attached to my last name.

The attention of every wolf in the room was glued on us, awaiting Lucas's answer to her question.

"Secret and I are soul-bonded," he announced. The official way in which he said it made it seem like it should be followed by *you may now kiss the bride*. A murmur spread through the room. "She is a McQueen and has a rightful place as a pack leader. However, as we have only just begun to *date*, calling her the new queen is a little premature." He chuckled, and the wolves politely laughed with him.

This was bizarre to say the least.

"I do expect all of you under my rule to treat her with the respect of a princess being courted by your king." There was no laughter in his tone, though being called a princess out loud certainly made *me* want to laugh. He was dead serious, and I knew every wolf in the room would respect his wishes.

He looked back to an expectant Genevieve. "The private room, please."

"Of course." She led us through the crowded room with such ease she did not so much as brush against anyone else.

I was willing to bet Genevieve always landed on her feet too.

Chapter Seventeen

For dinner we were served plate-sized, blue-rare Kobe beef steaks. They must have each cost more than what a family of five would spend on an average dinner, and they were bloody delicious. Literally. I sat with my eyes closed and sucked the juice from each thick bite of meat. It might not have been as satisfying as fresh, warm blood but my werewolf half was pleased with the offering.

I lingered in the soft red haze that followed a delicious meal, but deep in the pit of my gut my stomach growled for something more. For the time being I would have to ignore that urge and settle for an AB positive nightcap when I got home.

"That was the best steak I have *ever* eaten." I paused between each word for emphasis.

Lucas put down his napkin and chuckled. "That barely qualified as a steak. That was still a cow."

"Then it was the best cow I ever had."

Desmond, who sat at a table near the door with Dominick, smiled with none of his usual stiffness. The smile was so honest it surprised me, but it dimmed the moment he saw I was looking at him.

I couldn't understand why he hated me so much. Was my simplicity beneath what he expected from a princess or a queen? I didn't think the same constraints of propriety applied to werewolf royalty as they did to human royalty. Especially if one considered that the Queen Mum was unlikely to strip off all her clothing on a full moon and run wild with her grandsons. I'd known I was a princess less than twenty-four hours, and no one had really explained to me what the expectations were.

Growing up, the only thing my *grandmere* had demanded of me was survival. I'd been born in Southern Louisiana, which is about as south as you can get in the States without a peninsula. She had told Elmore only what she'd needed to about me in order to secure my protection from the pack. I don't know how much he knew, but it was enough that he respected our privacy and made others do the same. When he died, *Grandmere* knew she could no longer trust our safety so close to the pack. She left her three children, including her teenage son, and we fled the state. In later years, when she explained to me why we had been forced to move, she'd never told me anything about the finer points of how packs were run.

Knowing now that Elmore had been a king and had passed his crown to his barely legal son rather than his eldest daughter—Mercy, my mother—or his middle child, my aunt Savannah, I could see where the unrest would begin.

Grandmere had taken me first to South Carolina, where we remained until I was four, before deciding this was still too close for comfort. Then we left the United States altogether, to a place she felt would be outside pack law. I spent twelve years of my life in the southern part of the Canadian prairies, living on a fifteen-acre parcel in a large, old farmhouse.

One benefit of this upbringing was that unlike the boggy American South, the soil of the Canadian prairie allowed for houses to have real basements. It meant I had a room in which I could escape from the blistering sunlight every day. The land we owned provided me a place to run freely at night, burning off the pent-up energy someone of my unique genetic mix built up.

Raising me had been difficult for my *grandmere*. She was, however, uniquely capable of doing it. Being the mother of three children who had become wolves, and a powerful witch of some renown, she had knowledge others lacked. A human grandmother, feeding me formula or putting my crib in a light, airy room, would have made mistakes severe enough to kill just by doing what one was *supposed* to do with a baby.

Because my mother, upon abandoning me, had the foresight to leave a note explaining what had happened to me, *Grandmere* was able to brace herself for certain things. She'd already been aware that having any sort of silver near me would be disastrous, but that wasn't an unusual problem for her since she'd had three werewolves come of age in her home.

It was the vampire blood that made things tricky. It meant I could not be exposed to sunlight and also that I lapsed into daytime sleeps that resembled death, complete with lack of breathing or pulse. Then there was the added difficulty of my lycanthropy being activated in infancy. In my youth and adulthood I had intuitively learned how to suppress the need to change forms. I buried the ability so deep within myself I didn't know if it was possible anymore for me to shift. It was thanks to the calming effects of my vampire blood this suppression was feasible. As long as I was well fed I never felt the need to go furry.

As a baby that sort of control had been impossible.

My *grandmere* had a very memorable baby photo of me on the mantle of her fireplace. In a crib amid the shredded remains of a sun-yellow jumper and cloth diaper sits a puckish-looking wolf pup, tongue lolling happily, feet much too large for the body. It was only because of this photo I knew I had the ability to change at all. I did not remember the event happening and had no memory of how agonizing the pain must have been for me as a baby.

My *grandmere* said it only happened monthly from my first birthday up until my second. Before I turned one, the wolf inside was too small to force itself out. After that year the vampire in me learned how to put the wolf on a leash.

She knew, too, I needed blood to survive. Not many babies are given pig or goat's blood in a bottle. Needless to say my upbringing had been unique. None of it, though, had trained me on how to be a princess.

I had, until now, existed on the razor-thin edge of two worlds, part of both and accepted by neither. I didn't know how to switch from feeling unwanted to being considered among the ruling class.

"I'd say *penny for your thoughts*, but I think I'd have to offer you more than a million to get everything that just went through your head." Lucas was leaning across the table with a tentative smile on his lips, waiting for me to come back down to earth.

"Sorry." I was embarrassed to have been caught so lost in thought.

"Where'd you just go?"

"I was thinking about my *grandmere*." I waited for the confusion that accompanied my French nickname for her, which was something she had insisted upon from her Louisiana upbringing and also something to set her apart from my grandfather's Irish heritage.

"Is she...?" he hesitated.

"Oh! No. She's alive and well in Southern Manitoba, probably bitching to herself about the late melt and what it will mean for her peas." I grinned to myself, picturing her in rubber boots and rolled-up overalls, stomping around in the knee-deep snow and thinking of what type of spell she could use to speed up the melt.

Manitoban winters dragged on for longer than six months at a time, but once they were gone spring was a barely noticeable blip before summer swept in hot and humid. I missed it sometimes.

"She isn't like us, though?"

No one is like me, I couldn't help but think. "No, she's not a werewolf. She's a pretty tough witch, though." I didn't want to make it seem like she was a helpless old lady. Far from it. Now in her early sixties, she was more active than ever and showed no signs of slowing down.

"And she raised you alone?" He was a little surprised by it. Werewolves, from what I understood, were fans of the *it takes a village* approach to raising children. I'd told him yesterday my *grandmere* raised me, but I guess he'd assumed she had help.

"Because of, uh..." I tried to think of something that wasn't a lie but wouldn't tell him more than he needed to know, "...the in-utero trauma that caused my lycanthropy to activate early?" Okay, so I failed to mention that said trauma was my newborn vampire father force-feeding his tainted blood to my mother and turning me into a freakazoid hybrid. Not a lie, really, more of an omission. "My mother was young, only seventeen, and my father was...dead." Again, not a lie, just a twist on the truth. "She didn't know how to take care of a baby that wasn't just a baby. She probably couldn't have taken care of me if I *had* been normal. She left me with my grandmother and never looked back." All of that was one hundred percent truth.

Lucas's face was stony. Even Dominick and Desmond at their own table looked more solemn than they had before. To me this was history. It was like telling someone about Brutus betraying Caesar. Or about the collapse of the Roman Empire. History wasn't personal, it was just facts about the past. So, in spite of the fact that this history was *mine,* it no longer moved me.

Lucas took my hand, and with his other he touched the side of my face with a soft stroke of his fingers. His hand was hot against my skin, which didn't surprise me given the raised core temperature of all wolves. "You will never lack for a family again," he promised.

Sadly, I didn't think it was a promise he could keep.

Chapter Eighteen

The Chameleon Lounge was more than just a restaurant. While the main floor served as an upscale dining experience, the upper level, buffered by soundproof walls and floors, was a dance club.

Lucas guided me up a staircase at the back of the restaurant with our two D-named bodyguards following close behind us. At dinner, Lucas had mentioned Desmond would be keeping an eye on me, but he made it sound like the normal thing for a wolf-lieutenant to do for a displaced princess. I didn't pry further, but it seemed like Lucas was assigning me a bodyguard I didn't need or want.

When we reached the club it wasn't at all what I expected. The walls were decorated with sophisticated red-and-black damask wallpaper, and every flat surface looked like polished black marble, from the dance floor to the bar to the individual tables.

All the lights were dimmed and covered by beaded black shades. Both the bar and the DJ booth were on raised platforms, while all the booths were sunk into the floor so they had to be stepped down into.

I wondered if the marble floors posed any risk to dancing patrons, but the question was answered when a man grabbed his date's hand and spun her around three times as if she were a top. She stopped on a dime, dipped backwards and then into his arms again. Weres had enough natural grace to not fear a floor like this.

Genevieve knew how to create a unique and dynamic environment for her customers. As soon as I thought of her I remembered a question dinner had forced out of my mind.

Instead of asking Lucas, I dropped back to fall into step with Desmond. I figured since he'd known about Melvin the wereferret, he'd probably know about Genevieve as well.

"Desmond?" The taste of lime filled my mouth, and I had to swallow it before I could think of speaking again.

"Miss McQueen." His formality jarred me. I wondered if his coldness had something to do with his orders, if by being aloof he felt he was better equipped to protect Lucas and me. But Dominick didn't seem to have any problem being nice to me. Perhaps when this night was over, Desmond and I would have a little chat about what exactly his issue with me was.

I carried on with the question I'd been about to ask. "What is Genevieve? I know she's not a wolf, and she's definitely feline, but I can't quite pin her down."

A laugh punctuated the air behind us. "Ah, and here I thought the idea was that curiosity killed the cat. What, I wonder, did it do to the big bad wolf?" Genevieve was a few feet away, leaning against the bar with a glass of champagne in her hand. Of course it *would* be champagne, and I was willing to bet it was Cristal. Nothing but the best for our hostess. "You are concerned about what kind of cat I am?"

She sashayed over to us on her towering heels. With that added height and the fact I was in flats, she stood much taller than I and stared down at me with a lecherous smile that suited her quite well. Lucas had disappeared into the crowd with Dominick, leaving me alone in Desmond's company.

"I was just wondering. Not concerned. You don't smell like any other were feline I've encountered."

"And you don't smell like the average wolf," she pointed out, making me swallow hard. "Though I guess that has something to do with the company you keep." In that one sentence Genevieve proved she was a woman to be respected and feared. She knew much more about what happened in this city than I'd given her credit for. "I must say, standing next to this knight of yours, you two certainly smell alluring together, don't you?"

I grimaced. Impossible. There was no way for her to know what I could taste from Desmond. He gave me a wary look, as if thinking the same thing. It was the first time I considered what must be happening to Desmond whenever he came near me. If I was really bonded to him the same way I was bonded to Lucas, which still seemed impossible, then how much was he suffering by ignoring it?

I couldn't help but ask her, "What do we smell like?"

She grinned and tossed her hair over one shoulder. "Key lime pie. It's on your breath, and it's not on my menu."

My whole body went rigid, but I did not reply.

"To answer your original question, Miss McQueen, I am an ocelot. One of only a dozen in the country, and I am their queen."

I nodded, absorbing her species and rank. "Thank you."

"No, thank you. It has been some time since I've been in the presence of a soul that is double bonded. You are quite remarkable." She tipped her champagne flute at me. Before I could get any clarity on what she meant, she was looking past me. "I see your king has found an acquaintance. I will leave you now, but please drink whatever you'd like tonight. It's on me." And then she was gone.

Turning to Desmond, I noticed how hard-set his jaw was, his eyes looking anywhere but into mine. "Double bonded?"

"She shouldn't have said anything. It wasn't her place. Trouble-making cat." He glared in the direction she had gone.

"*Double* bonded?" I asked again, more insistent this time.

"Secret," he said, dropping the formality but none of the stern tone. "We can't discuss this here. Lucas will explain when—" His eyes located the spot Genevieve had been looking at moments earlier, and he was suddenly quiet. "Oh," was all he said. Then, "Are you a jealous woman?"

I couldn't ignore that. Even as I was saying, "No," I was turning to see what he was so distracted by. The *new acquaintance* Lucas had made was a willowy brunette wearing a minimalist taupe shift dress. His hands were on her waist, her back against his front, and they were dancing *very* close together, swaying in perfect harmony to the music.

My denial of jealousy stuck in my throat, blocking the growl that longed to follow. I shoved the urge back down into my stomach where it gurgled unpleasantly.

"So, what? Are soul-bonds the werewolf equivalent to... Hell, whatever." I waved my hands in front of me, trying to make the whole scene disappear while I failed to find words to express myself. I had the distinct feeling I was being played, and my naivety about werewolf commitment had been used against me. "This is ridiculous. First he's telling everyone that I'm on my way to being queen..." I looked pointedly at Desmond, who appeared worried, "...which I never *wanted*, by the way, and now he's out there grinding with some strange girl? And Genevieve is implying that *you* and I are soul-bonded too? But that's crazy, right? Even though you taste like biting into a fresh lime whenever I'm within a few feet of you." I was breathless from my ranting. All I wanted to do now was leave.

The willowy girl had snaked her hand up to Lucas's hair, and their hips were pressed so tightly together they might as well have been mating. His face was near her neck, and I was flushed with fury. Seeing them dance awakened a vindictive part of me that had no desire to go anywhere. Instead I wanted Lucas to know exactly how this rage felt.

"Calm down." Desmond grabbed my arm and pulled me closer to him so the crowd wouldn't hear us. "It isn't what you think."

"Fuck that." I took his hand in mine and turned to the bar behind us, ordering a tequila shot and another immediately thereafter. I drank both in rapid succession, their bitterness masked thanks to my proximity to Desmond. "You and I," I told him, looking right into his wide gray eyes, "we're going to dance."

This would be the perfect time to stalk off in a girly snit. I should have insisted on walking home and never speaking to Lucas again. A rational part of me knew he wasn't yet my boyfriend or my mate, and I had no real right to be jealous.

But as a woman who had been left by her date so he could dirty dance with another girl? Well that part of me was a lot less forgiving.

Desmond didn't fight me as I dragged him onto the crowded dance floor, and I was thankful to him for that.

When I took his hand and placed it low on my back, he hesitated for a moment as I felt an electric tingle jump from him to me. He placed his other hand on my waist as I wrapped my arms around his neck and pulled him in close. Sure, this was childish of me, but technically Desmond was still doing his job. There were few better ways to guard my body than by having it under his hands.

The song Lucas and the girl had been dancing to ended and

the tempo changed, picking up speed as it became a popular up-tempo dance number. I worried Desmond wouldn't be able to dance to it, but the hand low on my back held firm, and the other moved from my waist to grab hold of one of my arms. Before I knew what was happening, he bent me so far backwards my hair brushed the floor.

When he pulled me back up, his lips brushed my ear and he whispered, "Just try to keep up."

I turned to look at his face and he was smiling at me.

"Just try and stop me." With one hand in his, I swung myself out from his reach, then he spun me on the balls of my feet back into his arms. A small clearing on the floor widened to accommodate our theatrics, and several couples stopped dancing and stood back to watch.

Once he had me close, his hips pushed against mine, moving both of our lower bodies forward and then back in a sensual figure eight. I realized then that he was doing a modified version of a samba. He dipped me, this time backwards across his knee in such a way it would have probably broken my back if I hadn't let myself go bonelessly into it. Applause burst through the crowd. He grabbed both my hands and swung his leg back, dropped me to within an inch of the floor, then tossed me into the air before pulling me back towards the floor and through his legs. I found my footing on the other side with no difficulty and hurled myself at him. He caught me on his right side, his arm holding my hips up so I was almost sitting on his shoulder before I slid down the line of his body, his hands skimming my waist with emphasized awareness before my feet touched the floor. Our eyes locked as we fell into the more standard samba steps, in perfect time to the music.

I grinned at him, surprising myself by how much I was

enjoying his company. He was smiling back. By the time the song came to a close there wasn't enough room for a light breeze to make its way between our bodies. Over the new silence came a burst of applause and whistles.

Oh, right, the other people in the room. In the rush of endorphins and adrenaline that had accompanied our impromptu routine, I'd completely forgotten the reason we'd come onto the floor to begin with. Still in his arms, I turned to look at the faces of those around us who had taken in the show.

Clapping wildly along with them was Lucas. Next to him, applauding politely but with none of his vigor, was the girl he'd been dancing with. She looked downright bored.

Desmond kept an arm around my waist, and we thanked the crowd with an awkward bow, then he led me to the wolf king. Lucas was beaming, and when we reached him he put his arms around me, lifting me off the ground and out of Desmond's hands.

"That was marvelous! Where did you learn to dance like that?"

Actually, it was Keaty who had taught me to dance. We'd been investigating a dance studio where the council believed a rogue Russian vampire was offering more than lessons to his most promising ballet students. Keaty and I posed as a couple taking ballroom lessons to spice up our pending wedding ceremony. Long story short, the Russian met a violent end, and Keaty managed to teach me how to use my agility for something other than killing.

"I, uh, picked it up over the years." I was blushing.

Lucas clapped his hand on Desmond's shoulder. "Quite the show! I bet you never thought those dance lessons we took in grade school would pay off." This bit of new information surprised me. Had Lucas and Desmond really known each other since they were children? Lucas had told me they'd recognized each other before they were turned, but I'd sort of thought he was exaggerating. No wonder Desmond didn't want to discuss the possibility he and I might share a connection. He'd known since childhood his best friend was destined to be king and that certain sacrifices would have to be made.

A bubble of guilt swelled in my gut for forcing him into this scenario with me, even if Lucas seemed to be tickled pink by the whole thing rather than flying into a jealous rage. Nothing about the werewolves was what I had expected.

"Secret, Desmond, please allow me to introduce Sophia Sullivan." Her name sounded familiar, but I couldn't pin down why. He was directing our attention to the brunette he'd been dry humping. I no longer considered her willowy but rather lanky instead. Gawky, even, as if her long limbs were not really hers and belonged to a different body. I wondered what it was about her that had interested him when he hadn't given the stunning Genevieve a second glance.

"Charmed," Sophia said, giving a noncommittal wave and not offering to pick up either of the handshakes offered by Desmond or myself. Lucas laughed again, but this time it sounded forced. He was pardoning her rudeness, and I couldn't understand why.

"Sophia is the daughter of the Alpha in Albany, New York. Marcus Sullivan." He looked directly at me as he said it, his eyes narrowing for emphasis so he could be sure I understood him.

I understood all too well.

This rude wisp of a girl was the one I had killed a man for. This was Marcus Sullivan's ruined daughter. She didn't seem permanently scarred by her unfortunate past, unless being bitchy was a symptom of damage. When I'd left Albany, Sophia had been human, and it didn't take a supernatural detective to know that was no longer true. The smell of wolf radiated from her, and it wasn't just a byproduct of being near Lucas.

He had danced with her to keep the peace. He was showing the other wolves that, if they were to find out what I'd done to William Reilly, not only did he know, but he accepted what Marcus had to do.

At least that's what I thought it meant.

Lucas's heart was in the right place, but it didn't seem like Sophia was deserving of his kindness. She shifted her cold gaze to me just as I saw several large men moving to block all the doors.

"You're Secret McQueen," she said, her voice emotionless and flat.

"Yes." I wasn't really looking at her anymore. I was trying to figure out why the exits could no longer be exited. Something bad was coming.

"You killed Billy Reilly."

A few wolves nearby heard this, and it distracted them from what was happening at the doors.

"Yes," I admitted. "I would think that you of all people would be happy I'd done it."

"Happy? *Happy?*" Sophia's voice cracked, her lower lip trembled. Lucas stepped back from her as she jabbed a bony finger into my chest. Both he and Desmond moved to stand between me and the angry girl. She didn't seem to notice them as she continued her shrill tirade. "Billy was my fiancé, you stupid whore. You killed the love of my life."

It was like I'd been slapped in the face and dumped into cold water all at the same time. "Your father told me he'd raped you."

She barked out a harsh laugh. "*Liar*. My father knew Billy had proposed to me."

In the silence that followed, dark realization settled in for all of us. First on me, before it spread to Lucas and finally dug itself into Sophia. She grew pale and looked to have aged a decade in seconds.

"My father had my fiancé killed? No. No, that's not possible."

"By an outsider, so no one in the pack would suspect," I mused, ignoring her protests.

"But *why*?" She still hadn't accepted it, and who could blame her?

"Because," a deep, booming voice responded, "William Reilly was a lowlife junkyard dog, and you were meant to be a princess."

We looked over to see Marcus Sullivan step up onto the marble bar, surrounded by burly wolves who flanked him on the floor.

"And I," he continued, "was meant to be king."

Chapter Nineteen

Time had not been kind to Marcus Sullivan in the years since I'd last seen him. He, like all wolves, was muscular and lean, but age was beginning to show in the worn lines of his face and the smattering of gray in his black hair and beard.

"Marcus," Lucas shouted above the eruption of uneasy noise from the crowd. "What is this?"

"The end of your reign, pup. I won't be ruled by a baby-faced millionaire. I'm here to dethrone you."

Dominick emerged from the crowd to stand in front of Lucas, and other loyal wolves formed a circle around us. I was being protected by extension, but I saw uncertainty etch across Desmond's face. He looked at me, then Lucas, as if trying to decide who needed his protection more. He'd been asked to guard me, but his king was also in danger. He stayed next to me, but his gaze constantly darted back to Lucas.

I vowed to never leave my house unarmed ever again. Leave your gun at home for *one day* and look what happens.

"You're making a mistake, Marcus." Lucas took a step towards the bar, his voice calm and hands up, palms outward, showing he meant no harm. "If you declare yourself as a traitor, you'll be banished from the pack. You'll have no one you can turn to. You don't want that."

"Don't tell me what I want. I know what I want. You dead

and me as a leader in your place."

"You know the laws of succession. Desmond is next in line for the throne."

Desmond and I shared a look. My gaze flicked to the bar, where I could see a clear path between myself and Marcus. Desmond grabbed my arm and pulled me close to his side, shaking his head so his meaning was clear. *Don't try anything.*

From the bar, Marcus spoke again. "You lead like a friendly politician, Rain. You kiss all the babies and shake all the right paws. The pack doesn't need diplomacy, it needs leadership."

"Marcus, my family has led for generations. We might not be perfect, but we always do what's best for the pack. If you're unhappy, we can discuss it, but not like this." Lucas had stopped advancing. The tension in the room was so thick it was hard to breathe. No one but the two men dared to speak as everyone waited to see what would happen.

Sophia, in spite of what she'd learned about her father's betrayal, had gone to stand near him and away from the crowd protecting Lucas.

"It's time for a change. I am not alone." And all it took was a glance through the club to realize this was true. Marcus had at least a dozen men in the crowd, not counting his private guards or the men at the door. This was a coup.

"Marcus, don't be a fool. Think about your family." Like an expert police negotiator, Lucas was trying his hardest to defuse the situation without it coming to violence. His voice never rose above a soothing cadence, and his hands were still up.

I didn't for one second believe it would work. My mind was racing, trying to match this Marcus with the distraught father I'd met in Albany two years earlier. Had all of it been a lie? A ruse to eliminate an undesirable mate from Sophia's life? None of it was making any sense to me.

Marcus knelt on the bar and stroked Sophia's hair. She looked up at him with trust shining from her face. Maybe she believed he really had been thinking of her best interests when he had Billy Reilly killed. It can be so easy to lie to yourself when it means you don't have to accept a hard truth.

"My family." Marcus touched Sophia's cheek and smiled at her the way a doting father should look at his only child. I saw his hand move, but an instant too late, and was screaming "No!" as he snapped her neck and dropped her body to the floor like a sack of garbage.

Desmond was still holding me. I tried to break free, but he held me firm and whispered in my ear, "Not yet."

"And *her*!" Marcus pointed to me. "You would have our queen be a killer for hire? A woman willing to murder her own kind for wealth?"

I'd had just about enough of this crap for one night. Marcus had lost his mind if he was willing to kill a beloved daughter to make a point. He'd successfully proven he had nothing to lose, but it wasn't worth Sophia Sullivan's life. I could no longer hold my tongue. Desmond might be able to keep me from attacking, but he couldn't stop me from speaking up.

"That's a *lie*! You hired me under false pretenses to kill an innocent boy. Why should anyone trust a word you say?" I pointed to the heap on the floor that had, until very recently, been a source of irritation to me. "If your own daughter's life means so little to you, do the lives of your pack mean anything more?"

A few of the dissenting wolves turned to look at Marcus, whose jaw was clenched. I had expected a little more of the B-movie-villain banter he was proving to be so good at, but all I got was quiet rage. Tendons bulged on his neck, and his face reddened. He didn't say anything else to me and looked back to Lucas instead.

"They'll need to follow someone when you're dead."

He leaped off the bar into the crowd, and all hell broke loose on the dance floor. Weres, wolves or otherwise, are not the type to succumb to hysterics and make a madcap race for the exits. Nor are they the type to back down from a fight. Instead, men and women, friends and enemies, canine, feline or other, joined in the melee. This was no regular bar brawl, either. Everyone here meant business, making it a real fight to the death. I hadn't thought a royal uprising among wolves could be solved with polite discussion and treaty signing, but I also hadn't expected this level of violence to arise so quickly. The sickening sound of ripping flesh echoed through the room as limbs were torn from bodies. Once the smell of blood was in the air the madness really began.

People moved backwards from Lucas and Marcus in a wave, tumbling over one another and launching into attacks wherever they fell. When the floor had cleared around them, the two men stood facing each other. Lucas was rigid, his expression so pained I knew he still hoped for this to end without him fighting.

Desmond snarled as he yanked a man to the ground mid-attack, sending the inert body sliding over the slick marble floor. I doubted nonviolent confrontation was in the cards anymore.

"Marcus." Lucas's voice sounded tired, but there was an angry undertone that gave me a chill. "I've known you my whole life. My father trusted you. Please don't do this."

Dominick looked ready to jump in at any moment, but Desmond hadn't budged from my side. The power radiating off him made my skin tingle. We all watched Marcus to see what he would do.

The alpha of Albany swung his fist, connecting with the wolf king's cheek. The meaty smacking sound of flesh meeting knuckle was amplified above the rest of the melee. I'd never heard a punch sound so loud.

I moved, but Desmond was quick, pulling me back to him and crushing me against his chest.

"No," he growled. The word reverberated through my whole body.

Lucas hadn't budged. His face showed no change from the hit. Marcus flexed his hand and lunged again, but this time Lucas responded in kind, leaping into the attack. Their two bodies met midair with a crash of bone and skin. They snapped at each other like wild animals.

A seething mass of warm bodies crushed together like a sea of skin washing towards us. I held tightly to Desmond, trying to ignore the scent of blood the best I could. My fangs were extended, but I couldn't help that. I was a predator, and in times of elevated emotion, especially in the presence of blood, I could not force false humanity over my basic urges. I wanted to keep those urges in check, but when one of Marcus's guards came within arm's reach, I decided in the current situation it might be best to put my natural abilities to good use. Desmond was sucked backwards by the crowd, and I took the opportunity to make my attack. Throwing myself at the guard who was at least twice my size, I sank my teeth into his throat before he knew I had landed on him.

Going for the jugular was a concept both of my monsters understood and an urge I never allowed myself to indulge in outside of a fight. Thanks to the fact I did not feed on humans, and most of the monsters I hunted were vampires and therefore not a feeding option, I couldn't remember the last time I'd had my teeth gums-deep in a living neck. But this was a fight and people I cared about were at risk. I didn't think about the repercussions of giving into my own bloodlust. I had to use whatever skills I had in my power to help Lucas win this fight.

My fingers dug into his cheek with such ferocity that suddenly there was no resistance except for the wall of his teeth, and I knew my nails had burrowed right through the skin. It was my last coherent thought.

I broke the flesh on his neck as easily as biting into a ripe apple. Sucking the waiting artery into my mouth, I ripped it open. I might not eat this way normally, but it wasn't because I didn't know how. Every predator knows the way to kill. Death is a part of who we are. By repressing this side of me I had long been denying a core part of what I was. With an open artery in my mouth, it was impossible to deny that something in me loved this. The guard's blood poured down my throat, and he stopped trying to fight me off.

I drank and drank, the empty well of hunger inside me filling up and running over. I felt full, satisfied and strong. I felt incredible, indestructible. Everything in the room sounded and smelled clearer. I could hear the individual curses and threats of everyone else fighting. I heard Genevieve, her lilting contralto voice never rising with alarm when she warded off an assault. The guard and I landed on the floor once he'd lost the ability to stand. I hadn't noticed falling.

Someone ripped me off the dead werewolf, and I kicked the fallen body hard. I flailed and tried to pull free of the hands on me. Firm fingers pressed hard against my throat, and panic set in as I realized for certain this was not someone who intended to help me. I thrashed wildly, throwing my elbows backwards and kicking my feet in hopes of connecting with my attacker's groin, assuming he must be a male.

The fingers on my captor's hand began to shift and alter themselves until they were at the grisly halfway point between wolf and human. I'd heard some wolves had the ability to selectively shift with no full moon, but I'd never seen it in action. I would have taken more time to be impressed, but the claws dug into the skin of my neck.

I could taste blood in my mouth again and was hyperaware that it was my own. As I gasped for air, my throat made an open sucking noise that wasn't a sign of anything good. I couldn't fight back, not from this position and not with a hole ripped in my neck. I went limp and let my breathing stop. My head sagged to the side like a rag doll. I was hoping the idiot would think he'd nicked something vital and would move on. The ploy was rewarded when he dropped my would-be corpse to the floor.

All the noise around me was silenced by the serene white noise of healing. I was in a self-induced oblivion where nothing mattered but getting better.

My cheek rested in a puddle of sticky, coagulated blood so thick, when a huff of breath escaped my lips it made no impression on the rusty red pool. From where I lay, I could see the carnage of the battle littered across the floor. Discarded high heels and shredded clothing were scattered amid the lost flesh and fallen bodies. The once-black marble was now a dimly lit skating rink of gore. I was nose to nose with the man I'd killed moments earlier. I regretted not getting a look at whoever had attacked me so I could make them pay.

I felt the sharp, painful process of my skin knitting itself back together to make my neck whole. Strong hands landed on me and I almost lashed out to attack, until I registered that the blood in my mouth—my blood—tasted like limes.

The hollow silence slipped away, and now the din was

overwhelming. Screaming and crashes, the sounds of battle. Desmond took me away from the body on the ground, and I heard Lucas yell, "Get her out of here!" before he was swallowed up by the crowd.

Dominick—small, blond and unassuming—snagged a man twice his size off Lucas and threw him across the room.

There was blood everywhere and on everyone, so I knew seeing the whole front of me soaked in it wouldn't alarm anyone. With all the blood and body parts flying, I no longer knew who was on our side or who was winning the battle.

Shoving me roughly from behind, Desmond ushered me towards a now-unguarded door.

"We can't leave him." I tried to turn us around.

"We *have* to leave him. He can't fight his best and worry about your safety at the same time. Although if he saw what you'd done to that guard I don't think he'd be worried for very long." We had arrived on the main floor. With everyone upstairs, the restaurant was now empty.

"But—"

"Secret!" He spun me around and looked me in the eyes. I was thankful my feeding had sated the vampire hunger enough for my fangs to retract. "In spite of what Marcus thinks, Lucas is a strong and ruthless fighter. This is a skirmish, not a war. There is no doubt Lucas will win. But if something were to happen to you so soon after we found you... I can't let that happen."

I let him push me outside with no further argument. It was starting to rain, but there was no way for us to get to the car, which was parked below the Chameleon. Even if we could find it, we didn't have the keys. They were still with Dominick upstairs.

The night air held no evidence of the death and destruction

happening only one story up. There were no screams and no sounds of crashing glass or snarling, gnashing teeth, only the steady, slick sound of cold spring rain. It made me more nervous than if we could hear what was really going on.

"I know a safe place." I began to run, and he followed right behind me, never missing a beat.

The events of tonight made me wonder if there were any genuinely safe places left in the world.

Chapter Twenty

If I'd been able to, I would have taken him to Calliope's. Unfortunately, I was the only exception to the steadfast *no lycanthropes* rule she had. Time didn't pass in her reality the same way it did in ours, so shape-shifters were not governed by the cycles of the moon there. In Calliope's reality any strong emotion could motivate a shift. Since shape-shifters were not used to uncontrolled shifts and the damage they could cause when in a state of panic was extraordinary, Calliope didn't allow them to enter.

My apartment had no such restrictions. Even vampires didn't need my invitation to enter because that particular rule only applied to human homes.

I was safe at home, though, because of the council, Keaty and the myriad of protection spells placed on my apartment by both my *grandmere* and Calliope. While *Grandmere's* magic was good, having the protection of a half-god had a certain cachet to it.

I unlocked the exterior door with trembling hands and led us into the foyer that connected my apartment to the street entrance, knowing safety was awaiting us only a few feet away.

Once inside, I locked and dead-bolted the door. It wasn't just Marcus's rogue wolves I was worried about. Peyton was still out there planning something nasty. I couldn't let my guard down to put all my focus on the wolf problem, because if I did that, it would be the moment he'd come for me.

I looked around my small apartment, seeing it as Desmond might. The door opened into the living room. There was a closet on the left-hand side of the doorway that was overwhelmed by my shoe collection, and a table to the right for keys and mail. In the living room there wasn't space for a full couch, so instead I had a matching loveseat and armchair, both upholstered in a sun-yellow floral print.

No one really got my thing with yellow. The color adorned the fabric of my furniture and the paint on the kitchen walls. I had a framed photo of sunflowers hanging on the wall over the loveseat so the first thing I saw each evening when I rose was their cheery golden faces. At least half of the clothing I owned had a lemon or buttery hue. I was subconsciously drawn to the shade. When you've never been allowed to see the sun, you have weird attachments to it. Vampires had their lives before death, their *time before*, but I hadn't been so lucky.

On the wall opposite the loveseat was the fireplace. To the right of the fireplace was my television, and above it my sword collection. I had a medieval broadsword from the tenth century, an era when swords were made shorter and more usable instead of taller than a person and impossible to swing. It had been my twenty-first birthday gift from Keaty. Some girls went barhopping, I got weapons.

Below the broadsword was a sheathed Japanese katana. In an actual fight, it was by far the superior choice. I'd bought it in a tourist shop in Koreatown from a smelly fae ogre who was a little too happy to see it leave. The folded-steel blade was also the sword I'd used in the now-infamous subway incident no one would let me forget.

To the left of the living room was the kitchen, which was

currently dark, and down a small hallway was my bedroom. To the right past the hall closet was my miniscule bathroom, which had been done in gaudy pink fixtures. Given the size of the apartment, a tour was pretty unnecessary. A slow turn would do it.

"I really need to shower," I admitted, taking a moment to recognize my clothing wasn't the worst part of me. My cheeks and mouth were smeared with blood, and judging by how heavy my hair felt, it had begun to mat the curls together, which must have looked quite dramatic. My nails had bits of werewolf cheek embedded under them. Gross. I disappeared into my bedroom to fetch my robe, then returned to the living room, where Desmond remained motionless. "Make yourself at home. If you need to change, there are some sweats and T-shirts in the bottom drawer of my dresser that might fit you." I pointed down the dark hallway. "Help yourself."

Stumbling into the bathroom, I didn't bother to close the door. I shucked off my soiled clothing and turned the water on as hot as I could, then climbed into the shower.

I stood under the scalding torrent until the water was no longer pink with blood. It felt like hours and a few layers of flesh later that I finally set foot on dry land again.

I couldn't be bothered to dry my hair other than to towel off as much water as I could. My curls had always been fat and loose, not tight and frizzy, so I wasn't worried about them getting too out of control.

Slipping on the lilac silk robe, I wondered why I had ever bought such a stupid thing. It clung to me everywhere water was still on my body.

After exiting the bathroom, a cool wall of air greeted me in the living room, but there was no sign of Desmond. My loveseat was vacant and the television remained off. I didn't see him in the kitchen, either. I crossed the short distance to my bedroom and stood in the doorway.

He sat on the end of my bed, shirtless, wearing a pair of old, baggy black sweats that had been left by the only man I'd dated long enough for him to leave things behind. Several fresh cuts marred Desmond's chest, all of which were in the process of healing into pink scars. They would be gone by morning. His head was in his hands, and when he looked up I could see the weariness and frustration in his eyes. I assumed he was worried about Lucas until he spoke.

"I don't know what we would have done if something had happened to you tonight."

Again with this *we* business. It was the second time he'd said it tonight.

I got defensive, thinking he was being overbearing. "But you don't even *like* me. You can't stand to *look* at me. You don't think—" My temper was bubbling, but he was shaking his head.

"Lucas knew the minute he met me that when he became king of the pack it would be with me as his second. He knew it when we were only children. Because of his certainty, his family took me and my brother in, treated us like their own sons, and raised us to understand that kind of life in a way our own parents could not."

I could think of only one response. "Dominick's your brother?" It was difficult to reconcile the idea of short, blond Dominick being related to dark, olive-skinned Desmond. Not to mention their different demeanors.

He nodded and continued. "The reason Lucas knew I would be so important to him is that he and I share a variation of the same soul-bond you two share."

Puzzle pieces began to fall into place, forming the answer to my most lingering question. I sat on the bed next to him,

141

suddenly feeling rather queasy.

"So, what you're saying is... I mean the thing Genevieve said at the club...?"

"About the double bond."

"Yes. I take it she wasn't referring to the bonds between me and Lucas and you and Lucas."

He shook his head again. "No. She meant between you and Lucas, and you—"

"With you." I'd suspected as much from what Genevieve had insinuated, but it was different to hear it right from the wolf's mouth.

He looked at me, but I was staring at the empty armchair by the door. "I know how weird this must be for you," he said, his voice sounding weary. "I didn't believe it myself until the elevator earlier tonight. I could taste you so clearly it made my head spin."

I took a deep, shaking breath. "Me too." I was beginning to feel tired, and I knew it wasn't just from the fight. Sunrise couldn't be too far off and I would need to sleep soon, but I still had so many questions. "Is this normal?"

"We always knew it was possible. It's rare for kings to be soul-bonded to their seconds, but when it does happen it creates a powerful structure for leadership. We can read each other very well. But, with that, we knew the connection could either negate the possibility of Lucas being soul-bonded to a future queen, or it would mean that I might be connected to her as well. There isn't a science to soul-bonds. We honestly didn't know what would happen."

"So what is this, then?" I gestured from myself to him. "We're some sort of weird soul threesome? I mean, to be honest, I wasn't totally willing to accept that I was *destined* to be with Lucas, and now you're telling me I'm destined to be with both of you? Is that how this works?" Anger tainted the words, but I couldn't help it.

"I don't know."

"What do you mean you don't know?"

"All I know is since meeting you I can't stop thinking about you. And my best friend, my king, believes you're meant to be his queen. Normally you'd be with the one you felt bonded to. But you admitted you can taste us both, which means neither bond is stronger."

"Why didn't I taste you before tonight?"

"We wondered about that yesterday. We figured you were only connected to him, so we didn't question it. My best guess is because he's king, his influence over you was stronger. You'd never experienced the soul-bond before, so the first taste you got was from the most alpha wolf among us. It wasn't until you'd been away from him longer than a few minutes you were able to connect with me."

Sounded like a lot of guessing and not a lot of real answers.

"Did you know?"

"What?"

"Could you sense me yesterday?"

He was silent, his gaze looking at the wall next to my head. "Yes."

This frustrated me more. They both knew about what was happening, but had chosen to leave me out of the loop, making me feel stupid and unprepared. I stood and turned my irritation on him.

"I haven't *dated* in two years, and suddenly I'm *meant to be* with not one but two werewolves I've only known for a couple of days." I threw my hands up in the air in frustration. "If I hadn't tasted you both, if it didn't feel like electricity went through me when either of you touch me, I'd think this whole thing was *bullshit*." I put a lot of emphasis on the last word and directed it right at him, then dropped myself into the armchair.

"I didn't want to believe it either."

I sighed with a little more drama than necessary. "I fail to see how this is a negative for *you*," I snapped, then immediately regretted it.

Desmond snatched his bloody shirt off the floor and threw it at me none too gently. "Do you know whose blood is on that shirt?" I wasn't sure if he wanted a reply or not, so I smelled it. My heart sank.

"Mine." His was on it as well, but I knew that wasn't the answer he was looking for. I let the shirt drop back to the floor.

"Yeah, yours." He stood, picking it up and tossing it back across the room. With him this close to me, his anger rising, all the hairs on my arms prickled and a peculiar tingling danced across my skin.

"Desmond..." I remembered what happened the last time I had this feeling in such close proximity to someone I was soul-bonded to.

"I thought you were going to die. When that wolf got her nails into you and you went limp..."

So it had been a she-wolf who had attacked me.

"I was playing dead." I had to stifle a nervous laugh when I heard the words out loud. Desmond wasn't smiling at all, his hands shaking, and in one fast motion he grabbed me by the shoulders and yanked me out of the chair with such force my head spun.

"You asked me what the negative is for me? When you went limp, I saw every chance I had for happiness die with you. I could stand ten feet away from you for the rest of my life and nothing, not sex or money or power, could match how that feels. Do you *get* that?" He gave me a shake for emphasis.

I braced my hands against his chest. Where my fingers touched his bare skin, it felt like the dark hair there was made of electric wire. I jerked my hand back for a second knowing he must have felt the shock, but I couldn't not touch him. I needed to have my hands on him.

All sorts of very human thoughts were running through my head. *This is Lucas's best friend. Isn't Lucas my boyfriend? No. Is it okay to sleep with someone and say my metaphysical connection to him made me do it? Okay, that's actually a pretty good excuse.*

This close to him, I saw his eyes were not true gray but rather a washed-out violet, which was a pleasant surprise, giving his already striking face a little extra uniqueness. He loosened his grip on me, and I stood flat on the ground again.

"Yes," I said.

His hands were still on my arms, and I felt like I was on fire and freezing to death at the same time. I shivered. He rubbed my arms with the familiarity of an old habit, warming me with his touch but making the heat move lower as well. My body shuddered.

"Yes?" He had forgotten the question.

I was amazed we even remembered our names with this much static electricity dancing between us. All I kept thinking was, *he wants me.* And right then what I wanted more than anything was to be wanted. Maybe it was weak of me, but it would make me feel safe and protected, if only for one night.

We were staring at each other for so long I thought my entire being would unravel in his hands. In one breath I was wondering if I'd gotten the signals wrong or imagined the chemistry that was setting fire to the air. Was I misreading

145

anger for passion? In the next breath his mouth was on mine.

I knew now how Lucas had felt when I'd surprised him with my kiss earlier. Though I had anticipated Desmond and I were on the brink of something, I was left breathless by the force of him crushing me against him in the cage of his arms. My hesitation didn't last. Unlike my comparatively tame embrace with Lucas, neither Desmond nor I were fully clothed to begin with and the bed was not across the room. It was only tripping distance away.

He was kissing me so hard his teeth clicked against mine, and for a few ragged moments it felt like we were trying to consume each other. My lips were bruised by the intensity of his mouth, and small noises I wasn't aware of making emerged from the back of my throat. I deepened the kiss, wanting more from it than a mere kiss was capable of giving. I clawed at his back, trying to rid him of a shirt he wasn't wearing. Logic had flown out the window long ago, replaced by wanton need. My body was pressed so tightly to his I couldn't breathe without feeling the pressure of his ribs grazing mine.

A major problem I'd encountered in having functional relationships with human men was my overabundant enthusiasm in the bedroom. At first they thought it was great, albeit a little rough, but ultimately they could never keep up. I had a lot of stamina, and it wore human men out too quickly. Judging by the way Desmond held me by my thighs and lifted me like I was weightless, I didn't figure longevity was going to be a problem here.

Desmond stumbled onto the bed, and it groaned under the weight of us. I straddled his chest and stooped low so my mouth never had to leave his. He was kissing me so hard it hurt in the good way. There was so much need and intensity it made me rub myself against him harder, insisting on more.

His hands moved down my back when he found he no longer needed to hold me to him, and his fingers fumbled, sliding over the slippery surface of my robe. Instead of fighting with the garment, he tore apart the silk and discarded the remnants.

"I needed a new one anyway."

He growled when my lips left his, then flipped me over so he was on top, the weight of him very comfortable, making my mind race with promising ideas. I arched my hips upwards and dodged his kiss so I could look him in the eyes. My heartbeat was wild, matching the rhythm of his own. Taking his face between my palms while I made him meet my gaze, I tucked my feet under the waistband of the sweatpants and pushed them down.

With my legs secured around his waist, he pressed hard against my pelvis. I let out a shuddering breath. Everywhere our skin touched was like fireworks going off, and just as with Lucas earlier I could barely control myself.

"Yes." I licked his bottom lip.

I released his face, and he didn't hesitate before pushing me down into the mattress with another bone-jarring kiss. My legs loosened their grip and his hips arched backwards for a moment before he entered me. This time he withdrew from the kiss first, his fingers tangled in my hair. The look on his face was so intimate my heart tripped. There was a peacefulness to him I'd never seen before, like all the pain he'd been carrying around since we'd met had vanished. I could have stayed like that forever to watch him smile at me, because everything about his sweet, dreamy look made me believe I was completely wanted. I touched his cheek and drew him close, feeling him slide inside me with an aching slowness.

I gasped, clawing at his back, trying to keep him there to

maintain the electric fullness that made my body spark like a lit firecracker ready to explode. He pulled out and I whimpered.

"More," I insisted, and he chuckled in reply, pushing back into me. "Oh!" He put his whole weight against my body as he found a rhythm that met the demands of my writhing hips.

As his pace picked up, my hand clamored for the headboard and something solid to brace myself. My eyes fluttered shut and rolled back, and my spine arched into the rising sensation. The flavor on my tongue was so tart and overwhelming it stung. Behind my eyes bright green flashes started to appear, first as a dim glow, but with our rising fervor they blossomed and flared into sparkling pinpricks in shades of lime and chartreuse.

One hand left the headboard, twining in his thick hair, which was damp with sweat. At first I just raked my fingers through the soft brown waves, but as his teeth grazed my clavicle, tonguing the dip at the base of my throat, my grip tightened so I held the strands in a clenched fist. It did nothing to slow him down, and his mouth closed on one of my nipples. My lips parted in a soundless moan as he put one of my legs over his shoulder and found a way to get that extra inch inside me. I thought I was forming words until I realized the sound coming out of my throat was a howl.

One of the metal posts on the headboard snapped in my hand as we both came. Desmond collapsed on top of me, growling. Both of our chests were heaving, and we were slick with sweat.

He wrapped his arms around my waist and rested his head on my stomach, his hair tickling my still-sensitive breasts. His violet-gray eyes studied me, and he smiled in a way that promised to stop my heart. He climbed up the bed to lie next to me, and I let myself be folded into the safety of his arms. I nuzzled against his chest and breathed deeply, inhaling his musky wolf scent with its overtones of bright citrus.

It was past sunrise now and my body could no longer ignore its most basic need. With Desmond's arms around me and the sound of his heartbeat in my ear, I succumbed to sleep.

Chapter Twenty-One

I woke up alone.

Confronted with a flood of memories, I reached my hand out to touch the empty space on the bed next to me. I raised my head and looked at the rumpled sheets.

The clock told me it had been hours since Desmond and I drifted off, and I'd slept through the day. It wasn't impossible for me to wake during daylight hours, but my nocturnal schedule meant I was typically asleep when the sun was up. It worked better that way, since the evil day star drained my energy like crazy.

I grabbed for my robe, but the shredded bits of a silk explosion were all that remained. Desmond's bloodstained clothes were no longer next to the bed. The only evidence of him was the smell lingering on my skin and sheets.

I dressed without much thought to what I was putting on—a thin tank top, a black hooded sweatshirt and my second favorite jeans. I guess they were my first favorite jeans now that my other had met a bloody and tragic end.

I padded barefoot into the living room and my heart stopped.

Holden was sitting on my loveseat with his arm casually stretched across the back. He wasn't looking at me. Instead, his cold gaze was fixed on two werewolves, one sitting in the armchair, the other leaning against the fireplace. Lucas and Desmond weren't looking at me either. They stared back at Holden.

Oh holy mother of fuck. This was *bad.*

All three of them seemed to hear me enter at the same moment. The wolves looked at me, but Holden remained still, speaking first. "Secret, if you needed guard dogs, I'm sure Sig could have arranged something for you."

Desmond growled at him, but Lucas just kept looking at me, his jaw set tight.

In the pit of my stomach something twisted. I was anticipating I would feel guilty for what Desmond and I had done, but instead I was overcome with a relief so strong it washed away everything else I might have felt.

"You're okay." I let out the breath I hadn't known I was holding.

"Yes. Marcus and some of his men got away. Genevieve's club is a little worse for wear, and there were casualties on both sides, but I think he has been subdued for now." His eyes flickered from me to Holden. If he knew about Desmond, which he must considering the whole apartment smelled like us, he wasn't going to say anything about it here. "Mr. Chancery here insisted he has business with you." There was something disbelieving in the way he said *business.*

Chancery? Wow. I hadn't heard someone say Holden's human surname in years.

"Um." Having all three of these men with me in one small room, I felt naked in spite of layers of clothing. "How long has everyone been here?"

"Desmond, as you know, has been with you all day." Lucas's tone was smooth and unreadable. "I called him when things were secure, around seven this morning, and he assured me you were safe." Desmond was staring at me, and I didn't dare meet his eyes. "He told me you were exhausted, reasonably, and suggested we allow you to sleep through the day. He stayed with you to make sure you were protected." This time a little anger seeped in with the last word.

I looked at Desmond and smiled weakly, unable to put the warmth into it I would have liked. He didn't smile back, but his eyes had lost the hard edge they used to have around me.

"I arrived after sundown, letting myself in," Holden added, "and found both your wolves here."

Desmond made a noise of disgust when Holden said *sundown*. Of course they were perfectly aware he was a vampire. The hostility was evident. I couldn't tell which part bothered Lucas more—that I'd slept with Desmond or a vampire having such easy access to my apartment.

"Holden is my liaison with the vampire council." I figured honesty here couldn't hurt. Lucas already knew I worked for the council. "They wouldn't allow just anyone access to them, and because of what I do I need to be able to communicate with them directly. Holden..." I indicated the stone-still vampire, "...uh, Mr. Chancery? He's my guy on the inside."

I looked at Holden, trying to ignore the twist of a smirk on his lips and his small derisive snort. I hoped he was not willing to out me as a half-vampire for the sake of it. I'd trusted him for six years and had to believe I could trust him still.

"Close enough. Who are the dogs?" He validated my explanation, then negated any goodwill I had garnered him all in the span of a few seconds. I was surprised they hadn't made some sort of introductions since Holden had obviously told them his name. He must have just arrived. I was also impressed he was asking for introductions at all considering he was already aware of who they were, having watched them kidnap me two nights prior.

Holden was a snob like most vampires. He believed werewolves were at the bottom of the supernatural totem while he and his kind were at the top. Vamps wouldn't even feed on weres if they could avoid it. They considered lycanthropy a contamination in the blood. Sig had told me that, one of his little side comments that made me wonder how much he knew.

"Lucas Rain is the werewolf king of the Eastern states." I inclined my head towards the grumpy blond werewolf in the chair adjacent to the loveseat.

Holden nodded to Lucas. "Your highness." I had never heard a royal address sound so belittling. It's amazing what two hundred years can allow you to do with inflection alone.

"And Desmond is..." I struggled for a moment, searching for the most appropriate way to introduce him. "Lucas's second-in-command."

"Well, well..." Holden met my eyes, "...quite the lupine social climber these days, aren't you?"

"At least one of us is making an advance." I instantly wished I hadn't brought up his stunted progression in the council. I was largely to blame for his stasis, and drawing attention to it in front of those he considered lesser beings was a low blow.

Lucas and Desmond watched the exchange without interruption, and then Lucas rose to his feet. He came to stand in front of me, looking down with a small smile.

"You're okay," I said again, hardly able to believe it even with him this close.

"Of course." The warmth of his tone made it seem like there had never been any doubt, and perhaps there hadn't. What I didn't know about werewolves could fill volumes. Was last night's fight to the death tantamount to nothing more than a big-dog pissing contest?

No, I couldn't believe that. Marcus's intent had plainly been to kill Lucas. That Marcus was crazier than a Batman villain and had murdered his own daughter didn't make me feel any better about the rivalry. He would stop at nothing to take the throne away from Lucas, and maybe my soul-bonded wolf king was being foolish not to take the threat more seriously.

I ground my teeth but didn't know if it was out of frustration or worry. Holden was watching only me, dismissing the wolves' presence as if they were nothing more than furniture. I tried to catch Desmond's eye again, but he had decided to use the vampire as an excuse to ignore me and was putting his role as my bodyguard first.

I sighed more heavily and looked at Lucas again.

"Can I have a word with you?" I said, which caught Desmond's attention, his eyes flicking a quarter of an inch towards me. "In private."

Lucas's gaze traveled to my bedroom door, and I shook my head. "Out in the hall." The smell of the bedroom would be a dead giveaway. It was one thing to suspect Lucas already knew what had happened last night, but there was no sense in literally rubbing his nose in it.

"Okay." He opened the door and stepped back to let me exit first. Holden edged partway out of his seat, and Desmond took a half step towards him and growled.

"Boys, do you think you can call a truce for three minutes? I'll be right outside, and I doubt he and I are going to kill each other." I cast a wary glance at Lucas. Nothing in his face supported or contradicted me.

Holden and Desmond said nothing, but returned to their uneasy staring contest.

I stepped into the tiny hallway that separated my

apartment from the street entrance stairs, and was only a little surprised to see Dominick standing there. What *did* surprise me was discovering how relieved I was to see the grinning blond werewolf alive.

"I'm glad you're okay."

"Ditto. Things got pretty gnarly in there." Judging from his smarmy smirk, he wasn't too shaken up by his near-death experience. "Did you take good care of my brother?"

I flinched and it must have shown because Lucas's face became serious, and Dominick stopped smiling.

"He's inside," Lucas said. "Can you give Secret and I a moment, please?"

Dominick nodded and ducked into my apartment without another word, shutting the door behind him. Alone in the closet-sized hallway with Lucas, I was very aware of his physical presence. He was easily a foot taller than me, and standing this close to him in the cramped space, I had to force my gaze up to meet his eyes. With no one else around, I was anticipating the full wrath of his anger.

And why shouldn't I? I'd betrayed him.

No matter how I'd justified it in the heat of the moment, Lucas had staked his claim first. It had been he, not Desmond, who told me about the soul-bond, and it had been he who led me proudly before his pack as a potential mate.

What had I, his would-be queen, done in return? I'd left him in danger and used the rush of fear and near death to excuse being unfaithful to him before I had proven myself worthy of his respect.

I reminded myself, flipping the proverbial coin, *he* had been the one who kept the secret of my soul-bond with Desmond to himself in order to monopolize me. And he had been the one who asked Desmond to protect me, knowing the bond would make it impossible for Desmond to let anything happen to me.

I was beyond conflicted. Did I feel bad about sleeping with Desmond? No. I didn't regret it for a single second. And why should I? Two days ago I hadn't known either of them, and now I was thrust into a world where people thought I was a princess and part of my destiny was to be with the men the fates had chosen for me. So I'd slept with someone I felt a strong attraction to, but I felt bad because it might hurt someone else.

I hadn't asked for any of this. I didn't want to be a princess and I didn't want my future mate selected by supernatural forces. Denying that I felt something for both Desmond and Lucas would be a lie, but when and if I picked one of them, it would be on my terms. As it was, I wanted to have them both, which made me think it might be easier to choose neither and just stay single.

"Lucas..." I began, but wasn't sure what to say next.

He met my eyes and all the tension in his melted away. Suddenly I was in his arms and he was holding me so tight I couldn't breathe. I molded myself into the embrace, moving my arms around his back, which relieved the pressure on my lungs.

I laid my face on his chest and breathed in the warm, musky, living smell of him. Thoughts of staying single had vanished the second he touched me. His body was hot under my face and hands, and I resisted the urge to cry from relief no matter how badly I wanted to. My blood-tinted tears would give too much of me away.

"I wasn't sure I'd ever see you again." He spoke into my bed-tangled curls. "I don't know what I would have done if we lost you." His use of the plural mirrored Desmond's last night. "Desmond told me he thought he watched you die last night."

So they had been talking before I woke up. How much had

Desmond told him?

"I'm sorry," I whispered into the softness of his shirt, apologizing for nothing specific.

His hand looped into my hair, wrapping strands around each of his beautiful, long fingers. I was willing to bet his parents had made him play piano, violin or guitar. Something to make good use of such tapered fingers.

He used my hair to tip my head back without being rough about it, then bent to kiss me. It was not like our first kiss at all. There was no politeness. Instead he kissed me with the intensity allowed only for situations like these. We had both thought, however fleetingly, the other might have died last night. The desperation and yearning in the way we kissed said more than we could convey with words.

Lucas backed me against the wall with a loud *thump*, and I was forced to stop his probing hands before I let us go further.

"Lucas, about last night..." I felt the foolish need to be upfront with him even now with his wide palm under my shirt and his mouth at my neck. The hallway smelled like frosted cinnamon buns, and my breath was coming in short, panting gasps.

"Forget last night," he murmured into my skin.

The door to my apartment swung open and Dominick peeked out. Lucas and I both turned our heads to look at him, and I was relieved. Who knows how far I'd have gone without an interruption. History showed my self-control with werewolves to be somewhat limited.

"Sorry." Dominick bowed slightly. "We heard a bang and thought we should see if you two were at each other's throats. Guess we didn't take into account..." His apology drifted as he smirked at Lucas's hand placement.

Lucas righted himself and removed his hand from under

157

my top.

I remembered Holden with a blush, and realized he'd been able to hear every breathy detail. I grumbled at my own foolishness. The three of us returned to the apartment, and it was my turn to avoid Desmond's eyes. Instead I focused on Holden, who was showing a hint of a grin. Sure, he *would* find this amusing. Vampires.

Lucas, too, was reminded of the vampire's presence and Holden's reason for being at my home in the first place.

"I'll leave you to your business." Lucas leaned in so his lips rested against my ear. Holden would still hear him, but the illusion of privacy was enough. "I'm relieved you're safe after last night. I'm sorry you were put in danger. I know it put you in an unusual situation..." God, I wish having my life in peril was unusual. "Anything that happened as a result is understandable. Emotions were running high, after all." He stepped back and nodded.

Had he just *pardoned* me for having sex with Desmond?

My face flushed and not from embarrassment. I was enraged. My choice to sleep with Desmond had been made logically. Well, as logically as a decision can be made with someone's tongue in your mouth. And what's more, it was made at least in part because of a metaphysical connection Lucas himself had alerted me to. I balled my hands into fists. Of course I didn't want him to be mad about it, but would he expect Desmond to forgive him if he, Lucas, had been the one to bed me first? I doubted it.

He frowned and arched a brow. My anger must have confused him. Hell, it confused me. Didn't I want him to be okay with it?

"Just go." I indicated the open door. Out of the corner of my eye I saw Desmond smirk, a flash of humor so quick it was almost imaginary. At least someone found this situation funny. I suppose it wasn't often anyone blew Lucas off.

I wanted to smile back, but it would ruin the effect of my incensed and unceremonious dismissal of the king.

After the werewolves left I felt like a fog had lifted from my senses, and I was able to see and think more clearly. Just being near them threw me off my game, and I was going to need to find my sea legs with this soul-bond thing if I had a hope in hell of surviving in a relationship. I couldn't handle being so out of sorts.

I sat in the armchair Lucas had just occupied and stared at the vampire on my sofa. "What are you doing here? Sig gave me his orders. The Tribunal doesn't expect me to have captured Peyton yet, so what do you want?"

"Aside from getting you in trouble with your wolves or catching you *in flagrante*?" It was apparent he found the situation hilarious, but I wasn't laughing. "I came to help."

I considered Holden to be my friend, and most days I liked him a hell of a lot. He was a great ally but was usually only around when it benefited him. I leaned back in the chair, watching him carefully. I didn't think he was lying.

"Secret." His voice was tight with impatience, which was a rarity for a vampire. "I know things have been, for lack of a better word, *strained* between us since my bicentennial." That wasn't a sentence you got to hear every day. "But we're still the people we were when Sig assigned me to you."

I laughed at him. If I was the same person I had been six years ago, I would be dead by now. The Secret of six years previous was a dim-witted sixteen-year-old with only the vaguest idea of how to keep herself alive.

"Okay, maybe not the exact same."

"I get what you're trying to say. Don't strain yourself with the niceties. They aren't your strongest gift." I looked out the small window to the street outside. Feet passed by in a rush. Human lives without the slightest clue of the strange world existing all around them. How many of them would Peyton kill before I stopped him? "I really could use your help."

"Any ideas of where to start?"

"I have one. But you're not going to like it."

Chapter Twenty-Two

"I don't like this," Holden agreed.

We were standing in front of the seventy-sixth precinct police headquarters. It was a squat, ugly, concrete building made of two rectangular floors of offices and interrogation rooms, and a basement level for holding cells. The police cruisers were parked in a fenced lot behind the building.

"I told you." Starting up the stairs, I turned to look at him. "You don't need to come in. But *trust* me when I tell you no one in here is going to have a goddamn clue what you are. They're all human. Very, very human."

Begrudgingly he followed, hesitating at the entrance before walking in. An exhausted young woman sat at the reception desk and gave me a look of contempt when I cleared my throat in front of her. She softened when she saw Holden, and one of her hands flew up to fix the errant strands of her hair. As usual he appeared to have stepped out of a *GQ* article on making looking good appear effortless. An article he could have written once upon a time.

"How can I help you?" She ignored me completely.

I tried to draw her attention back to me by saying, "Detective Mercedes Castilla, please."

"Who should I say is here?" Now that she was looking at me again, all the friendliness leached out of her voice.

"Secret McQueen."

The girl rolled her eyes, believing it was a poorly constructed alias. I was getting pretty irritated with people who thought my name wasn't real. I was going to have to thank *Grandmere* for taking my mother's note literally when it said *keep her a secret*.

"And you?" She nodded to the vampire.

"Holden Chancery." He smiled, flashing fangless brilliant white teeth at her. She met his eyes and became a lost cause. He had her enthralled in an instant.

"Of course." Her voice had a dreamlike quality, totally entranced. If he told her to cluck like a chicken, she would do it. I'd seen baby vampires do some truly awful things once they discovered how to enthrall humans, but Holden had never been one to abuse the thrall for kicks.

The girl used her desk phone to announce us, then sat there grinning at Holden like a dog who had executed a new trick for the first time. Pitiful.

A few moments later Mercedes descended the stairs behind the desk and waved for me and Holden to follow her.

I had lied when I told him no one in the building would know what he was. Judging by the cold stare Cedes fixed him with the instant we sat down at her desk, she'd recognized straight away he wasn't human.

"Cedes," I said, a warning tone in my voice, "this is Holden."

She was familiar enough with the work I did to recognize the name of my liaison. It didn't do anything to make her like him, though. Mercedes hated vampires almost as much as the werewolves did.

"What brings you to my humble establishment?" She

leaned back in her desk chair and pretended Holden wasn't there. "I was hoping the next time I saw you it would be over cocktails and you'd be giving me the dirty details about Lucas Rain."

Holden made a sniggering sound that I tried to ignore.

"You know the girl, the one who said she was saved from a..." I lowered my voice, "...vampire?"

Cedes focused on Holden with a glare tainted by accusation, then looked back to me. She was a beautiful woman, but her job had etched her face with a shrewd, knowing patina that aged her more than necessary. She had almost-black eyes, and her dark hair was curly the way mine was not, with tight untamed coils. Her skin was honey bronze, but too many hours indoors without natural sunlight made it look sallow. The dark bags under her eyes and minimal makeup told me she was working hard on something. I just hoped it was something that could help me.

"Yeah, her name is Brigit Something. Stewart or Samuels. Something Anglo. Are you admitting you're the one who saved her?"

"Off the record?"

"Sure."

"It was me."

"Yeah, I knew that."

"I need to know if anything has seemed hinky since it happened. Anyone reporting attacks from similar assailants? Any bodies showing up looking a little *pale*?"

"You want to know if I suspect any vampire activity?" Her voice hushed. "Isn't that really more your box of crayons, Secret? What's going on?"

"I can't tell you. The fewer details you know the better. But you'd be helping a lot of innocent people if you could tell me everything you know."

Her face was grim. She laced her fingers together and leaned back. "Some big bad on his way?"

"Big bad is already here."

Exasperated, she directed her full focus on Holden. He met her eyes, but to his credit didn't use his powers on her.

"Now you listen to me, you pretty boy mosquito, because I'm only going to say this once. I don't care how old or powerful you are. If anything, *anything* happens to this girl here, I will find a way to rip your pulseless heart right out of your chest. *Comprende?*"

Without missing a beat he coolly replied, "Detective Castilla, your Secret is safe with me."

She blinked with surprise, and I groaned. "God, Holden. How long have you been waiting to use that line?"

"About three years."

"And in three years you couldn't find any room for improvement?"

"I like a good pun, what can I say?"

"Terrible." I shook my head.

Cedes, in spite of herself, was unable to keep from smirking at his awful one-liner. She might not like him, but he had done his best to endear himself to her without stooping to mind tricks, and I appreciated it. With the exception of Keaty, Mercedes was my only human friend.

"Please, Cedes."

"Okay. One of our undercover vice officers has been hearing that a lot of the girls are afraid to go with new johns. From what she's been hearing, there are rumors about some handsome john who pays girls double or triple the normal rate, but after they leave none can remember what he asked them to do or why they were paid so well for it. Same rumor mill says a few of the girls haven't come back at all. We had an anonymous call to come get a dead body, but when we got there it was gone. And we found a dead girl a few blocks away from Central Park. She was totally drained, but it was the fucking weirdest thing. It looked like she'd been ripped up by a wild dog before she was killed." Her eyes were all too knowing. "Since we don't know of any wild dogs loose in the city, you could say we're a little mystified."

I swallowed hard. A girl drained of her blood meant a vampire was involved. The girl being ripped up was something different, though. I knew of monsters that might tear their victims limb from limb for kicks, or demons who would remove a person's bones to suck out the marrow. I'd once heard Keaty mention a bog fae who used ribbons of human skin to make its clothes. But in the city, there was a much more likely option.

Werewolf.

Chapter Twenty-Three

The limited number of plausible options to explain the girl's strange and ghastly demise circled inside my head as Holden and I walked side by side into the night. Her being killed by a demented human was possible but on the very bottom of my list. How sad is it that in my world a human killer would be the best-case scenario?

My most fitting approximation of what happened was the girl had been attacked by a werewolf and left for dead. A vampire following the scent of blood and suspecting an easy kill had found her and drained her. Shitty way to die—presumably killed by one supernatural beastie and then killed for real by another.

Some people have no luck.

"What's on your mind?" Holden must have thought I'd stewed long enough.

"I'm thinking if someone is taking these girls, it isn't Peyton himself. But anyone from the council wouldn't be stupid enough to leave so much evidence. Whoever is taking these women must be a rogue working for Peyton." Alexandre was too smart to leave a trail or be out in the open, so he would have other rogues doing his dirty work—vampires loyal to him and his ideas.

"And the girl attacked by wild dogs?"

"Fluke? Just a really unlucky woman."

"Hmm." He didn't look convinced. Honestly, neither was I.

"We need to talk to Keaty. See if he's heard anything significant from his sources. Mercedes gave us a good starting point, but we need to know if anyone less human has heard something that could help us. If we find out who, or what, is picking up these prostitutes, maybe it will lead us back to Peyton."

"And you believe Mr. Keats will be able to assist us with this better than the council?" Holden remained unconvinced.

"Keaty has access to things and people the council can't get to. It's the reason you guys trusted him to do your dirty work to begin with. It's also the reason he was allowed to bring me to you."

Holden's mouth fixed in a grim line, but he didn't argue. He knew I was right. Keaty had friends in places both low and high, well, mostly low. But those contacts might be what we needed to find Peyton and whoever was feeding on the prostitutes.

I hadn't been to the office in two days, which wasn't all that strange. Keaty kept up the business end of things and only had me come in for non-council jobs when he needed an extra pair of hands. Since he hadn't been required to kill rogues for the council in six years, it left him time to explore a variety of other unusual cases. It was those unusual cases that had taken me to Albany and made me kill a young werewolf. I was definitely beginning to see how every action had a consequence.

Keaty's office was a cross between that of a Dashiell Hammett private detective and an NYU literature professor. I let us in through the fogged glass door with a quick tap to

167

announce our entry. He would have already heard my key in the front door of the brownstone. Centered in the room was an antique oak desk, with no computer or any modern convenience in sight. Behind him was a window that looked out on a brick wall. To the left and right of the desk were two walls stacked floor to ceiling with old worn books that had no discernible cataloging system. There was an ashtray on the desk and a bottle of scotch behind it. The story the room suggested was a web of carefully manufactured lies. Keaty was nobody's fool.

He wasn't wearing his glasses today, so he showed no physical signs of weakness. When it came to physicality, it was important to him to feel equal to those he hunted. You don't earn a reputation like the one Keaty had by flaunting your humanity. In the supernatural community Keaty was a ghost story, the kind that changed with every telling but was somehow always true. I knew too well he was not an invisible killer swooping in and stealing lives, just a gifted man who was skilled at his job. It was one of the reasons I tried to distance him from the monsters I dealt with. Eventually his luck would run out and something would kill him. I'd keep that from happening for as long as I could. Kind of karmic payback, considering he was the one who'd saved me from death to begin with.

Keaty rose and offered a hand to Holden. They shook cordially before Holden and I took our seats in a pair of high-backed leather chairs facing the desk. Keaty didn't make any passive-aggressive remarks about my absence and lack of check-in calls, but he did say, "I understand you had an interesting night."

I tensed because feminine decency first led me to believe he was talking about my unexpected intimacies with Desmond. Then it dawned on me that my romantic endeavors wouldn't interest Keaty in the slightest. "You mean the thing at the

Chameleon?"

"It was practically a massacre according to what I've heard."

"I'm sure Genevieve has insurance."

"Genevieve Renard has a type of insurance cash can't buy," Holden interjected. "She is owed favors by just about everyone in this city, both human and otherwise. She is a clever woman."

I smirked when Holden used Genevieve's last name. *Renard* was the French word for fox, which I knew thanks to my *grandmere's* insistence that I learn a second language. An ocelot named after a fox. If Genevieve was as clever as they claimed, maybe our names really do help define us. Mine was a royal pain in the ass.

"What brings you both to my office?" Keaty asked, interrupting my musings.

I wanted to correct him that it was *our* office, but I didn't think an argument of semantics with a vampire in the room would go over too well. My pride remained wounded for the sake of preserving his.

"Have you heard anything about these prostitutes with missing memories? Or the girl who ended up mauled and drained in the park?"

"Yes."

"Anything other than the basic details?"

"Yes." His attention moved to Holden, then back to me. For all his apprehensions about things that went bump in the night, Keaty would have made an incredible vampire. He loved to be vague and lacked the nuances for sarcasm the same way older vamps did. No wonder the Tribunal trusted him so much. "Is the council suddenly interested in dead whores?"

"No. But we are very interested in what is killing them."

Holden looked just as unmoved now as he had sitting in my apartment with the werewolves. I wondered if the only place he felt uneasy was walking with me to the Tribunal.

Keaty leaned back and laced his fingers together behind his head. He looked contemplatively at the ceiling, which had beautiful, thick crown molding and was a rich burgundy color in the center. I imagined he was thinking about blood when he looked at it.

"I think your best option would be to talk to one of them yourself."

I glared at him with no attempt whatsoever to mask my unhappiness. It was past ten now and I still hadn't eaten. I was cranky and more than a little bloodthirsty. My willingness to scour downtown New York for vampire-thralled prostitutes was wearing thin. It would be so much easier if someone would tell me what I needed to know rather than making me feel like Gretel following a trail of crumbs.

Keaty had no patience for the antics of a twenty-two-year-old vampire hunter and fixed me with a hard stare. "When I say that, I don't mean interviewing them as yourself, either. I mean if you want to find out what is happening to these girls, you'll need to find out firsthand."

Holden's eyebrows raised such a slight amount it would have been an indifferent change to anyone else. But I didn't miss the tiny curve of a grin on his lips. He knew what Keaty meant by firsthand.

Unfortunately, so did I.

Chapter Twenty-Four

I'd rather not get into the reasons behind why I own a pair of gold lamé hot pants.

I found this whole idea ridiculous, and the outfit, in my opinion, was too clichéd. I'd seen enough prostitutes, probably more than Keaty or Holden had, to know the hot pants and black halter were beyond unnecessary when it came to picking up a john in this day and age. The fact I was slight of build and a natural blonde meant I'd be an obvious target.

Maybe that's what I wanted.

I walked down 59th Street, past the looks of disdain I got by Bloomingdale's, and gathered more inquiring glances as I reached the area near the Queensboro Bridge. Across the river the lights of Long Island City glimmered more attractively than I thought the city itself was capable of. The East River swept by, and as I watched the water, I considered how many bodies I'd put there and how many had been dumped there by others. Bodies that didn't all deserve to be dead.

A short distance from the bridge a group of girls huddled together, most wearing tights and long T-shirts. The evening still had a bite of winter to it, but only one of them was wearing a coat. All five girls were smoking, and a permanent cloud lingered over their heads. Three were Latina with hair styled in dramatic braided rows and perms. One was a black girl with her hair in a misguided weave that appeared unnatural and uncomfortable. The look on her face was somewhere between exhaustion and ennui, and her lip jutted out in a pout. She wasn't inhaling any of the smoke from her Pal Mal. She just sucked it in and blew it back out, not taking any time to let it linger in her mouth. Her shirt had a silver tiger on it. The remaining prostitute was the skinniest white girl I'd ever seen. She had pale skin wrapped like cellophane around her jumble of elbows, knees and jutting bones. These girls had seen monsters that had nothing to do with my line of work. I felt guilty that some of the creatures of my world had crossed into theirs. They had it bad enough without vampires using them as a source of fast food.

As I approached I was thankful my internal temperature protected me from the bitter spring chill. The possibility of a late-spring snow was an unspoken promise on a night like this. I sidled up to them cautiously, my head bowed like a submissive puppy.

"Whatchuwant, you?" the largest of the girls asked. She was six inches taller than me and had to weigh over two hundred pounds. Her arms were crossed over her substantial chest, and she didn't look like she wanted any part of whatever I was selling.

It hadn't occurred to me on the walk here I would need any kind of a backstory. Foolishly, I had hoped the prostitutes would see me as one of their ranks and accept me into their questionable sisterhood. Then they would immediately start talking about the vampires who had taken others of their kind, giving me the answers I needed so I could call it a night. I could be such a dumb blonde sometimes.

"Uhh."

"Park Avenue is da other way, girly. You a long way from da

escort services of da Upper East Side, ya know?" This was from the black girl as she exhaled her ornamental smoke in my face.

The skinny white girl laughed but said nothing. It was clear she was the minority here and she knew it.

The big girl took a hard look at me and snorted. "You think you can come here? You think your pretty blonde hair gonna make us say *oh, Blondie, you can be one of us*? Hmm? You lost on your way to a strip club? Whatdafuckyouwant."

What I wanted was to give her a good reason to shove her attitude right up her ass before I did it for her. These girls were treating me with the same disdain young vampires did upon hearing my name for the first time. It pissed me off, but in her case she had a reason to look down on me.

A line of tears shone in my eyes, turning them into wide, wet orbs of sorrow. "I was working a few blocks east. Last week this girl on my corner got into a car. She never came back and they found her in the park all ripped up." My voice trembled convincingly. *The Oscar goes to...*

They looked unmoved, but I saw the two leaner Latinas bobbing their heads in enthusiastic agreement.

"Yolanda, like what happened wit Cleo, yeah?" The black girl was silenced with a raised hand from the larger girl. She was clearly the leader.

Yolanda's eyes narrowed, and she assessed me more seriously now. "Whatchyourname, girl?"

"Brigit." I used the name at the forefront of my mind after meeting with Mercedes.

"Brigit. Sounds like a fucking cheerleader."

The other girls laughed for a second before they settled into observant silence. In the darkness near the river, at least one vampire was watching the whole exchange. Holden's presence covered me like a thin, protective blanket. Thinking of Holden brought another vampire to mind. I wondered what Sig would think of this if he knew it was a result of the assignment he'd given me. I thought he might get more than a little pleasure out of my current situation. Doubtless, Holden would let him know about tonight's antics.

A car drove by and slowed, and I became the girls' last concern. I hung back, and the five of them launched into a well-oiled chorus of, "Hey, baby! How you doin', honey? You need a date? I'll show you a real good time." The whole thing made me queasy.

I was expecting him to pick one of the thin, prettier Latina girls, but to my surprise large, bland-faced Yolanda was chosen by the john. I craned my neck to get a better view of him, but the guy looked like any other hard-up, middle-aged schmuck who could only get pussy on a street corner.

The other four returned to huddle near me and gawked at me like I was a zoo display. They said nothing, just blew clouds of smoke in my face. I was willing to bet none of these girls were older than sixteen, yet each one looked about forty.

"Who's Cleo?" I broke the silence and hoped it didn't make me sound like a cop. I had crossed my arms over my chest and was pretending to be cold.

The two skinny Latinas looked at each other and said nothing, but each wore a grim expression. The white girl shuffled uneasily. The chatty black girl was my in, that much was clear. I stared at her, and she folded faster than a lawn chair.

"She used to be wit us, ya know?" the black girl said. One of the Latinas snarled when the girl started to speak, but it did nothing to stop the newly opened fount of knowledge. "It was like you said, yeah? She was here, she got picked up, but she *did* come back. Only she wasn't right."

"Wasn't right how?"

"Veda. You shut your fucking mouth."

Veda ignored her. "What it matter now, Misty, huh? Cleo dead, ain't she? What da fuck it matter now?"

I needed to be clear on what Veda had said. "She's dead?"

"Yeah, fuck man. Yeah."

"But she was alive when she came back to you guys?" I asked.

"She got dropped off in this like, limo. She got out and she was like, staggering, ya know? Like she was drunk?" Veda pantomimed the weaving and bobbing of a woman under the influence, then abruptly stopped and pretended to smoke again. "Cleo ain't no dummy. She knows you don't drink when you wit a john. Dat shit get you killed." Veda shook her head, heaving a solemn sigh as she pointed her cigarette at me for emphasis. This was the knowledge of world-weary teenaged prostitutes.

"But she was alive?"

"Fuck, girl, you deaf?" Misty said, but she didn't seem hell-bent on putting an end to my questions anymore, so I would take what I could get.

"It was weird, yeah?" Veda continued, looking from me to the other girls, who each nodded seriously. "Like, she was babbling some shit in a weird language. Like you see on dem Jesus shows where the guy touches their heads and shit?" Veda mimicked this by acting out a faith healing on the skinny white girl. The girl giggled when Veda touched her forehead and dramatically announced, "You be healed, bitch!"

"She was speaking in tongues?"

"What da fuck else she gonna speak with?" Veda rolled her eyes. I saw no reason to explain, so I let her go on.

"Anyway." Veda was enjoying being the center of attention even for such a small group. Her voice had begun to bubble with enthusiasm. I suppose being around Yolanda must have limited her opportunities to be noticed. "She went home after that an da next day Yolanda goes to check on her, right? 'Cause Raymond would be right fucking pissed if Cleo missed a night, ya know?"

I nodded as if I knew the full extent of their pimp's wrath.

"And?"

"And Cleo was dead."

"Dead how?"

"Fuuuuuck, Blondie, you ask a lot of questions."

"I've been told that before."

"Yolanda said it looked like she'd been dead for days," Misty interjected, looking for her own chance to be the group's source of knowledge. "Said she was all pale and shit, and looked like she had no blood in her."

I felt the blood drain from my own face. I knew all too well where this was going. "Did you have her buried?"

"Do we look like we can afford to pay for a funeral?" This obvious point had been brought up by the previously silent white girl, who had recovered from her faith healing enough to resume smoking.

"Did *someone* bury her?" My heart was pounding.

Misty looked guilty, turning away from Veda, who appeared ill at ease upon hearing the question.

"No."

"No?"

Veda glared at me and I shut my mouth. "We wanted to. We called the cops, right? Anonymous-like so that someone would take care of her?"

Now I could see where this fit in with the information Mercedes had given me. I nodded. They all bobbed along.

"But when the cops came, they didn't take a body. There was no news about it. It was like she ain't never even been there."

But she *had* been there. It was no longer a mystery what had happened to Cleo the prostitute. And I knew, too, what had happened to the girls like the one Mercedes had told me about. I'd thought the body in the park was too sloppy to be Peyton, and now it was clear to me why.

I looked at the girls and could tell they had sensed the change in my attitude. I wasn't hiding the horror on my face and was thankful they would have no understanding of its deeper meaning.

I had a clear grasp on what the base level of Peyton's plan was. At first I'd believed he was killing and eating the girls for food alone, because no one would miss a dead prostitute. But if Cleo had just been drained for a meal, her body would have still been there for the cops to find. She wouldn't have been speaking in tongues.

The signs described by Veda and Misty were those of a baby vamp before the change took effect. Drinking the blood of a vampire often caused hallucinations, violent fits, nausea and a number of other side effects. Then it caused death—one so fast-acting it didn't resemble a normal human passing. Lastly, it resulted in rebirth.

And with that birth came the hunger.

Peyton or one of his nest had turned Cleo into a vampire and then unleashed her onto the unsuspecting streets, sending her with a newborn's blind thirst to hunt her own people.

She would not be the only one.

Chapter Twenty-Five

There were a lot of swears and protests when the shiny new BMW rounded the corner and beckoned me to its passenger door. Veda and the other girls were trying to tell the driver he was wasting his time and a *skinny-assed* girl like me couldn't satisfy him.

I took offense to the last statement, knowing perfectly well my ass wasn't bony and some people seemed to enjoy it a great deal.

The girls put an end to their complaints when they got a look at the driver's face. Mercedes had told us some girls on the street reported the mystery john had been very good looking, so Holden's face must have set off alarms for them.

"Good luck, Blondie," Misty said with a sneer, her farewell acting as a eulogy.

I accepted my fate and got in next to Holden, mumbling, "Take me home."

"We aren't looking for Peyton?"

"We won't find him tonight. Take me home."

"What did they say?"

I turned to face him, trying to find a way to summarize what the girls had told me so he would experience it with the same gravity I had.

"They're the rats of London," I said at last, knowing no other way.

His jaw spasmed. "What do you mean?"

I rested my head against the cool glass of the car window. "Peyton isn't feeding on the disposables. I mean that's what we thought, right? He would go after the homeless and the girls on the street because they're easy targets. Food."

"Yes."

"But that's not it. He's changing them."

I didn't think vampires could get paler, but the new ashy pallor on Holden's face proved me wrong. "He's turning them?"

"He's making some of the girls vampires and sending them back into the street."

"But *why*? No vampire in their right mind would turn a prostitute. We won't turn anyone we consider unworthy."

"Don't you get it?"

He looked at me out of the corner of his eye.

"He's creating an army. They're plague carriers, Typhoid Marys. He will use them to create more or to destroy others."

"Oh Jesus." The depravity of Peyton's plan was setting in.

"He's going to make Manhattan a vampire city. He wants to come out of the dark."

"He wants to kill everyone."

"And he's starting with the lowest levels. The prostitutes will infect their johns. They'll infect their wives or girlfriends. It will spread. If we can't find him soon, we won't be able to stop it."

"But Peyton is a known rogue. One vampire alone can't make this work."

"He has to be working with someone. And he has to have

179

someone in the daylight too, but I don't remember him having a daytime servant. Only the really powerful masters can manifest that kind of control."

"Like Sig has Ingrid."

"But Sig is also well over a thousand years old."

"Two," Holden corrected.

I didn't have the energy to absorb the magnitude of that information. "And Peyton isn't even three hundred."

"He wouldn't be able to manipulate a human servant in the daytime. He could barely manage a Renfield."

I hated the phrase *Renfield.* After Bram Stoker's eponymous tome vampires had thought the name was too hilarious not to use. Much like Dracula used the poor, weak-minded Renfield, rogue vampires often enthralled someone into doing whatever they wanted over an extended period of time. They called them Renfields.

Daytime servants, on the other hand, maintained an illusion of free will, but always knew the needs and desires of their master. Furthermore, because of the bond it created with their master, the daytime servant could live for many centuries. They lacked the strength and power of a vampire but enjoyed the extended life.

Sig's daytime servant, Ingrid, was a stunning German girl he'd met sometime in the early thirteen hundreds. She was quiet and dutiful, but I was certain time had shown her things none of us could imagine, especially at Sig's side. I suspected, at over seven hundred years old herself, Ingrid was not a human of any small strength. I didn't like to be alone with her. There was too much in her eyes I didn't want to know.

Holden pulled the BMW up to the curb in front of my apartment. I had begun to shiver as the shock of the evening's events really sank in. If Peyton was going to try taking over the city, outing vampires everywhere and waging an all-out war on humanity, he wasn't doing it alone. And whoever was helping him had to be strong, mean and determined.

Of all the people I wanted to discuss this with right now, Sig was at the top of my list. But how could I have a casual chat with the head of the vampire council about my suspicions? Would Sig want to know what a half-breed vampire killer thought?

Holden seemed to be reading my thoughts, because he put a hand on my thigh and said, "Let me go to the council. I'll request an audience with Sig and see if he has any thoughts about what you've discovered."

I nodded solemnly. It would be better if Holden went. Perhaps it would help him curry favor and find advancement in the ranks of the other vampires if he brought them the information. I couldn't begrudge him the desire to advance among his own kind. I knew I never would.

I opened my car door, noticing an unfamiliar but pristinely well-kept '72 Dodge Challenger parked near my building. It was a charcoal gray color I rarely saw on cars, let alone vintage muscle cars.

I was about to ask Holden if he remembered ever seeing it before when I noticed that my living room light was on. I might not remember cars, but I definitely knew I'd turned off all my lights before leaving.

Someone was in my home and it wasn't someone I'd invited.

Chapter Twenty-Six

"Holden." I leaned back towards the car, but my eyes remained focused on my window, which rested on the same level as the sidewalk. My living room was the only one in the apartment that allowed natural light in, and as such also the only one that let light out.

"I see it."

"Are we expecting anyone?"

"Keats?"

"Keaty would have called first. He knows better."

"The wolves?"

I raised my eyes, looking away from the window when it didn't yield the answers I needed. I hadn't considered Lucas or Desmond, but now that Holden suggested it, it seemed like the most obvious answer.

My face flushed, and it didn't escape Holden's notice.

"That would make sense."

"Do you want me to come in with you?"

If it was either of my wolves, then having Holden with me would only serve to make things all the more complicated. The uneasiness of earlier this evening was still fresh in my mind, and I doubted the boys would have forgotten it either. I was also more than a little annoyed that they would invite themselves into my home, and I didn't want Holden with me when I made that clear to whoever was inside.

"No. It's got to be one of them, that makes the most sense. You can go."

"You're sure?"

"Go and see Sig. We need to know what he thinks we should do and how we should act on it. I need to know if he still wants Peyton alive, given this new information."

Holden scoffed, and I knew he doubted the Tribunal's opinion would change regardless of any new details, but being allowed to kill Peyton would go miles to help ease my mind.

"Tell me as soon as you know anything. Please."

He nodded and I closed the car door at last. In my lit apartment there was a whole other world of problems for me to deal with. I was starting to think I'd never find an end to my troubles.

It wasn't until I was standing alone on the sidewalk, watching Holden's car drive away, that I felt the full force of a body slam into me from behind and realized how right I was.

The blow was accompanied by snarling and snapping next to my ear that made my whole body go cold. I remembered being in the club yesterday with a man's throat in my mouth, only then the animal noises had been coming from my throat instead of next to my head. It was a feral, distinctive sound, that of a hunter with prey only a bite away.

I was being immobilized by someone's full weight, and they were trying to eat me.

I let out a howl that was less a horror-movie victim's scream and more the noise of a wounded animal, but was the most natural utterance I could manage in the heat of panic. How could I have been stupid enough to let down my guard for a fraction of a second, knowing Peyton was in the city waiting for a chance to conclude our unfinished business?

"I thought you were so strong," the mouth near my ear said.

The fact human words were coming out when the previous sounds had been so guttural was enough to snap me out of my internal chastising. As the voice and words sunk in, I put together that the speaker was young and female. Had one of Peyton's new lackeys found me?

Using her new calmness as an opportunity to rear back, I smacked the back of my skull hard into the front of her face and knocked her off me with the suddenness of the gesture. It never ceased to amaze me how people's cockiness could lead to their undoing. Getting to my feet as quickly as possible, I spun and crouched in a fighting stance, preparing for her next attack. I was wishing, not for the first time that week, I hadn't been forced to go without a weapon. As much as I'd have liked to be armed, there wasn't any place to hide a gun when you were wearing an ensemble that barely hid your lady bits.

Recognition slammed into me with the force of a hammer when I saw the face of the young woman who had attacked me.

She looked almost exactly as she had when I'd sent her running from me in Central Park with her broken heel trailing behind her, only now a stream of blood was coming from her nose where I had broken it, and she no longer seemed afraid of me. The girl Mercedes said was named Brigit knelt close to the sidewalk, primed like a lethal predator waiting for her moment.

She was as pale as she'd been that night, but it wasn't fear making her that way. Her new pallor was visible beneath the fake bronze of her skin. She was wearing a gauzy white summer dress that looked all wrong in the chill of spring.

Brigit was dead.

I knew from what Mercedes had told me I *had* saved her that night. She'd left Central Park alive and made it home in one piece.

So how was it she was now a baby vampire, staring at me with the clear objective of killing me when only a couple nights ago I had saved her from the monster she had now become?

It couldn't be a coincidence.

All of these thoughts flooded my head in a matter of milliseconds. Before I had time to voice any of my questions out loud, Brigit sprung out of her crouch and hurled herself at me a second time.

She no longer had the element of surprise, though. Now she was not a clever stalker but an inexperienced killer launching an attack against a trained and lethal opponent. She would not best me again.

I grabbed a fistful of her hair when she got close enough and used it to yank her body to the ground, where it landed with a hard, fleshy crash. I knelt on her chest, using one hand to hold her head back. With the other I held her chin so she couldn't try to bite me.

"Who was it, Brigit?"

Some of the fight went out of her, but the voice was still bitter. "You *know* who it was. He told me. He told me it was *your* fault. He would have let me live, but he needed to show *you*."

"Show me what?"

A shimmer of blood-red tears built in her eyes. Her desperation to see me dead had begun to drain away, but beneath the killing urge was a blind rage I couldn't ignore. "He said he needed you to know you wouldn't be able to save us." She swallowed her rage. I could feel her throat contract under my palm. "Them," she corrected, removing herself from among

185

their ranks. "Every human you try to save he will turn personally. So you would know."

I fought back my own tears and violently turned her head to the side in my haste to check the skin. There it was, as sure as I knew it would be. The uneven, broken-toothed bite of a psychopath.

"Oh, Brigit." There was only sadness in my voice now.

"Secret?"

Brigit and I were not alone on the sidewalk anymore. Without budging from my place on top of her, I looked to find Desmond standing a few feet from us. The scene must have been quite alarming to an outsider. I was still wearing my gold hot pants, hooker shirt and four-inch heels. My eyes were done with a heavy dose of black makeup to complete the effect. I was kneeling on the chest of a cute blonde girl whose face was covered in blood from her tears and busted nose.

I would have liked to tell him it wasn't what it looked like, but I really didn't know what he was thinking.

"Please help me," I pleaded.

"Of course." Without hesitation or questions he was beside me, waiting for me to tell him what I wanted next. I wondered, had it been Lucas in my apartment rather than Desmond, if he would have been so compliant.

"Is that your car?" I nodded in the direction of the Challenger.

"Yes."

"Are you going to kill me?" Brigit choked out sobs, making a pretty pathetic new vampire now that the urge for revenge had gone out of her.

"No," I said. She and Desmond both looked shocked by the response. "I'm going to take you to someone who can help you."

I held Desmond's gaze this time and hoped he knew enough about the paranormal to understand who I meant.

"The Oracle?" His tone was hushed.

"Yes."

"But we can't go to her. It's against her laws."

"Please." I pulled Brigit to her feet, still holding her arms in case she was a better actress than I gave her credit for. "Do you know how to get to her?"

"Of course. It's just down the block, but I'm telling you we won't get in."

My mouth was set in a tight, determined line. I couldn't explain it to him, especially not in front of Brigit. "Just trust me."

Chapter Twenty-Seven

My apartment on West 52nd was walking distance to the coffee shop, but with a bloodied vampire in tow, driving made things a little less complicated. I was thankful the busiest hour for coffee lovers had passed and the Starbucks was relatively vacant. When Brigit and I vanished in the doorway, Desmond was left alone, but with so few patrons it was unlikely any of them noticed there had been two girls with him. I felt bad leaving him there without any answers, but Brigit's docile state wouldn't last long. The hunger would take her before the night was through. We were lucky Peyton had thought to feed her before sending her after me, otherwise she wouldn't have made it to me. She would have gone after the first available blood source instead and another innocent would have been dead.

Rather than finding ourselves in front of the cash counter at Starbucks, we were standing in the foyer of a majestic house. *House* wasn't the right word to describe where Calliope lived. Mansion would have been much closer to the truth, but even that didn't really fit. Her estate transcended the laws of physics binding other homes to a fixed size. It had a limitless number of rooms that could expand and recede to accommodate guests as necessary. Whether it was used to heal those who were injured or safeguard new vampires too unstable to be among the public, Calliope's home was whatever it needed to be.

The foyer was larger than my entire apartment and probably larger than Lucas's mammoth bedroom. The floor was covered from end to end in overlapping Persian rugs Calliope had acquired at bargain prices when there'd still been a Persia.

An immense variety of portraits all depicting hauntingly beautiful women hung from the walls. It wasn't until my fourth or fifth visit that I realized every painting in the room was of Calliope. Done by the most famous artists in the world, she was portrayed in every era and style, from Renaissance to Impressionist to Pop. The crown jewel of the group was a Warhol painting of one of the women Calliope had claimed to be in her many lives.

The room was dimly lit in colorful jeweled splendor by dangling Tiffany lamps casting kaleidoscope shadows over the floor. Color was a mainstay of Calliope's world. The rugs, lamps, paintings—all a dizzying array of red, blue, green and pink. Scattered along the walls were large, plush leather armchairs that made the ones in Keaty's office look like they were for children.

Slumped in one of those chairs was a small, pale teenaged boy wearing a Pizza Hut uniform. His eyes were hazy and unfocused, but he was alive. And judging by the smell of him, completely human.

I wasn't the only one to smell his true nature. Brigit's eyes widened and darkened to the oily black of a hungry vampire. Her nostrils flared and her fangs were out before I could yell, "Calliope!" It was lucky I was still holding Brigit by the hair, so when she lunged for the boy, she was yanked back to me by the leash of her own body.

On cue, Calliope entered the room.

As entrances go, Calliope rarely did things subtly. She swished through the door in a flourish of red material. Her hair was done in tumbling black waves held back by ruby stickpins. She was barefoot, and trailing behind her was a snow-white tiger. Seriously.

"Secret!" Her voice sounded like a song, and she never seemed unhappy to see anyone, regardless of how they came to be in her presence. "You've brought me something. I was expecting you."

I couldn't help but smile. "Of course you were." She was the Oracle, after all.

Brigit turned her attention from the boy to the woman who had just walked in. To a vampire's heightened senses, Calliope was a confusing jumble of fragrance. She smelled intoxicating and alluring, but there was a pungent edge of warning to her blood. Something in the fiber of her being warded off potential predators.

"Who is this you've brought me?"

The tiger smelled my legs and then the hem of Brigit's dress. It bared its teeth at her, growling, and she knew enough to stop struggling against me.

"Brigit is new. Unsanctioned. Alexandre Peyton turned her to make a bit of an overly dramatic point." My voice wavered as I spoke.

"You feel responsible for her?"

"Yes."

She didn't need to hear more. She came to us and put one arm around Brigit, releasing her from my hold.

"We'll get her settled in no time, don't you worry. Then you can get back to that handsome wolf of yours. No sense in leaving him there too long. Wolves and caffeine are a terrible combination."

The tiger preceded us out of the room, and before exiting I

remembered the pizza boy.

"Uh, Cal?"

"Yes, love?"

"Is the boy okay there? I mean...he just heard all that, and—"

"He didn't hear a thing. He's busy forgetting some things before he goes home alive and well-tipped." She wore a devious little grin, which on her was far too beguiling.

I was often curious if one of her forms had been Helen of Troy, because it didn't take much to imagine an entire war occurring for the right to love her.

We left the boy in the room alone and began our long walk down a very dark hall.

In the room where we settled Brigit, unnatural sunlight dappled behind the curtains. It made my chest constrict from panic and longing. The sun was an illusion, a kindness she provided to those who would never see it again in the real world.

Judging by the tan coloring Brigit's features, she had been a bit of a sun worshiper in her human life. From my chair in the corner of the room, I wondered how many other parts of her life she wouldn't be allowed to enjoy now because of me.

I felt as guilty for Brigit's current situation as I would have if I'd turned her myself. It made me sick to know she would never see her family again. She could no longer enjoy whatever macrobiotic food lifestyle had kept her so thin. She couldn't go to the beach in the Hamptons this summer or date a normal human boy.

Her life had ended, but in more ways than it would with a normal death. With human passing you lost everything, but you weren't there afterward to know it. When you became a vampire, you had to mourn your own losses.

It was that awareness of the missing parts of one's life which often drove new vampires mad, turning them into killing machines. Coupled with the strength and power inherited from their master's blood, it was difficult to combat the initial reaction to vampirism.

I was genuinely grateful I had never had to experience it.

Calliope had chained Brigit to the bed with satin-covered silver. It wouldn't burn her, but it held her in place. I was pretty sure it was fairy-wrought silver too, so the extra enchantment helped.

The Oracle was standing next to the bed, humming a strange song while she unpacked bags of blood from a small red cooler. My stomach growled.

Without batting an eyelash she threw one of the bags to me. I took it with thanks and bit into the bag, drinking its contents like a juice box. The blood was cold, but I wasn't going to pick nits when I was being fed for the first time that night.

"So, tell me about this man of yours."

"You're the Oracle, Cal, I was hoping you'd tell me."

She was holding one of the bags to Brigit's mouth. The girl ripped it open with her teeth and shook it like a wild dog, spraying blood all over the bed and herself. Calliope sighed and threw the bag into a wastebasket, then took Brigit firmly by the chin and looked her right in the eyes.

"Secret and I are talking, little one. Do not think your youthful insolence will play here with the big girls. You will take this blood and live, or refuse it and die. That is the choice. Be a good vampire, behave and don't make trouble, and you will live. Ignore what I am telling you, and the next time you see Miss Secret over there, it will be when she is delivering your death warrant. Do. You. Understand?"

Brigit's eyes were wide, her face splattered with the discarded blood. She looked insane, like she couldn't be reasoned with, but she nodded her understanding. It gave me a chill when Calliope got serious because it revealed something inside of her that was old, strong and very frightening.

She held another bag to Brigit's mouth, and this time the girl took it, tearing it open with a dainty bite before glutting herself on the contents. The Oracle was looking at me, waiting for me to continue.

"Do you know about soul-bonding?"

"Ahh." Her face collapsed and she let out a heavy sigh. "It's that time now for you. I thought we had longer."

"You knew?"

"You need to understand. There are certain things in your life that *must* happen to you. I cannot always warn you about them because you are so stubborn you will try to keep them from happening."

"You knew I had a soul mate?"

"Common human understanding is that everyone does, is it not?"

"Human understanding and romanticizing really don't apply to my life."

"I suppose not. Although the love triangle transcends human romance. There were plenty of them with the old gods. But I digress. In your situation you should know things, romantically, are not going to be easy for you."

"Duh."

"I don't only mean the wolf king and his lieutenant."

"That's the only love triangle I'm currently a part of."

She smiled, but there was a little sadness to it. "The wolf is one half of who you are. There is another half. A whole other arena for trouble."

My face must have gone white because she raised another bag of blood to give me, but I waved it away. "You're saying—"

"I'm saying what I've said. Your love life will be complicated, to say the least."

I barked a laugh, shrill and short. "If it gets any more complicated than it already is, I think I'd rather do without."

"We shall see."

Brigit mumbled something into her now-empty bag, and Calliope freed it from her mouth. The girl licked blood from her teeth and lips, then looked at me before speaking. "You are a vampire."

"I am."

"But you smell like a wolf?"

Calliope regarded me carefully, wondering if she would need to help Brigit forget more than usual.

"I've been told that."

"Are you like him, then?"

"*Him* who, Brigit?"

"The one who made me?"

"Peyton?" I asked, and she nodded. "We are both vampires, if that's what you mean."

She shook her head and scrunched up her eyes the way an annoyed little girl would, obviously frustrated. "No. The wolves. Do you have wolves like he does?"

My stomach was suddenly in my shoes. Calliope gave me a mournful look and brushed some of Brigit's blonde hair off her face.

"Pet wolves?"

Brigit shook her head again. "Werewolves."

I stared at Calliope, but her face told me nothing. If she understood more about this than she was telling me, she wasn't showing it. I rose from my chair and went to stand next to Brigit.

"Peyton has werewolves? How do you know that?"

"Three of them grabbed me off the street in the middle of the day and took me to this old building. I guess it was a theater, it had a big screen..." Her eyes began to tear again. "I tried to run, but one of them held me and made me watch as one of the others changed. They told me if I tried to escape, they'd feed me to the wolf."

"What theater?" I asked.

"The vampires woke up when the sun went down," she continued, not hearing my question. "Peyton came. He asked if the wolves had taken good care of me. Until I met you, I didn't believe in vampires. Or werewolves. I didn't think any of this was real." Brigit turned her face away, a bloody tear rolling down her cheek.

I knelt on the opposite side of the bed so I could see her face, and waited for her to look at me.

"Brigit..."

"After he killed me he told me everything would be better if I found you. He said once you were dead I'd be free. Free from what?" Red tears streamed down her face. "Can I be alive again?"

I shook my head. "No. But if you can tell me where he is, I'll make sure he pays for what he's done to you."

She sniffled and wiped her face against the pillow. When she saw the bloodstained smear on the case she began to cry again. Incoherent mumblings crossed her lips, but nothing that helped me.

"Where is he?" I asked again.

Calliope placed a hand on my shoulder and gave a gentle squeeze.

"Maybe we should give her a break. It's been a difficult night. She can answer more questions later," Calliope whispered.

Admittedly, Brigit wasn't in any condition to give the responses I needed, but it pained me to let up now when I was this close to getting the information I needed. I stood, prepared to leave, when I heard Brigit murmur a word that sounded like Orpheus. That got Calliope's attention, her body going rigid and eyes widening.

It also told me where I would find Peyton.

If Brigit was correct and Peyton had werewolves working with him, then there was no time to waste. A rogue vampire with plans to overthrow a city was bad enough. But I knew of one werewolf who would be foolish enough to join forces with him, and it made everything that much worse.

This ended tonight.

Chapter Twenty-Eight

"It's Marcus."

I was back outside on 52nd, and Desmond was trying to keep up with me as I barreled down the street, wanting very badly to be back in my apartment.

"Marcus?" He was confused and had every right to be. "Is this about the other night?"

"No. Yes? No, I don't know. But—" I stopped mid-stride and turned to face him. He nearly collided with me due to the abruptness of my stop. "I hunt vampires."

"I know. You're working with the vampire council. You mentioned it."

"Okay. Well, they sent me to hunt a really bad one who seems to have it in his mind he can take over New York if he infiltrates our population from the bottom up." He looked puzzled but didn't ask for explanations. "We, Holden and I, couldn't figure out how it could be possible since this vampire isn't powerful enough to have a daytime servant."

"A what?" He unlocked the passenger door, opening it for me before going around and letting himself in the driver's side.

"Someone to do his bidding in the daytime."

Desmond's face looked a little ashy. "They can do that?"

I nodded and continued. "This vampire, Peyton, he and I go

way back, and it's because of him that girl attacked me."

"Did you kill her?" He wasn't accusing me, just asking.

"No, I took her to the Oracle. Calliope can help her come to terms with what's happened to her."

"Calliope? You're on a first-name basis with the Oracle? And why did she let you in? I thought she hated weres."

"She doesn't hate weres!" I was vexed and wanted to defend Calliope because she wasn't here to do it herself. "Things just work differently in her world than they do here."

"Her world? But if that's the case, why would she see you?"

"I sort of have...special privileges?"

"Why?"

I couldn't blame him for questioning me on this. Everyone who knew about the Oracle was aware her hospitality didn't extend to the lycanthrope community. Of course they would assume she hated weres, it was the easiest explanation. To suddenly discover she allowed exceptions? Well, it wouldn't make sense to me either if I wasn't the exception in question.

"Because of the vampire...council." I'd almost said *blood*. What I wanted most in that moment was to tell him everything. To have someone who genuinely cared about me and wanted to be with me know everything about who I was. But I'd kept my secret *very* secret for such a long time. In twenty-two years only my mother, grandmother, a vampire, a bounty hunter and an immortal oracle knew what I really was. Of those, one had abandoned me, one I'd run away from, two used me to kill my own, and the last had seen my future but wouldn't tell it to me.

How could I tell my sort-of boyfriend about it when we had enough complications to deal with from my being soul-bonded to him and my *other* sort-of boyfriend? Telling them both I was also half-vampire wouldn't help our existing situation. Or maybe it would help things a lot by removing them both from my life posthaste.

"What does this have to do with Marcus?"

I took his hand, and he placed his other one on my cheek. Being with Desmond lacked the complications of being with Lucas. Desmond wasn't a king. He was just a man who wanted to be with me instead of a man who wanted me to be his queen. How did this get so difficult so fast? And could Calliope have been right when she said it would only get worse?

"When Marcus attacked the club he was vying for the throne."

"Yes."

"And if he'd gotten it, he would have killed those loyal to Lucas and the Rains."

"Most likely."

"With the pack of his choice, Marcus would be outside of question. Those willing to leave Lucas would have been morally ambiguous to say the least. What if Marcus told them to follow a vampire? To embrace their urge to hunt and take their rightful place outside of the shadows, in a position of power greater than humans. They would do it." Our short drive from the Starbucks had brought us back to a parking space near my apartment building.

Desmond let out a huge breath, and my mouth tingled with the limey taste. "Marcus wants to help Peyton turn the human race into slaves."

"Starting with one of the biggest cities in the world. Can you imagine if the rogues of other cities saw this? Even if they didn't succeed, think of how many innocent lives would be lost in the attempt. Peyton has already killed or turned some of the prostitutes. He's starting with the people who don't matter, but by doing that he can infect so many more before people begin to notice."

"The girl who attacked you?"

"She was somebody someone will miss. She was someone who mattered. He killed her because I saved her life. He wanted me to know I wasn't capable of protecting anyone. I killed one of his children that night and in return he took a life I'd saved."

"He has something against you personally?"

I nodded with renewed weariness. We were out of the car and making the half-block trip back to my front door. He draped his arm around me, and I leaned my face into his chest, breathing him in. He had given me his jacket after I'd left Calliope's, which protected me from prying eyes, and I was grateful for the illusion of modesty.

Desmond would need a little more of my personal history if he was going to understand why Peyton hated me so much.

"When I came to New York I was sixteen, and saying the city was overwhelming is an understatement. I had it in my mind that because a vampire attack had caused my mother to abandon me..." *shit was that too close to the truth?* I continued in a hurry, "...I would kill every vampire I met."

"You were sixteen?"

"I was an idiot."

He smirked at this.

"I did pretty well for myself at first, actually. But that was because the vampires I was finding were new, stupid and reckless. I'd been here a few months and was feeling pretty big in my britches, and then I found Alexandre Peyton. Or I guess he found me. I didn't have the same reputation with vampires that I have now, but he still knew about me. He must have heard about some little girl trying to kill vampires and decided to have fun with me. He found me while I was hunting, and before I knew what was happening he was on me, feeding from me. Killing me."

Desmond's grip on my shoulder tightened. Having arrived back at the apartment, neither of us had sensed any dangers lurking within and had locked the door behind us. We faced each other in my living room.

"What happened next?" he asked, standing in front of me. He slipped his hands under the lapels of the jacket, his bare palms rubbing over my shoulders, pushing the garment off me and onto the floor.

I let out a shaky, uneven breath as his hands continued their path down my arms.

"He was cocky. He was so sure he had me beaten he stopped feeding. He started to tease me, make me feel foolish for believing a little girl could kill the monsters under her bed. That's what he called me, *little girl*. It's what he still calls me, though he knows better now. He went in to take the last of my blood, and that's when I hit him. Did you know vampires can heal almost anything, but they can't regrow teeth?"

He arched his eyebrow.

"It's part of the reason vampires have retractable fangs like cats' claws. Because it's their weapon and their only way to feed, it must be protected whenever it's not being used. Fangs are only exposed when a vampire is taken by the bloodlust or when they are provoked in anger. Or when they're aroused."

Desmond was less than a breath away, the tips of his finger trailing up and down my arms. I put my palms against the softness of his sweater and dragged my fingernails down to the waistband of his jeans.

"What happened next?" He lowered his mouth to the exact spot on my neck Peyton had once tried to rip out, and licked the place where only the memory of a scar existed. I shuddered, and my body pressed anxiously against his as our wandering hands moved lower. Keeping my own fangs from extending was only possible because I'd just fed.

"He was ready to feed..." as I said it Desmond nipped my neck and I let out a little yelp, "...so he was vulnerable. I kept hitting him until I knocked out one of his teeth, and that's when he let me go."

Desmond's arms were around me and his mouth was traveling from my neck to my chin. I was running out of time to tell my story. "I..." My breath quivered as my fingers found his belt and struggled to undo it with the lack of space between us. "I was lucky. Peyton was a rogue, and Keaty had been looking for him too. Keaty found me that night and saved me. He trained me and made me who I am now. But Peyton never forgot, and he's been meaning to repay me for the last six years."

"He won't get the chance." Desmond spoke the words right into my own mouth. "I won't let him."

Finding I was lacking any further words, he pressed his lips to mine in the same moment I freed the belt from his jeans and worked my way through to the cage of his zipper. His kiss was hot, devouring, and we didn't get to the loveseat before he pushed me down onto the carpeted floor. Within seconds he relieved me of my own ridiculously small pants and was in me with such force it arched my back off the ground.

I knew what I had to do soon, and because of that I was willing to let Desmond take me over completely. This might be the last time we'd be together, and it was the only way I knew how to say goodbye to him.

I closed my eyes and fell into the fierce rhythm of his movements so he would not see me cry, thankful the heavy makeup on my eyes would hide the pink tinge of my tears.

I never wanted this moment to end. Once it did, my whole world would come crashing down.

Chapter Twenty-Nine

I sat on the lawn in Central Park, wearing a now-familiar wedding gown, its front still stained with a palm print of my blood. This time there was no one with me, no wolves chasing me and nothing but the silence of the night.

I shifted the layers of the gown so I could sit without being uncomfortable, then lay back to look at the stars. As I watched, the sky grew brighter and bluer until the stars faded out and I was left blinking into the screaming light of day.

My arms went up to protect my face, and I huddled in a ball of wedding gown, waiting to burst into flame at any moment. It took me cowering for awhile before I realized I felt only the warmth of day on my skin rather than the fire of incineration.

"Do you miss it?" said a small, female voice.

I saw Brigit, with her bronze skin and glowing blonde hair, beaming at me, looking healthy and alive.

"How can I miss what I never had?" I asked, unable to keep the sadness out of my words.

"I miss it." She ran a hand through her hair, and large blonde clumps, scalp still attached, came off in her fist. She held them out to me with a defeated expression, and the golden strands disintegrated between us. I reached out to her, but before I could, her eyes boiled and melted and her skin began to slip off her like thick wax. Everything that left her body turned to ashes, and I was staring at a pile of rubble where the pretty girl had once been.

"It's because of you, you know?" Lucas was standing behind me, but he wasn't dressed in a tux. He was no longer coming to our wedding. He looked down at me, then offered me a hand to help me to my feet.

"I didn't change her."

"No. But everything will change because of you."

I took a step closer but stumbled on something. Casting my eyes downward, I recoiled in horror. Desmond lay at my feet, his body red with blood. Looking back to Lucas, I saw he too was covered in blood so thick it ran down his hands. My dress was soaking in it, turning everything from white to red. The whole gown was crimson and bloody.

"It's all because of you," Lucas said.

"No. Not this."

"Aren't you afraid of the daylight?"

"I'm not afraid." But my voice trembled.

"Then go." He put a hand on my shoulder. Desmond's body was gone and Brigit's ashes were no longer there. Instead of the gown, I once again wore my own clothes and a gun was in my hand.

We stood in front of an old movie theater, its façade worn down and grimy from lack of upkeep. The shadow of the marquee blotted out the sun. I could see everything better now. Lucas gave me a sad smile.

"You must go or it will all fall apart."

I was about to ask him *what*, when he too was gone, and the doors of the theater opened like a yawning mouth waiting to swallow me whole.

My eyes snapped open, and I took a moment to get my breath back.

I was lying on the carpet in my living room, which was an incredibly stupid and dangerous place for me to have fallen asleep. Next to me, snoring softly with his arm cast across my bare stomach, Desmond slept peacefully. On the other side of the room, rays of light were sneaking through the window, illuminating the chair below. It wouldn't be long before the sun reached me.

I recalled the dream and Lucas asking if I was afraid of the daylight. There was no way to lie to myself now. Not only was I afraid of the sun, I was shaken to my core at the thought of what I had to do next.

Watching Desmond sleep, I couldn't keep from seeing how good his olive skin looked in the natural light of day. What was he doing in my dark life?

Blinking at the bright window, I knew I didn't have much time. The sun didn't have the muted hue of early morning. Looking at the clock over the fireplace, I confirmed it was almost one in the afternoon. I was glad I'd fed at Calliope's, because it meant I'd been able to rouse myself when I normally would have kept sleeping. Like a kid on Christmas morning, my anticipation was the only other thing that had gotten me up. The real miracle was that Desmond hadn't awoken. I gently removed his arm from my belly, wishing I could stay with him longer, but knowing it was out of my control. I had to leave now before the urge to go back to sleep got too strong.

I got to my feet and padded naked through the apartment to my bedroom. Once there I was calmed by the comfortable darkness and set to work preparing myself. Donning my jeans from the day before and a long-sleeved black turtleneck, I dug through the closet looking for anything suitable to wear outdoors. Bless *Grandmere* for still being concerned about my health, even knowing what I was, because every Christmas she sent me sensible grandmotherly things like scarves, hats and gloves.

I had to be thankful for the cold season of the year too. In summer I would not have been able to encase myself so completely. Living in New York was a saving grace itself, because no one would wonder at me for traveling the sunlit streets under a black umbrella.

I wrapped a dark scarf several times around my face and pulled a hat low over my ears so only my eyes were visible. Leather gloves covered the exposed skin of my hands, and I added a long black peacoat over everything for an extra layer of protection. Under the coat I had two guns tucked into the back of my jeans, and the pockets were laden with extra silver bullets, the clips preloaded for me by my fae weapons dealer so I didn't have to touch the bullets. I had on knee-high black boots over the jeans, not wanting to risk an exposed slash of ankle. And because I couldn't feel too protected going into this situation, I slid a long, sheathed silver blade, the handle double taped for my protection, into one of the boots.

Back in the living room I stood next to my doorway, watching Desmond sleep. Part of me hoped he would wake up and try to stop me from going, but he only muttered something incomprehensible and stirred no more.

Bringing Peyton in alive would have been easier with help, but the job had been tasked to me and I wasn't willing to risk anyone else's life to get it done. I needed to do it alone, and the best chance I had to succeed was to attack in the daylight when he would be dead to the world.

I stooped and gave Desmond a delicate brush of a kiss. I

hoped, if all went right, it wouldn't be our last.

Then I was gone.

Chapter Thirty

Outside, daylight smashed into me like a fist. I felt discombobulated and dizzy. My vision swam, unaccustomed to the brightness of a sunny afternoon, and under the layers of clothing I broke out in a cold sweat. This was the kind of fear I didn't know how to deal with. The sun was not an enemy I could fight. I'd spent my whole life hiding from the light, and now I was willingly walking out into it.

I opened up the umbrella, and the black material blotted out the worst of the light as I stepped out onto the sidewalk. Stumbling down the street like a burdened drunk, I kicked myself for not thinking about sunglasses. I'd never owned a pair—I'd never had a need for them before—but with the glaring shine of afternoon burning my nighttime retinas, I was blinded.

The urge to sleep was so incredible my body and feet felt like lead. I hoped Brigit hadn't been mistaken about the theater, because if I could at least find myself somewhere dark, my body might regain enough strength to give me a fighting chance.

I tilted the umbrella to keep the light out of my eyes and continued my pathetic trek towards the only location that made sense. There was a place halfway between my apartment and Central Park that had once been a luxurious theater called the Orpheum. A fire in the 1980s had killed several people and led to its subsequent closure, but because it was considered a historical building debate raged on for decades as to what should be done with the place.

It was remiss of me to not think of it sooner as a perfect nest. Of course it would appeal to vampires—it was full of darkness, death and tragedy. Furthermore, the nasty appeal of the place would sometimes attract someone foolish enough to sneak in who would then find themselves as unexpected supper guests for a hungry clusterfuck of undead.

After a few blocks of lethargic progress, I stood on the corner opposite the theater. It managed to look foreboding in the bright light of day. The *ph* of the Orpheum's sign had fallen down years ago so I read it as the *Or eum*, which was probably Latin for *terrible fucking idea*. Many small round bulbs that once lit the marquee had been smashed by vandals, so only those out of easy reach were still whole. The marquee itself had lost most of the letters that had once announced its closure, so instead of saying *Closed for Business* only a half dozen black block letters remained with no semblance of meaning. The windows of the main double doors were painted over with black, and through the shattered panes the boarded panels behind were visible.

I limped across the street and stood in front of the doors. Deep in my chest was a sensation I'd only experienced before a meeting with the Tribunal. Both there and here, my fate was in someone else's hands. Beneath the marquee the sun was blocked out, as it had been in my dream, but I hadn't yet begun to feel refreshed. Instead a chill seeped into my bones and unease spread like a dark shadow through my whole body.

No turning back now. I'd come this far and I had no choice but to continue. Touching my back, I reassured myself I still had my guns. What lay beyond these doors was the truest kind of *get it done or die trying* situation. If I didn't take Peyton alive, he would see me dead. There was something comforting about knowing the outcome would be black or white with no room for gray.

With my own death at the forefront of my mind, I pulled on one of the handles, and it yielded, swinging out towards me. Part of me was expecting the squeal of angry hinges, some sort of loud announcement of my arrival, but the door opened with nothing more than a swishing sigh of air being sucked inward.

The atmosphere inside was that of stagnant darkness, and the air was cold and still. I entered the old lobby of the Orpheum, crossing the aged red carpet and moving past the empty ticket booths into the large arena of the movie theater itself.

It had once been a theater for stage productions and operas. The ceilings rose in high arches to amplify the acoustics and were painted in detailed murals depicting choirs of angels and devils combating over the souls of the patrons below.

On either side of the room were three private boxes. Each had once held a collection of seats, but according to local news coverage those had since been removed and taken to storage or alternate theaters. I stood under the archway that led into the room and took in the entirety of the scene, smelling the air for goons who I knew waited within.

I removed my scarf, hat and gloves and tucked them beneath a nearby seat so they wouldn't reveal my arrival too soon. I kept the jacket on, unwilling to leave my extra ammunition anywhere out of arm's reach. Removing one of the guns from my waistband, I held it as my only comfort.

I smelled the group of guards before I heard them. Pressing my back against the wall, I ducked behind one of the heavy, red velvet curtains and waited without breathing. There was laughter and a chorus of booming male voices that didn't falter as they passed me. I had gone unnoticed.

There were three of them and their scents were muddled together, but the whole group reeked of wolf. I must have escaped detection because they were used to smelling their own kind. I was willing to take any small kindnesses the universe was offering me right then.

They moved upward to one of the boxes and settled there. I waited until I heard the scraping of metal chairs being rearranged, followed by the dull creak of settling bodies, before I pushed back the curtain to get a look at where they were. Their voices were coming from a box closest to the movie screen.

These were the daytime guards of whichever vampires were hiding beneath the theater. Given what I'd learned from Brigit, and how it fit with my own assessment, I also believed they were working for Marcus. I didn't recognize any of their voices from the brawl at the Chameleon, but that didn't mean they hadn't been there.

I surveyed the main floor of the theater to make sure I hadn't missed any guards. Since I was here to take Peyton alive, I didn't want there to be unnecessary casualties. There were plenty of ways to render a man useless aside from killing him, and I was proficient in most of them. I may have been a killer, but none of the guards had done anything to warrant being murdered.

If I could find Peyton and get in touch with one of the daytime servants of the council, this whole ordeal could be finished without any bloodshed.

Trying to take on three werewolves at the same time wasn't an ideal option if I wanted to finish out the day without a body count. I needed to split them up and hope one of them would tell me where to find Peyton. It might take a little persuasion, but broken fingers healed. So did bullet wounds.

I slipped away from the curtain and back into the lobby.

The lethargy of day was wearing off as a wave of adrenaline overcame me. I spotted the sign for *Second Balcony and Left Boxes* and stole towards it in the shadows of the unlit room.

I'd never been more aware of my wolf than when I stalked down the hallway towards the sound of their voices. I ducked into the box one over from theirs and stayed low to the ground. Snippets of their conversation were now audible, and I sat and listened, waiting for a good moment to make my move.

"Christ, Jackson, chill out. You're making me all antsy."

"Sorry." The voice sounded young and strained with worry. "It's just, I mean, this is creepy, isn't it?"

"Creepy?" The man who responded gave the word a mocking tone. "What's so fucking creepy?"

"Knowing there are vampires, like, below us?"

"Get a grip, kid. Boogeyman ain't gonna get you."

One of them let out a huff of air, and the trio fell into silence. Muffled chewing noises and the squeak of Styrofoam were the only sounds in the theater.

Staying low to the ground, I used my heel to drag a heavy metal bar towards me. It looked to be the post that once held a bank of seats in place, judging by the discolored seat-shaped rectangle on the floor around it. The bar rolled closer with the slightest metallic ringing, but still I held my breath and froze.

Their munching continued.

I picked up the bar, and when I heard one of them clear his throat, I shuttled the post over the edge of the box. The fall seemed to last an eternity before the clatter of metal meeting a concrete floor reverberated through the room, bouncing off the ceiling and back into the wings.

"What the...?" Chair legs squealed on the floor of the guards' booth. "Jackson, stay here and keep an eye out. Come on, Al."

Two of the guards stomped down the stairs back to the lobby. Once I could hear them below, I slipped out of the box and into the one next door. Before the young werewolf could call out, I clamped my hand over his mouth and dragged him to the floor.

"Shhh," I warned. My gun was drawn and glinting in the dim overhead light of the box. "Don't make me use this."

His bright green eyes were wide, and his pulse quickened. He managed to nod against the force of my hand. Jackson was so young it made me sick to have to scare him like this. Sure, he was guarding Alexandre Peyton and probably worked for Marcus Sullivan, but he didn't look more than twenty years old. I doubted he understood the implications of keeping the company he did.

"Where is Peyton?"

His brows knit together, confusion clouding his features.

"The vampire," I clarified. "Where is the vampire?"

At that his eyes widened with understanding. He nodded again and mumbled something into my hand.

"If I let you talk, do you promise not to call them?" I held the gun to his temple. "You don't want to call them."

His head bobbed, and I lifted my hand one finger at a time, praying he would keep his word.

Jackson let out a whoosh of air and sucked back a breath. "Who are you?" he asked, but to his credit he kept his tone low.

If he didn't know who I was, then there was a good chance he hadn't been at the Chameleon. There was hope for this one yet.

"It doesn't matter." I pressed the gun harder against the wrinkled skin of his forehead. "Just tell me what I want to know and this won't get messy."

His mouth formed a surprised O, but still he didn't shout for help. The weapon did seem to be distracting him from answering though, so I pulled it away. The entire frame of his body relaxed noticeably. From below I could hear shuffling feet and irritated voices as the men continued to look for the source of the disturbance.

"The coffin room is under the theater. I've never seen it, so I don't know exactly where, but there's a door behind the curt—"

I covered his mouth with my hand again upon hearing the withdrawing voices of the two other guards. Jackson's eyes looked huge with terror.

"Who do you work for?" I needed to make this quick.

Lifting my hand enough that he could move his lips, I let him continue. "Work for?" He looked confused.

"Why are you here? Werewolves guarding a vampire doesn't make sense."

"We're not guarding the vampire. We're here to protect our alpha. He's guarding the vampire."

I was pretty sure I knew the answer to my next question already, but I needed to know for sure. "Who's your alpha, Jackson?"

"Marcus Sullivan."

"And he's underground too?"

Jackson nodded. "He and the queen sleep down there."

"Are there other guards?" Footfalls were echoing upwards. My time was almost up.

"Yes. Six."

I showed him the gun again. "How many?"

"Six, I swear." He swallowed hard, his Adam's apple rising

and falling with an exaggerated bob. Male voices were closer now. I couldn't just leave Jackson to tell them I'd been here, but there was also no way I could take on the other two guards and keep the young wolf subdued.

"Thank you. I'm sorry." I saw his confusion at the words, but a moment later the butt of my gun connected with his temple, and he was out cold.

For the next part of my plan to work, I needed to be quiet and quick. I hopped onto the edge of the balcony, teetering as I balanced on the thin rail before leaping off and into the box where I'd originally hidden. An instant after I landed I heard one of the other guards swear.

I slipped back into the hallway where one of the guards stood with his back to me. The other was out of sight, but I could hear him trying to revive Jackson. I leaped onto the guard I could see and snaked my arm under his chin, jerking backwards to cut off his air supply. It would have been a perfect sleeper hold if I'd been six inches taller. I'd still be able to knock him out, but it was going to take a little extra elbow grease.

A wheezy moan escaped his lips and his body went slack under mine, tumbling to the floor. The whole process took mere seconds. If I could have left then without dealing with the third guard, I would have been happy to, but I doubted he would just ignore the fact that his two comrades were suddenly out cold.

"Bitch."

Yup, that's what I figured.

I got to my feet and squared off against the redheaded guard who was now all that stood between me and the basement.

"I don't want to hurt you," I said.

"That's a pity, because I want to hurt you."

I stepped backwards, careful to avoid the fallen werewolf who was now snoring on the floor. At the same time, I leveled my gun at the remaining guard. I had no intention of firing it, but he didn't need to know that. Nothing says *guess what, I'm here* like gunplay.

"If you leave now, nothing will happen to you," I promised.

He laughed. "The queen should have finished you off when she had the chance."

Jackson had mentioned Marcus's queen earlier, and now this wolf seemed to be suggesting she'd had a chance to do me in. I was still wondering who they were talking about since there was no queen in the east, but I was pretty sure his words meant she was the one who almost killed me at the Chameleon.

"I think you'll find it's a lot harder to finish me off than you might imagine."

"We'll find out." He lunged for me, but his foot snagged on his fallen friend's arm. He didn't fall, but the stagger gave me enough time. I didn't waste the effort to incapacitate him painlessly. Instead I smashed my gun into the back of his head.

Knocking Jackson out had made me feel bad. Bringing this guy down brought a smug, satisfied smile to my lips. I surveyed the floor and the three unconscious figures and let myself breathe a small sigh of relief.

The easy part was over.

That taking on three full-grown werewolves had been the *easy* part made me want to vomit.

Chapter Thirty-One

I dragged the inert bodies into the box and used the braided curtain tiebacks to bind their hands and feet and tether the three of them together. Once I felt sure they wouldn't easily be able to free themselves if they woke up, I went in search of my quarry.

Access to the basement was through a trap door behind the tattered gray movie screen. When the Orpheum used to host plays, the door had probably been for easy access to the stage for surprise entrances or dramatic death scenes.

Now it would once again play a part in a very different kind of death scene.

I took a long, deep breath and pulled my cell out of my jacket pocket. I'd only been gone an hour but Desmond was likely awake by now. Part of me wanted to use the phone to call Keaty and ask for backup. I couldn't make myself do it. Maybe it was because Keaty had saved me the first time I met Peyton, and now that I was facing him for the last time I had to do so by myself.

It was stupid, but I had to know in six years I had become the kind of hunter who didn't need help to kill a three-hundred-year-old vampire. Since meeting Peyton I'd killed others older and stronger than him, but something about the Cajun vampire made me feel as foolish and weak as the sixteen-year-old he'd once bitten.

I looked at the phone once more before putting it back inside my pocket. Pulling my jacket around me, I balanced on the balls of my feet at the edge of the gaping black hole. I only smelled mold and dampness, the scents of the dark, no vampires or wolves.

I jumped.

It took my eyes a few moments to adjust to the total darkness and a few more to take my surroundings in. Below the stage, mildewed sets and props lined either side of the walls. Glass from broken stage lights dusted the floor, making a sound like dry leaves on autumn sidewalks whenever I put my foot down.

Raising my face, I sniffed the dank air, trying to sense anything alive over the pungent odor of decay. Then, as faint as a whisper, I detected something real, something with a beating heart.

I sidestepped the glass the best I could and moved in the direction of the smell.

A short distance down the hall the ceiling dipped low into a small crawlspace that led to a maze of storage spaces and dressing rooms. I crouched, bracing my hands against either wall, and tentatively sniffed the air again. The scent was stronger here, so I dropped to all fours to follow it down the rabbit hole.

Several dozen feet of squat, tight space later the tunnel tilted upwards and began to grow larger. I could rise to a hunched standing position and used it as an opportunity to grab my gun, preparing myself to step into the open.

I ducked low to the ground, shrinking as far into the shadows as possible and taking advantage of my superior breath-holding abilities. I listened for crunching glass behind me, or anything to suggest someone ahead was aware of me and waiting to confront me at the mouth of the tunnel. All I heard was the echoing thrum of the subway as it careened through a station a few blocks away.

The sound of my own heart was a quiet, fearful thump. As far as I could tell, no one was coming. I sniffed the air again, trying to distinguish the different smells.

There was a mishmash of lupine aromas. Too many to give myself an actual head count, but enough to make me a little queasy. Jackson had told me there were six guards, in addition to Marcus and his queen. I was hoping he hadn't lied.

I slumped back, holding my gun to my chest and keeping my breaths steady against a wave of panic. What was I doing here? This wasn't a nest of rogue vampires or one errant wolf. This was a dissenting pack, and until this moment I had only been viewing their leader as a pawn between me and my goal of bringing Peyton to the council.

Yes, Marcus *was* a puppet in Peyton's larger plan, but I hadn't put enough thought into the coup he was plotting. Within the werewolf community there were those who believed choosing a ruling class through family lines was outdated. I didn't fully disagree with them, but I also respected that Lucas would only ever do things for the benefit of his pack.

Furthermore, I didn't think for a second Marcus intended to make the wolves a democratic society if he usurped Lucas's throne.

But those who believed his campaign of false promises would protect their leader with their lives, and I had been a fool to underestimate the scope of his following. These werewolves were more than just guards. They believed they were warriors for a righteous cause.

I would have given anything at that moment to berate

myself aloud, but that was out of the question.

Well, moron, if this is the end, at least you can feel good about splurging on silver bullets.

I pulled out the second gun and checked the clips on both. I slipped extras into my boots as well as the back pockets of my jeans, then I switched off the safety on each weapon.

Right now, I needed to know if Jackson had been honest about the number of guards. Once I knew what I was up against, I'd be able to figure out how to get around them. The ultimate goal was to capture Peyton. The plan for the moment was nothing fancier than *don't get caught.*

Who's afraid of the big, bad wolves? The light of the main room was bright, but it didn't spread into the whole hall. There was an edge of black shadow along the wall, and I used it to stay out of sight, but it let me pass by the room and see who was within.

Dogs playing poker was the first thing that came to mind. Six bulky men crowded around a folding buffet table, using Doritos in place of poker chips. They looked so benign I almost laughed. There was a low metal trolley stacked with folding chairs and another table, all flat. They must have used the rolling frame to bring the furniture in. The passage was wide enough for coffins, even in the cramped areas. It was hard to imagine the guards carting caskets and card tables down that wee hallway, but the goods had to get here somehow.

None of them appeared to be carrying weapons. What was it with monsters assuming nothing out there made bigger bumps in the night than they did? Daylight hours were limited in early spring, and I'd wasted much of the morning sleeping, but with them unarmed there was still a chance I might reach my intended target before night fell. Once Peyton awoke, one of us wouldn't leave the Orpheum alive, and I needed us both to have our lives when this day was done.

I had to remind myself that even this far from the sun's reach I too was weakened by the day, and there was no way I could easily take on these guards, plus however many others were in the room beyond with Marcus and his *queen.*

I didn't believe in God, at least not in the sole-being, grumpy universal father-figure sense of the term. But if he or any of the gods from which Calliope descended were paying any attention this spring afternoon, I was praying to them to show me how I could come out on top in this situation.

My mind was racing, gaze darting around the hallway. They hadn't picked up my scent yet, but that luck wouldn't last, and I needed to figure out of how to handle them, sooner rather than later.

If I went in guns blazing, I could take out half of them before they got the jump on me. But then I risked being ripped apart by three werewolves—not the end to the fight I was hoping for.

There was no other way to get from where I was standing to the door behind them unless I suddenly developed the ability to fly or become invisible. Myths about vampire abilities aside, flying wasn't something any of us could actually do. I wondered if there might be a rear entrance to the room, but judging by the layout and the cramped passage that had led me here, it seemed unlikely.

What had I gotten myself in to? I was beginning to think the first option was my only available course when I noticed something on the wall a few meters down the corridor. I took my eyes off the men and slunk deeper into the darkness.

Mounted on the wall was a silver box. My heart pounded. I could not be this lucky. I opened the hinged cover and squinted into the box's interior. Sure enough it was exactly what I expected it to be. Before my eyes were dozens of breakers, all with faded labels that once explained the power of each switch. I scanned them and saw a heavy double-pronged black switch with the word *MASTER* still visible.

I cast my eyes upward and smiled. Maybe it was time to start believing in divine intervention after all.

Let there be dark.

I flipped the master switch down.

Chapter Thirty-Two

Had I found myself in a nest of vampires, the sudden fall of darkness wouldn't have been noticed. Perhaps a musing of *oh, the lights appear to be out,* but it wouldn't have affected them in any negative way. They could see just as easily in the dark as in the light, and it was a gift I was pleased to have inherited from my father's blood.

Werewolves, on the other hand, only have the benefit of heightened night vision when they're in their wolf form. Even then they rely more on the senses of smell and hearing. One of the problems of being a werewolf, apart from the obvious issue of bursting out of your skin and becoming a wolf every month, was most of the strengths you had in wolf form did not translate to your human body.

Strength and sense of smell remained, as well as keener hearing, but a werewolf in human form couldn't see in the dark. At least not without a considerable period for adjustment, and that was what I was counting on.

From the main room a chorus of voices rose in alarm. Chair legs squealed on concrete and one baritone seemed to float to the top of the din, taking control of the madness before it boiled over.

"Simon," the voice said, "go check the breakers. Something probably just overloaded the system again. James, I need you and Hollis by the King's door with me. No one gets in or out."

"I can't see my hands, let alone the door."

"It's three feet away from you, you fucking moron."

Fish in a barrel.

I listened to the commotion as they tried to organize themselves inside the room and waited for my moment alone with Simon.

Stealth was not the reason Simon the werewolf had been hired for his job. He trundled down the hall with the grace of an elephant in a canoe. If he or the others had any sense of what was waiting for them, it didn't show. He was almost face-to-face with me before he took the breath that told him I was there.

His eyes flared as awareness dawned on him, and his mouth opened to raise the alarm. I clapped my hand over his mouth, holding the gun to his chest to add emphasis to the threat. I didn't want Simon to die. I couldn't sacrifice my newfound luck. I'd gotten this far without killing anyone, and I hoped that wasn't about to change.

He was beginning to panic. One of his fists swung blindly and hooked me in the ribs. My breath came out in a whoosh, and before he had a chance to swing again, I smashed his head against the rock wall and stood over his collapsed body, breathing hard. I held my breath until I heard a small hiss of air escape his lips.

Had this been a comedy of errors, the guard in charge would have sent out one guard at a time to check on the one before until they were all out cold. But this wasn't going to be that easy.

Earlier I had hoped to be invisible, and now I'd been granted that wish. I stepped over Simon's inert body with my gun still at the ready, and moved into the main room.

The scene was almost comical in its ridiculousness. Werewolves, now only five of them, staggered around the room with outstretched arms, tripping on furniture and over one another. They were swearing and barking out orders that got lost in the din of so many simultaneous shouts.

"Jesus, Simon! What's taking so long?" the main guard bellowed from the far back corner of the room. He was freakishly tall, close to seven feet, and as broad across the chest as my torso was long.

It wasn't the size of him that worried me the most, though. It was how calm he sounded—unhappy but not alarmed. He would be my biggest obstacle between this room and Marcus, but all the other guards stood between me and him, and he wasn't budging from his position.

I safetied my gun and put it back in my waistband. In this kind of darkness a gun would only work against me, and until I took out a majority of the guards I couldn't use it. The flash of the bullet exiting the chamber would illuminate my position and give me away. Plus, if I was smart about this, I might not have to use it at all.

The first two were easy. They fell as quickly as Simon had in the hallway, each subdued with a basic chokehold before they could cry out. I was going to have to thank Keaty for teaching me that particular move. Most of my training was lethal, but the sleeper was proving to be a great silent, non-fatal alternative to a broken neck.

With two of the remaining five guards down, I no longer had the cacophony of raised voices to mask my approach. I moved silently through the darkness towards the two guards by the locked door—James and Hollis. James went down quick, like the others, but when I grabbed for Hollis my arms came up empty. He had feinted out of my grip with surprising speed and grace. He swung at me, not able to see me but aware of my general position, and his punch landed squarely on my collarbone.

This hit was more painful than the one landed by Simon, and I couldn't stop the cry of pain that escaped my throat. The femininity of the sound must have taken him by surprise, because Hollis's next swing hesitated and glanced off my shoulder.

"A girl?" Hollis sounded worried.

"I don't care if it's a baby, you morons. Pay attention! A girl is just as capable of killing you. Think of the queen."

Now that they knew I was here I didn't see a point in playing it subtle anymore. I grabbed Hollis's head again. He was staring right into my face, but his eyes were unfocused, not seeing what was right in front of him until I snarled.

The sound was ragged and frightening even to me. It was the snarl of an animal that had no natural sense of fear, a hollow, almost rabid noise of warning. His eyes widened and his mouth went slack. He tried to pull away, but my grip was firm and unyielding. He would not escape me again. Hollis grabbed my arms, scratching at the skin in desperation. I growled deeper. The big guard was moving out of the back corner now, and I twisted Hollis in my grip, using one arm to hold him by the neck as I pulled out a gun and flicked off the safety. I aimed it at the main guard who was only a few feet from us.

Hollis went limp and I let him fall to the floor. Now it was just me and Andre the Giant. I'd been lucky to find the breaker switch, so I guess it was asking too much to make the biggest, scariest bastard in the room an easy target. If I'd been able to take him out first thing, I'd be waltzing into Marcus's room right now.

Instead I was leveling my gun across a two-foot gap and

pointing it at his abdomen. Geez, this guy was massive.

His eyes had adjusted to the darkness, because he was staring straight at me.

"I know you," he said, no fear in his voice in spite of the incapacitated figures littering the ground around us. "You're Lucas's new mate. You're the girl all this trouble is about."

"I hardly think I'm the reason Marcus and Alexandre Peyton are trying to take control of this city."

"Oh, no?"

I was hoping my flicker of uncertainty went unnoticed, because I was getting more and more unnerved by how calm he was with my gun pointed at him. He inched forward, and I loaded another bullet into the chamber.

"What do you think you'll accomplish by killing Marcus? Do you think he's the only one who threatens you and your king? Take my advice, *princess*"—never had the word sounded so condescending—"stay out of Lucas's life. Stay away from the big dogs."

"I'm not here for Marcus. He's just a bonus."

"Ha." The sound was humorless. "You're here because Peyton wants you here."

"You expect me to believe that someone like you knows a damn thing about Alexandre Peyton's plan?" I stepped backwards, but he kept coming. He was advancing slowly, but there was no mistaking the minute movements. I steadied my hands and raised my gun a few inches so it was even with his sternum.

"I know more than you can imagine." His voice told me otherwise. The bravado was gone, replaced with wavering uncertainty. I'd hit the nail on the head. He had no clue about Peyton's plans.

"You don't know anything," I said.

He snarled and moved to close the small space between us.

I shot him.

I might have wanted to hear him out if he'd claimed to be privy to what Marcus's plan of action was, because it was feasible the alpha could have trusted him. But I didn't believe for one second Peyton would let a werewolf, even the leader of the guards, be privy to his real agenda. I doubted Marcus himself knew the details of what Peyton had in mind.

If this had really been the plan, the vampire would have wanted me here at night when he could kill me on his own. He was such a ham he'd want it to be showy and over the top, and he wouldn't want to miss it. Opening the doors to Marcus's bedchamber in the middle of the afternoon would not be a part of anyone's plan but my own.

Alone at last, I gave a hard tug on the door they'd been guarding. "Little pig, little pig, let me in." The door was locked from the inside, and through the wood I heard someone scrambling. Then the door swung open abruptly and I staggered backwards, almost tripping over one of the still forms on the floor.

Marcus stood at the end of a bed, butt naked, with a shotgun pointed at me. After dispatching nine unarmed guards, I hadn't expected anyone to have a weapon. We locked eyes from across the room, and my heart skipped a beat as he pulled the fore-end towards him with a deafening click.

"Pleasure to see you again, Miss McQueen. It's a shame you can't stay." He aimed at my chest and fired.

Chapter Thirty-Three

Either I was dreaming again or I was dead.

I was lying in bed, naked. A tangle of buttery-soft sheets that smelled like sun-dried linen kept me modest from the waist down, and a male arm covered my breasts. I rubbed my face against a downy pillow, breathing in the smell of sunlight that made my eyes water.

Lucas, naked next to me, opened his eyes and fixed his blue irises on my brown ones.

"I've never been here," I whispered.

He wiped a tear away from my eye. "Pink?"

"Yes."

"Hmm." When he stuck his thumb in his mouth, I cringed. "Blood?"

"Yes."

"Where are you, Secret?" *Where*, not *what*. His question surprised me.

"Not here."

He pulled me near, and the line of our touching bodies made my skin explode with heat. He buried his fingers into my hair and brought my face close to his.

"This is real," he told me.

"No."

"You are dying."

"I am?" I hated dreams. Especially when I knew I was dreaming, but I couldn't make myself behave like I should. I kissed him and tried to push my conscious sense away so I could just be naked in bed beside him. His hands slipped down to the small of my back, and he returned my kiss with renewed vigor.

Then he seemed to register what we were doing and pulled back. We were always stopping short of the good stuff.

"Secret, focus."

"I *was* focused." My eyes were closed, my mouth trailing down his neck.

"No. You need to tell me where you are."

I kissed his clavicle, grazing it with my teeth. "I'm with you."

He was getting frustrated; I could tell by the heaviness of his sigh. "You are dying."

"You're killing me," I quipped.

Before I could make another pun, something in my stomach twisted and pain seared through me. It started as a throbbing ache, and I made a whimpering sound. I looked down and saw the cream-colored sheets turning red.

"Like my wedding dress."

I began to cough violently, expelling something hard from my gut. It clicked against my teeth, and he reached between my lips, pulling out a bullet.

When I scrutinized my own body, I saw a gaping hole beneath my ribs where blood was spilling out. Pain rocked through me like angry waves battering a ship at sea, and my breath was sucked from my lungs. I looked to him for help.

231

"Lucas? Why?"

He grabbed my face to keep me from looking at the blood. "*Where are you?*"

I screamed back, but only because it felt like I was being ripped open from the inside.

"The Or-Orph-pheum." I was beginning to shiver, my teeth chattering. "Lucas?" I looked at him with pink tears streaming down my face as I fought to breathe. "I'm so sorry. I want to be here."

"You will be."

"I'm dying."

And then he was gone and I was alone in a widening pool of my blood. Pain shot through the whole of my being, and I knew I wasn't dreaming anymore.

"She's coming to," Marcus said.

I felt fingers withdraw and realized they had just been inside my body. A pitiful, keening noise echoed in the air. It too had just been inside me.

Red fog slipped from my eyes, leaving me looking at a low ceiling in a poorly lit room. Everything came back in tiny shards. The Orpheum, the guards, Marcus and the gun.

Another agonized sob escaped my throat. On instinct I scrambled for a weapon, but my hands were empty and when I tried to move them they were heavier than anchors. I could barely lift them from the floor. My rib cage was punctured, just as it had been in the dream. I didn't need to see the hole to know it was there; it felt like someone was shredding me open from the inside. There should be more wounds from the spray of the buckshot, but I could only feel the one. I tried to take a deep breath but was left sputtering. Only the left side of my chest rose when I tried, and there was a build up of pressure on the right side that made it feel like my body was caving in on itself. I whimpered, but even that hurt.

Marcus came into view, still nude, standing over me with an expression of triumph on his face.

"You bleed slowly. You've been out for hours."

In all that time he couldn't find a robe?

Something else sunk in. *Hours*? "N-night?" Saying the one word felt worse than any torture I'd ever endured. My throat was raw, and though every breath I took seared through me like a blitzkrieg, I couldn't stop my labored panting.

"Oh she is clever, even as she dies," someone else spoke up. This voice was more familiar than Marcus's and sent a chill through my body and turned my bones to ice. No. Not this. "Her blood does smell delicious, doesn't it?"

"No." I couldn't even breathe without wanting to black out, but still I tried to sit up. Dots of white light swam across my vision, and I was forced back down by a wave of nausea. Every inch of me thrummed and reverberated with the swell of hot, liquid pain, the way a thumb pulses after being struck by a hammer. "No."

"She's quite adamant, *non*? Apparently it is not night. Shall I return to my rest, then?" The vampire was laughing as if the whole situation was the funniest he had ever encountered. His face came into view over me.

I blinked several times to be sure it was really Peyton. He had not aged at all in six years, which was to be expected, but there was something different about him all the same. His hair was a dull rust color and fell in waves around his face. He peered down at me with soft brown eyes that reflected the laughter of his voice. When Peyton had been turned he'd probably only been sixteen or seventeen years old. He had the face of a boy on the verge of becoming a man and forever caught in between.

He was lovely, with a youthful roundness to his features. The paleness of his skin against the coppery hair made him look angelic. It was his smile that made the angel fall from grace and gave away the devil inside.

He stepped over me, placing one foot on either side of my legs, and crouched low, not kneeling so as to avoid getting my blood on his pants.

"Secret, it has been a long time, hasn't it?"

"Not." My lips quivered, and I tried a few times to take a deep breath to finish the sentence. "Long." A new sensation rolled over my body, replacing my torment with a cold nothingness. "Enough."

"Haha!" He gave me an assessing once-over. "I am pleased Marcus and his queen abstained from finishing you off until nightfall." He caressed my injured side, and I cried out again. "Very pleased."

Peyton had always been a fan of playing with his food. It was one of the things that got him in serious trouble with the council before he'd gone rogue. His idea of *play* was more in line with the Marquis de Sade than sports and rec. Funny, but even on the verge of bleeding to death on a concrete floor, I still wasn't in the mood to be penetrated by a sadist. Especially not when I had a gaping chest wound waiting for him to explore.

"I was interested to know how you came to be here in the daytime, my little dhampyr. But Marcus's queen was able to provide me some enlightening insights." His gaze was crawling over my body. "It seems the queen knows quite a lot about you, Miss McQueen." When he looked at me, the malice in his eyes glittered like the joy of a child. Then he glanced to the side and fixated on someone else. "Isn't that right, Ms. McQueen?"

While he spoke I had begun to drift, the fog of

unconsciousness settling over me again, trying to protect me from the impossible hurt of being awake. I barely had time to be confused by his change of titles before someone jabbed a thumb deep inside the bullet wound on my side. I wailed, much to Peyton's obvious delight, but the sound was dismantled by my ravaged throat and lungs and came out as a stuttering whistle. When I looked at the queen to whom he'd addressed with my own name, I couldn't have hidden my shock if I'd been totally uninjured.

Kneeling next to me, as naked as her mate Marcus, was a beautiful woman about forty years old, with hair as curly as my own. Only hers was the dark brown color inherited from my grandfather. Her father.

"Mom?" She looked older than she had in the pictures I'd seen, and far less jovial. I looked from her cold face to the finger she had pressed knuckle-deep into my flesh, her nail scraping against my rib bone. "Mom." Then I began to scream again.

Chapter Thirty-Four

"Mercy, perhaps you could live up to your name a little, *non*? I thought perhaps we'd lost her that time."

"A little pain won't kill her. She's a monster."

"We're all monsters here, Mercy," Peyton said, laughing still.

When I came to, my breathing was so ragged and uneven that if I were not awake to hear it, I would have thought it had stopped altogether.

It dawned on me why they kept sticking their hands in my wound. It wasn't only to inflict pain or for the pleasure it granted them. It kept my natural healing abilities from closing the hole, which was why only one gash remained open while the others had vanished. Continually jamming the bullet back in kept me from healing myself.

My mother's finger was no longer inside me, and I was grateful for small kindnesses.

Peyton was still on top of me, tapping my face to lure me back to consciousness.

"They will s-st-stop you," I said, but the threat lost any weight when a full-body tremor rattled my teeth.

"Who? The Tribunal? Yes, I can see they tried very hard to get me. Sending you alone." He touched my cheek. "This was not about my death. This was about *your* death. If they wanted me dead, I'd be dead."

I closed my eyes, unable to continue looking at his smug, victorious smile. He was wrong. He had to be wrong. I was here because Sig believed I could do this, however misguided he'd been. They didn't want me dead.

Well, Juan Carlos wanted me dead, but he was hardly a majority vote.

No, this isn't how Sig would have wanted me to go out. I couldn't believe that, not after everything I'd done for him and the council. The Tribunal owed me something better than a death at the hands of Alexandre Peyton.

"Wrong," I insisted.

He patted my cheek again, but this time it was more of a slap. "You are a foolish believer in the Tribunal even as they leave you to die. You are not one of them. They do not care if you live or die. You are meaningless to them. No one will miss you."

From somewhere in the room I heard my mother laugh. "I should have killed you when you were born. I don't know why I gave you to my idiot mother."

Hearing her use such contemptuousness for the woman who had raised her and taken in her unwanted baby, the woman who had been the only light of kindness in my childhood, stirred something hot and angry in me. Rage proved to be a temporary distraction from the pain.

"Not dead yet." My vision swam and the threat of blacking out was almost realized before I resisted the urge to slip back into the dark tides of inertia. If I didn't find something in me that could fight back, I would die here and become nothing more than a fading afterthought to those I loved.

I didn't know if I loved Lucas or if I loved Desmond. I didn't know what Calliope meant when she told me I would be the center of more than one love triangle, or if I loved anyone at all. What I did know was if I bled to death beneath the Orpheum, I would never get a chance to figure out who I loved. I would never see Keaty again or stand next to Holden in my tiny kitchen.

I would never run through the woods of my *grandmere's* property or feel the sweet, tingly allure of the full moon in my blood.

If I didn't fight back now and find some part of me willing to live, I would never do anything at all ever again.

With my mother across the room and Peyton occupying himself by telling me how little I mattered, my body had started fighting the injury. With a sensational amount of suffering on my part, muscles pulled themselves together, blood clotted where it once ran free and inch by inch the bullet was forced out, until it fell silently into a pool of my congealing blood. The surface wound was slower to heal, but I could feel it knitting itself, pore by pore, back into a smooth whole. I was, for once, glad to be so covered in blood. They wouldn't notice right away that I was no longer leaking.

Fate had smiled on me. If I hadn't taken Brigit to Calliope's, I might have avoided this mess, but I also wouldn't have fed. The blood I had taken at Calliope's was probably the only thing that had kept me from dying, and now it was singing through my body, burning a path of energy and strength as it went.

Every part of me was attuned and hyper aware. I felt whole again, more awake, and I could appreciate my situation more completely.

Once I could feel things other than the gaping hole in my side, I was able to register something hard digging into the small of my back right where Lucas had touched me in my dream. It took me a fraction of a second to realize that it was my second gun.

They must have dragged me into the bedchamber after Marcus shot me, because if they'd lifted me they wouldn't have missed it. They had removed the blade and bullets from my boots, but they hadn't turned me over and looked for a second weapon. All I needed to do now was wait for the right moment. Soon Peyton would stop belittling me, grow weary of the games, and want to feed, and that would be easier if I was sitting up.

That's when I'd make my move.

Until then I needed to focus on what he was saying and act like my pain kept me teetering on the edge of delusion.

"Not dead yet," I repeated, this time a little louder.

"She's got a lot of you in her." Marcus laughed. Mercy didn't seem to think it was so funny.

"She is nothing like me."

"You've got that right," I said under my breath, but loud enough they all heard it. "Thank God."

"God? You think God had anything to do with an abomination like you?" Her anger was palpable. I could only imagine what she felt, but from what I knew of her history, I could piece some of it together. I was a living, breathing reminder of her first love, of a more innocent time, and of his death. I reminded her of him with the color of my hair and the infection in my blood. Everything about me assaulted Mercy McQueen with memories she didn't want, and it made her blind and weak with fury.

Apparently my mother's greatest weakness was me, but not in the way of most mothers. It wasn't her love for me that made her weak; it was her hatred.

"I think..." I faked a gasp for air, "...that God tested you and you failed." I laughed, short and merciless.

No one else seemed to see the humor.

"If you don't finish her soon, I'll do the job for you," Mercy said to Peyton.

"That won't be necessary." His words were polite, but his tone was full of loaded threats. Mercy's face, the beautiful face genetics had seen fit to pass on to me, understood what was unspoken, and she sat next to Marcus.

"Good dog," I said. It almost sent her barreling across the room at me, but Marcus grabbed hold of her and kept her in a sitting position.

"Ah..." Peyton shifted his focus back to me. "There is still a little of the Secret I know and love in there."

"Secret," Mercy huffed, her tone incredulous. "What kind of name is Secret? Who names someone that?"

"You. You told *Grandmere*, in your letter."

"I did *not* tell her to name you Secret."

"You said *keep her secret. Grandmere* couldn't think of anything else so she took it literally." The sentence was rather full, so I coughed at the end for several seconds, then moaned.

"That batty old witch."

"Like you could have done better."

"I was going to name you Harmony."

I laughed so loud it took them all aback. Even Peyton's expression was quizzical. "I think *Secret* suits me a little better when you really think about it."

"I don't think about it. I don't think about you. He's right. No one will miss you when you die, not even your mother."

"I have no mother."

"I wish that was true."

"As touching as this familial bonding session is," Peyton interrupted, rolling his eyes, "the junior Miss McQueen and I have some unfinished business to attend to, and I'd rather like to get it underway while she's still plucky enough to *really* enjoy it."

"You bit me once." I fixed my eyes on his. "I hope you remember it well, because it won't happen again." A note of challenge hardened my words, and I counted on him rising to the dare.

"You seem very sure of that."

"Doesn't really matter what I think, does it?"

I was no longer faking my pain, but no one seemed to notice. Tension was simmering to a boil between me and the redheaded vampire. To an outside viewer I looked profoundly outmatched, and my death should have seemed certain.

But I had learned a long time ago at the hands of this same vampire, no death is one hundred percent certain. Not until it's all over and someone's a pile of ash, or someone else no longer has a pulse.

And I was counting on still having a pulse when this was all said and done.

As for Peyton, I no longer cared what the Tribunal wanted. He would die tonight.

"You think you can kill me?" I said with a defiant sneer. "I'd like to see you try."

"Insolent girl!" The humor was fading with every syllable. I was getting to him, and that's what I had been counting on.

Peyton grabbed a fistful of my hair and used it to pull me up with him as he rose to a standing position. After lying on the ground for so long it took me a moment to get my footing, and that's when he went for my throat. I made a decision then, and

I could only hope it was the right one.

Instead of escaping Peyton, I pulled the gun from the back of my pants and pointed it in the opposite direction. As the vampire's fangs punctured my artery, I started with a full clip and emptied half of it into Marcus Sullivan's head. I pivoted my eyes in time to see him fall dead at my mother's feet, surprise still etched on his face.

"Guess you're not the queen now, bitch."

Chapter Thirty-Five

The moment Marcus's death registered with my mother it felt like a dozen things happened at once. Too much was taking place simultaneously for my brain to process most of it, and my vision had begun to swirl.

I turned the gun on my mother but before I could shoot, Peyton's fangs sank deeper into my neck, undeterred by the previous gunfire. As his teeth dove farther he must have severed a nerve because my whole arm went limp and my hand fell open against my will. The gun clattered to the floor, leaving me unarmed and helpless. Peyton's hands splayed across my back, and he used my sagging frame to his advantage, dipping me backwards in a way that would have looked romantic if he hadn't been sucking my blood.

With my eyes rolling back I could see the empty antechamber and wondered, for the first time, what had happened to the unconscious guards. The mountainous corpse of the head guard was still slumped on the floor, but none of the others remained. I didn't want to dwell too long on what might become of werewolves who'd failed to protect their alpha and his vampire partner. Before I had time to further ponder their absence, my mother let out a loud, anguished scream and hurled herself onto Peyton and me.

In her short flight across the room her hands transformed.

The fingers disjointed, twisting and shifting with sickening crunch-pop noises I could hear over her shrieks. Her nails elongated and became claws. It was with these deformed appendages that she attempted to lash out at me from on top of Peyton's back. Those monstrous hands, I knew with perfect clarity, had been the same ones she had buried into my neck that night at the Chameleon.

The weight of the two of them brought us all crashing to the ground. Peyton was locked on to me in a feeding frenzy, like a shark maddened by the scent of blood, only he was attached to me at the neck, drawing out my life one swallow at a time.

My mother was shrieking and growling, slashing at whatever she could reach. Peyton's back was being torn to bloody ribbons, but he no longer seemed aware of anything except for feeding.

Pinpoints of light appeared in my vision, and they danced and shimmied all across the room. One of my mother's swipes hit me across the face, and her claws opened the skin of my cheek, but I was in shock from having lost too much blood. It felt like something wet and breezy that stung my face.

"You killed him! You killed him! You killed him!" Her words were jumbled together, repeated over and over until they no longer had any meaning, and she was just making impotent, pained noises.

I opened my mouth to make a quip back at her, but a bubbling, gurgling sound came from the base of my throat instead. If I couldn't be a smartass, chances were good I didn't have much time left. Mind you, if I could still think about being a smartass, perhaps I wasn't a lost cause just yet.

As my vision started to taper out and my hearing became more tinny, I swore I heard someone shout my name.

"Secret!" It sounded like Lucas.

This had to be a sure sign time was running out. Hallucinations couldn't mean anything good.

"Secret!" This time louder, closer, more adamant. It seemed too real to ignore, but with a three-hundred-year-old vampire latched onto my neck, I didn't have the luxury of turning to look.

Rolling my eyes to the side, I imagined I could see a large group of people crowd into the room.

"Huhhhh." I was trying to say *hi* in a last-ditch attempt at my lunatic form of humor, but it came out as a sort of death rattle. "Oh," I added, when I realized the words were not what I wanted them to be.

Snarling echoed through the room, but more masculine than the sounds my mother had been making.

"Get the wolf." This voice was so familiar my pulse quickened with relief, which only caused Peyton to clamp down harder.

"Hol..." I stopped trying to talk and gurgled a scream as Peyton buried his face into the open wound of my neck, and his teeth grazed bone.

Holden moved faster than the werewolves and was already grabbing for Mercy before Dominick, Desmond and Lucas had crossed the antechamber. Lucas was still growling as they surged forward and fell onto the writhing mass of pain on top of me. The four of them had all swept in so quickly I was only half willing to accept they were real.

With Desmond and Lucas so close I expected I'd be able to taste them, but I couldn't and it chilled me.

Lucas edged past Holden, ripped my mother off the pile and hurled her at the far wall, where she collapsed onto the floor in a heap, not moving. Desmond and Holden were trying to pry Peyton off me without success. He had bitten me down to the

245

bone and wasn't showing any signs of letting up.

I locked eyes with Desmond, and in that moment the whole tableau froze. The look on his face was so much more tormented than it had been the night at the club. His expression made me think I was as good as dead, because no one looked at you like that if there was hope. In spite of the fact we were staring right at each other, he was giving up. He looked defeated, crushed and totally hopeless. It broke something inside me.

"No." It was the one word I was capable of saying no matter how bad things got. My brow furrowed at him, and I tried to shake my head, but I couldn't for obvious reasons. "No." My voice may have been small, but the look in my eyes made my point for me.

Desmond released the breath he'd been holding and turned back towards Holden and Peyton. Holden was using all of his strength to drag Peyton off, and I could feel the skin of my neck tearing looser and separating from bone as they struggled. If they continued on this course, my neck would be ripped wide open by the time they succeeded in pulling him away.

"You mustn't yank him like that." A female voice, clipped, with an unidentifiable accent. It was familiar, but I couldn't place it. "He's locked on to her. If you continue, you will only succeed in killing your half-breed friend."

Lucas recoiled, but Holden was less compliant.

"Warden." This was said in a warning tone that carried commanding weight. She was addressing Holden by his title, his low rank, which implied she was superior to him. "You *will* release the rogue."

Holden hesitated, but he let go of Peyton. It was only then Peyton seemed to become aware there was anyone aside from me in the room with him. He unhinged his jaw and raised his head from my neck to look around. His face was smeared and dripping with my blood.

"Ew," I said, and the room spun, making me wonder how everyone managed to stay standing. I tried to raise my hand to cover my throat but found none of my limbs would do what I wanted them to. Paralyzed by blood loss, all I could do was lay there and watch the theater of the absurd unfold around me.

Someone new came to stand over me. She had gold-toned skin and thick, straw-blonde hair, with eyes so green I thought she was part cat. The eyes were what gave her away, too even and calm to be genuinely human. Ingrid. Sig's daytime human servant.

She gave me an appraising look, appeared to be satisfied with my place among the living for the time being and turned to whoever else she had with her. Snapping her fingers twice, she indicated the bewildered vampire on top of me.

"Alexandre Peyton, you are to be requisitioned by the vampire Tribunal and held for investigation and punishment based on the charge of abandoning the laws of the council and attempting to expose the secrets of vampire society to the general public. Do you acknowledge and accept this decision?"

He snarled at her. I'd never seen a human address a vampire in such a cavalier and condescending manner. Ingrid obviously believed she had no reason to fear Alexandre Peyton and was making sure he knew it.

"I take your lack of response as acceptance. There will be hell to pay should the Tribunal's pet not survive. Sig is especially fond of the half-breed. He won't like it if she dies." She cocked her head to the side. The expression on her face was that of a Harvard scholar speaking to an insolent puppy who had just peed on her rug.

From behind her a collection of vampire wardens

descended on us. They jostled me against the hard concrete floor as they grabbed Peyton and pulled him off me. He began to thrash like a hooked fish when he realized Ingrid wasn't just speaking out her ass.

"Take him to the Tribunal," she said, her voice monotone and bored. When they had removed him from the room, she looked at me again, then cast her gaze to the three werewolves and the remaining warden, Holden.

"Someone may want to give her some blood. She's not looking well. I suspect she wouldn't be too picky, given her situation." What she meant was that any healthy vampire would have rejected werewolf blood outright. As smart as Ingrid was she didn't know anything about me other than what the council did, that I was half-vampire. Her dismissive title of *half-breed* was more accurate than even she was aware.

"Warden," she said to Holden, "you will come with me."

"No."

The room shifted and I felt my whole body getting heavier. Everything was quieter and people's voices were taking on the slow, drowsy quality of a broken tape recorder.

"She's my responsibility. I won't leave her. She's my responsibility." He was kneeling by my head, stroking my blood-soaked hair.

"This won't escape the Tribunal's notice."

"They made this decision for me."

She snorted and left without another word.

"Someone needs to help her," Holden said, presumably to the wolves, though his eyes never left mine.

"*How?*" This from Desmond.

"She needs blood." Lucas sat next to me, clamping a hand over my shredded neck. It took several seconds before I noticed his touch.

"Like an IV?" Dominick was still hovering nearby.

"No." Holden shook his head. "No, she needs to *drink* blood."

"Why?" Dominick asked. He was the only one unwilling to accept the obvious answer.

"Vampire." It was my last word before everything went dark.

Chapter Thirty-Six

When I woke up it wasn't from any kind of prophetic dream or restful self-indulgence. I came to in the back of a moving car, only somewhat aware of my head being in someone's lap and that same someone stroking my hair.

"Where...?" I began to ask, but my throat felt as if I'd been swallowing broken glass and I couldn't say anything more.

"Shhh," was the response.

I looked up and saw a bandaged wrist, and beyond that the drawn, tired smile of the wolf king.

"Lu..."

"Shh," he said again, more insistent. "The vamp—" He stopped himself, grimacing. "Holden told us we need to take you somewhere. Desmond says you can see the Oracle, so we're taking you there."

After a tentative pause I touched the bandage on his wrist, relieved I was able to move my hand well enough to do so. I knew what it meant, what Lucas had done for me. He'd given me his blood so I could live. But it also meant he knew the truth now, or at least a variation of the truth as he chose to understand it.

"Sorry." I made the word a complete sentence and gazed at him with heavy sadness. How could he look at me the same again? I was sure I would lose him and Desmond both when this was all over. It made my chest feel tight at the thought of going back to the lonely life I'd had before their romantic complications mucked everything up.

"It's okay." He brushed my hair back from my face. "I'm keeping my promise."

I didn't know what he meant, but I wondered if he must be referring to the dream I'd had when I was dying, which made me wonder how much truth there was to my daytime reveries. If Lucas and I really had shared a dream and that's how he'd found me, there was more to this soul-bond...

My head swam, overwhelmed by too many thoughts happening at once.

I smiled and he returned it, but neither of our expressions was happy. I drifted out again and when I awoke he was gone.

This time I was in a bed not my own, and the golden light of morning draped across the comforter. On instinct I recoiled from the light, but it didn't take long to realize it wasn't burning me.

It took even less time to realize every single bone in my body, every inch of skin, every joint and muscle was awake and screaming with pain. I had been in fights before, and I had been left in bad shape, but never in my life had I knocked on death's door twice in one evening only to have him send me away both times.

I'd be overjoyed by the knowledge I was alive if I wasn't so painfully aware of it.

"You're up!"

The cheeriness of this voice was almost as bright as the artificial daylight and hurt nearly as much. I winced in the direction of a chair next to the bed.

"Brigit?"

"Hi!"

The blonde vampire was perched next to my bed, radiant in a cobalt blue sundress, her hair long and straight, held back by a sapphire-colored headband. Even as a vampire she looked like she should be spending the day on a beach in California. It pleased me to see her looking so happy, but I couldn't focus on it for long. My body hurt too much.

"Calliope?"

"Yes." Brigit understood the unspoken question, confirming I was at Calliope's mansion. "Holden brought you in. He was with the wolves. The cute one you were with when I came here and another one. He was cute too." She grinned, flashing her pageant-queen teeth at me. "They couldn't come in, you know the rules."

"No wolves."

"Right. It's really too bad. I mean, I like Calliope and all, but you'd think in a place that can adjust to the needs and wants of those who live here, there might be a cute serving boy or two." She flipped her long hair over her shoulder.

"Brigit, why are you here?" I closed my eyes against a new wave of pain.

"Oh. Oh! Yeah, I guess last time you saw me it was that whole awkward trying-to-kill-you thing." Brigit rolled her eyes, as if to say *what can you do.* "Calliope set me right. She introduced me to the council and they said I'm okay, but I need a liaison until I've proven myself in the real world, you know?"

"Liaison?" My heart sank.

"And that blond guy, Stick?"

"Sig."

"Sure, him. He said you were my liaison. And I had to stay

with you until you got better."

This bolted me up, which I regretted when a wave of nausea threatened to pull me back down. I moaned and sank deep into the thick down duvet, shutting my eyes tight enough to block out the light, hoping Brigit and my pain would be gone when I looked again. Instead, when I reemerged from the blankets, Brigit had been joined by Calliope.

The immortal looked downright casual, dressed in jeans and a rose-pink cashmere sweater, with her dark hair in a high ponytail. She was smiling at me in the manner of a concerned mother. A real mother, not the one who had tried to rip my face off. Reminded of what Mercy had done, my hand flew to my cheek, grazing the skin for any trace of open wounds.

Calliope shook her head. "All healed. Everything on the outside is healed."

"Still hurts."

"It will for awhile. You almost died."

"Twice."

"Yes. And getting shot certainly didn't help you deal with the open neck wound. You're very lucky the wolf king was willing to feed you."

"He's a king?" Brigit interjected. "Cool!"

Calliope gave Brigit a frustrated but patient look. The young vampire sat back in her chair and stayed quiet. The Oracle was on the end of the bed, her hand gently resting on my foot.

"I'm sorry he couldn't be here with you. He wanted to be. He and his lieutenant both. They've been waiting all day in the coffeehouse for you, ever since you arrived. I send Brigit there every so often to tell them you're okay, but I don't think they'll believe it until you're with them again." She lowered her eyes.

"You know the rules, though. It could be very—"

"I know. It's dangerous."

"But someone is here to see you."

I pressed my unharmed cheek into the pillow and smiled in spite of myself. "Holden."

Calliope frowned, patting my leg with maternal comfort. "No. Someone else."

If it couldn't be my wolves and it wasn't Holden, I was out of guesses for who could be waiting to see me. I didn't think Keaty could come to Calliope, seeing as he wasn't afflicted by any sort of supernatural ailment.

"Send them in?"

She reached out for my hand, giving it a firm squeeze. "You have to go to him. I won't invite him in."

It was night in the courtyard. Time could exist in parallel ways in this realm. The sun and the moon could share one sky, and it could be daytime in one room and night in another. The sound of cicadas filled the air and stars sparkled overhead in constellations that had never been seen from the New York skyline.

Calliope led me to an overstuffed loveseat and eased me back into a more comfortable position, me wincing every inch of the way. Calliope claimed I was healed, but I'd never felt less whole in my life. I felt like I was one sneeze away from breaking into pieces.

"Where *is* Holden anyway, if he's not here?"

"He brought you here and left shortly after that. He didn't tell me where he was going or if he'd be back." She stood close to me, hand resting on the top of my head.

"Then who came?"

"I did."

The voice was soft and even, coming from the darkened edge of the courtyard. Calliope and I both looked in that direction, and she took a few steps away from me. A figure emerged from the shadows, and Sig walked with long paces towards where I sat.

It was rare for me to see Sig outside of the Tribunal, and to find him in Calliope's realm was an extra shock. Overdressed in comparison to how I'd last seen him, he now wore black dress pants and a black T-shirt tailored so perfectly it looked like it was painted on. He was still barefoot, though, and I wondered how he managed it living in a city like New York.

He stopped in front of Calliope, ignoring my presence for the time being.

"Oracle."

The corner of his mouth twitched with a smirk that vanished so fast I might have imagined it. Calliope's face was stony.

"Good evening, Sigvard," she replied with cold detachment, crossing her arms over her chest.

It was my turn to suppress a grin. *Sigvard?*

"Thank you for bringing her to me. Are you sure we cannot have this discussion inside?" This time the laughter in his tone was unmistakable.

Calliope rolled her eyes. "Don't make me regret this, Sigvard. She is important. Too important to play these games with. You need to protect her better. Especially considering..." She cast a glance towards me and then back to the Tribunal leader.

I didn't like being talked about when I was sitting right here. I may have been hurt, but my ears worked just fine.

"Don't keep her long," the Oracle threatened, and turned back towards the house.

Sig watched the immortal go, not bothering to hide his smile now, looking quite pleased with himself for how irritated he'd made her. "She hasn't changed."

"Why won't she invite you in?"

"She's a little mad at me still."

"Still?"

"I said something to her during the Italian Renaissance, and I gather she's still annoyed about it."

"What could you possibly have said to make her mad for more than four hundred years?"

He sat next to me, leaning back in the chair and looking up at the sky. "Who knows? To an immortal four hundred years isn't that long. Calliope is much older than I am, but she's still a woman, and even immortal women are capable of holding irrational grudges."

"What did you say?"

He smiled at me. "I told her I didn't love her."

I stared at him, trying to process the meaning, but I couldn't grasp the enormity of the two oldest, most powerful beings I'd ever met having once been a couple. "Oh," was all I said. "Why did you tell Brigit I was going to be her liaison with the council? You have to be a warden to be a liaison to baby vamps."

"You were promoted."

"I'm not a vampire."

"You are many things, Secret."

We stared at each other. He'd combed his blond hair back so I could see nothing but his glacier-blue eyes.

"You know."

"Yes," he replied. "I know everything."

"And the others?"

"Daria and Juan Carlos cannot know the truth. Not ever."

I let out a breath I hadn't realized I was holding. "Thank you."

"I've given you this position because the rest of the council cares very little about the daily lives of wardens. When you just worked for us, you were constantly drawing attention to yourself." He sighed. "If you are *one* of us, you will stop being considered an outsider, and it will be less likely for you to fall under serious scrutiny."

"And that starts with me babysitting Miss Vampire USA?"

"She is a vampire because of you."

"I didn't make her."

"Did you not? Really." Sig arched a loaded eyebrow at me. "If you hadn't taken Peyton's fang, or killed his rogue spawn *without* permission, would Miss Stewart be a vampire today? It may be ripples in a pond, Secret, but your actions have their consequences."

I looked at the stars so I didn't have to admit he was right. "Brigit isn't why you're here. And I doubt you came to check on my health."

"This is true."

"So, what? Why come across dimensions just to get me out of bed?"

"Would you rather I came across dimensions to get you *into* bed?"

I frowned at him.

"No, then?" He chuckled, then rose from the seat so I was

staring up the full six-and-a-half-foot length of him. It was a daunting view. "I came to give you your next job."

His announcement reminded me of the last job he'd assigned me, and phantom pains stabbed through me at various key places.

"Peyton. What happened to him?"

"We are taking care of that."

"He's alive?"

"As alive as a vampire can be. Though I'm certain he wishes he were not. He will say nothing about what he learned of you from Mercy, I've seen to that. You did excellent work. Ingrid was very complimentary, which is rare for her."

Apart from telling him how well I was able to bleed out, I couldn't imagine what kind of compliments Ingrid had paid me.

"And my mother?"

Sig's calm veneer flickered. "She escaped. Your wolf king sent someone back so she could be dealt with under the covenants of the pack, but she was gone. I'm sorry."

I took a moment to think about that. Mercy McQueen, the mother who hated me enough to sell me out to her mate and his vampire associate, was still out there somewhere.

"What do you want?" I was exhausted, weak and so sore the slightest shift made me feel like I was being compressed by the Death Star trash compactor. What I wanted more than anything was to be in a bed with Lucas or Desmond beside me, and to feel whole again. I did not want a vampire protégée or more responsibility from the council. I certainly didn't want whatever job Sig had felt the need to hand-deliver to me before I'd been given a chance to heal.

He withdrew a small black envelope from his pocket and placed it on the seat next to me. It looked different from the white linen envelopes I usually got from him. "I am so very sorry." He bowed down and placed a hand on my cheek, staring at me for a long time with such intensity I was unable to turn away.

"She was never really my mother."

"That's not why I'm sorry."

He dropped his hand and walked away. Before I could think of a proper response he had disappeared into the shadows and was gone.

I picked up the black envelope and flipped it over in my hands several times, tracing the outline of the wax seal with my fingertips. The seal was an engraving of a peacock feather.

Never in the six years I'd worked for the council had Sig met with me alone to give me the name of a target. I almost always received them from Holden. It felt too intimate to receive my orders straight from the hands of the Tribunal's leader, and I was instantly suspicious of the envelope.

My heart was pounding inside my rib cage like a frightened bird trying to use its body to invent freedom where there was none. I took a deep, rattling breath and broke the seal on the envelope, but paused before opening it.

This was big. It was important. Sig wouldn't have brought it to me this way if it weren't. Something in me understood that when I opened the envelope the whole game changed. When I opened it nothing would ever be the same.

I released the breath and slid out the stiff white card inside. On it, in Sig's sharp, looping scrawl, a name was written in mottled black ink.

That name was Holden Chancery.

About the Author

Sierra Dean is a reformed historian. She was born and raised in the Canadian prairies and is allowed annual exit visas in order to continue her quest of steadily conquering the world one city at a time. Making the best of the cold Canadian winters, Sierra indulges in her less global interests: drinking too much tea and writing urban fantasy.

Ever since she was a young girl she has loved the idea of the supernatural coexisting with the mundane. As an adult, however, the idea evolved from the notion of fairies in flowerbeds, to imagining that the rugged-looking guy at the garage might secretly be a werewolf. She has used her overactive imagination to create her own version of the world, where vampire, werewolves, fairies, gods and monsters all walk among us, and she'll continue to travel as much as possible until she finds it for real.

Sierra can be reached all over the place, as she's a little addicted to social networking. Find her on:

Facebook: www.facebook.com/sierradeanbooks

Website: www.sierradean.com

E-mail: sierra@sierradean.com

Twitter: @sierradean

Her blood is his lifeline. His love could be her salvation....

In the Blood
© *2011 Abigail Barnette*

Call girl Cassandra Connely drifts through life in a haze of guilt and sedatives, burdened by a deadly mistake from her past and plagued by nightmares of horrific, clawed creatures. Her newest client is a mouth-watering distraction, and she finds herself intrigued by Viktor Novotny's eccentric...tastes. Until he touches her, and her nightmares become real.

One look at the woman in the hot red dress, and Viktor rests assured he will hang onto his humanity at least one more night. In the century since an attack turned him into a vampire and killed his wife, regular sexual encounters are his only defense against becoming a mindless Minion. Yet when Cassie agrees to be his companion—and meal—for the evening, she stirs his soul in a way he hasn't felt since his lost lover.

Viktor's haunted eyes pull at her heart, but Cassie cannot bear to feel anything, ever again. When she flees his apartment, though, she is in more peril than she knows. Tasting her blood without completing their union has left Viktor hungry for no other but her. And vulnerable to the very Minions that wait to drag him into the void. Worse, Cassie is their next target...

Warning: Contains explicit love scenes that will make your blood boil over, including a brief m/m encounter, ill-advised (but oh-so-sexy) use of sharp objects, and hypnotic kisses that could—just for a moment—make you imagine you are Viktor's lady of the night.

Available now in ebook from Samhain Publishing.

What happens in Atlantic City…changes everything.

The Naked Detective
© *2010 Vivi Andrews*
Karmic Consultants, Book 4

The "gift" that makes Ciara Liung the FBI's prized secret weapon makes her existence more like a curse. Unable to bear human contact, she lives as a hermit, immersing herself in the water that gives her peace and amplifies her power.

Her new FBI handler, though, only believes what he can see. The problem? Her gift—the ability to psychically locate stolen jewels—only works in the nude.

Special Agent Nathan Smith can't believe he's expected to babysit some psychic finder. Psychic…right. An undercover op gone wrong may have left him a desk jockey—and Ciara's charms are more distracting than he cares to admit—but he's a field agent at heart. She's working some kind of angle. It's just a matter of time before he unravels it.

Sent to Atlantic City to recover a ruby necklace for Monaco's royal family, both finder and Fed are pushed outside their comfort zones, and discover more than they ever believed possible. And when a trap is sprung, they realize they stand to lose much more than a sparkly stone…

Warning: This book contains gambling, go-go dancers, public indecency, and every brand of trouble a troubled psychic can get into in America's Playground.

Available now in ebook from Samhain Publishing.

SAMHAIN
PUBLISHING

www.samhainpublishing.com

Green for the planet.
Great for your wallet.

SAMHAIN
PUBLISHING

It's all about the story...

Romance

HORROR

www.samhainpublishing.com

CPSIA information can be obtained at www.ICGtesting.com
Printed in the USA
LVOW101658200312

273977LV00002B/49/P

9 781609 284671